SOMETIMES STUDENTS DIE

A NOVEL

ANDREW S. CIOFFI

Sometimes Students Die

ISBN: 978-0989715652

First Edition

Mokkou House Publishing

백지장도 맞들면 낫다

"It is better to lift together, even when it is a blank sheet of paper"

Korean Proverb

Dedication

To the thankless many who make this their profession

Special Thanks

To my family, especially my wife and kids,
and to Chris for all the help with editing

Table of Chapters

PART 1

CHAPTER ONE
STUDENT EMERGENCY

We don't have funerals on campus for these kids; the lawyers won't let us. We have "grief counseling." It's a pretty bad day when you have to beg for one around here.

❖

"It's Dean Freeman," she said, interrupting. "Line 1." He never called. She rarely interrupted when I was with a family, if ever. That meant that I had to interrupt, too.

"I'm so sorry, I have to take this..."

"Pete... It's Min. He's gone." I could hear it in his voice. He meant *that* gone. The words were rehearsed, I could tell. Or I wasn't the first person he told. Who has seen this enough that those words could be so robotic? Other words, mostly instructions, followed, but those were the gut punch.

Dean Freeman... He never was one for a delicate touch. She did tell him I was with a family, too. Either he was afraid of what he was feeling, or he was just crossing something off the day's agenda.

10:14 a.m., dead student, suicide, call advisor.

10:16, email faculty.

As deep down as I could have hoped, he felt something near what I was feeling.

People tell me I'm good at what I do. I often wonder why they say so. I like to think that it's that thing inside... The one that made me think, in that moment, that the family I was with would have wanted me to cancel on whoever sat in their place if I got the same call for their son. "Student emergency" is what we called it. I wish I could have told them it wasn't one of those times when we stretched the term. The tears in my eyes must have spoken clear enough. They were only in town for the weekend, too. We'd have to finish over the phone.

I'll never forget when I met this kid. International student orientation was an afterthought at best. They put out some sticky mess of a *General So-and-So's* chicken for lunch. I remember, in fact, the exact moment when I first saw him. With a plate full of that and some Philadelphia maki in his lap, he said "I'm excited to try this *American* food." He meant no offense. That was the way everything was with him, even if he said the wrong words. He usually said the wrong words.

These kids were "full pays," though...international students. At least that's what Admissions called them. But, man, Min was full of something else. His classmates were all brighter, and that's not a knock. Not on this one. There were students in that group that were ahead of some of our faculty. We always recruited well overseas. Min was plenty bright, and he had passion. He had gusto. It was like everything was some miracle; like everything was an upgrade. You could see it in his eyes, the way he talked, the things that reminded him of his home, some of the funniest questions a kid could ask... He used to say that the sky was so big here.

This was a school, with a gym and a theater; we had a day care; there were ice cream socials in the res halls, late night breakfast on reading days; there was an anime club. We shouldn't have had to have protocol for this.

Twenty eight. I'm only twenty eight... Four years out of grad school and Min's not my first. Think about that. Think of all of the advisors at all of the colleges who can say the same thing. But he was unlike any other. For one, and being as removed as humanly possible, there was the matter of his status. Min was Korean, from Japan. His father was a salaryman. They were rooted there, like the Zainichi, he would say, whatever that meant. I suppose it meant he didn't really fit in there, either. Anyway, there were parents more than six thousand miles away from a dead son and some mid-level administrator was supposed to relay that message. As much as I liked him, I was pretty happy to find out that it wasn't going to be me. The thing is, the way these Deans have to work, if there wasn't some checklist about this, there would be now.

The other thing, the one that I wasn't professionally or emotionally prepared for, hasn't stopped choking me up. I'll let you read his note, I still can't:

Mr. Cahill,

It would be an honor if you would escort me to my funeral. Please tell my parents what you can. They never believed in me, but I think, when you meet them, you will understand.

You said you always wanted to go...

Minho

His note came to me by way of an email later that morning. Someone had to retype that. Fuck... Chief took the real note from his room in a plastic baggy. "What a scene," they said. And that was all they said. I'm not sure I wanted to know how it happened. In fact, I didn't. I could have known, but he was too good. It was too soon. I wanted no part of what was in that room. I didn't need this kid's blood staining the way I was supposed to remember him to his family. Jesus Christ, I still can't believe he had me considering going.

That's me, by the way, in the letter from Min, if that wasn't obvious. Peter Cahill. "Mr. Peter," he called me. I don't think he understood why that made me chuckle. A little about me... I'm a bit soft spoken, but I can project in a classroom. Public speaking is one of my strengths, but I

4

always lose sleep the night before. Let's see... I love samurai movies. Sushi. I hate coffee. I've never done drugs. Drugs scare me. So do bees. When someone sits in the handicapped spot on an otherwise perfectly empty train, I want to say something, but I usually don't. I did once. Turns out, she had MS. Imagine the egg on my face. What else? I talk too much, though I'm terribly shy. Sometimes, I can be a bit of a one-upper. Those last two things are because I'm from a big family. I'm slightly overweight, but not hugely, and I'm tall enough that I can usually hide it well. My hair is kept short so I don't have to worry about it in the morning, and my beard is kept year round so I don't have to shave. I don't wear dress shirts and I hate ties. I'm always neat and presentable, but am built for, in a word, comfort. All told, this makes me an unlikely sort of advisor, I guess. At least for that place.

I would say that my office was pretty cool. I guess it would have to be, given the amount of time I spent there. It was all part of the plan. Some of the other advisors were so...professional. Students don't want that. They want to talk to the guy with Star Wars toys on his desk; the guy with the tattoos and an earring; the one who knows what they're listening to; who always spends the extra few minutes asking what they're up to for lunch. Min always asked, I mean every time he came in, if I knew that the painting on my wall was Japanese. The Great Wave off Kanagawa, by Hokusai. I did know. Every time I heard the story about his summer trips to the sea with his family, it was for the first time. He really liked the sea, and he always told me that he wished he could

5

swim. Min never left my office without bowing. I really had always wanted to go.

So I'm a college advisor. Like...academic counseling. Sometimes it really is like therapy. But not really *real* therapy, you know. Sometimes it's pretty prescriptive: picking classes, signing forms, fielding calls, making referrals. Other times students tell you that they can't stand their roommate's boyfriend, or they come out to you because of the Safe Zone sticker on your door. Advisors are the first people blamed and the last people thanked on campus. To be one, you need a good thick hide and the patience of a saint. Every now and then, a kid - we don't call them kids, we call them students, but this was the kind of day for exceptions - comes along and reminds you why you love your job.

This wasn't ever the plan. I was an Engineering major at a college that was less prestigious than my high school History teacher thought. Turns out, their program was just fine, and I did just fine, Engineering just wasn't for me in the end.

It's "ok" to change your major. Any high school senior that knows what they want for the rest of their life and then sticks with it is either playing things too safe or is following in someone else's footsteps. The last thing that Min wanted was to be an International Business major. Guess who was paying the bills. Guess who drilled into him that he would never write manga, like he wanted, or become a sushi chef, open a kendo school, or design video games.

The one part of my job that I hate, other than playing politics, is answering the phone. One ring means it's an internal call. Those I don't mind. Two rings means it's an off campus call. You never know how angry the parent on the other end is going to be. It's weird, but we are - by "we" I mean advisors - usually better with angry parents in person. The confrontation makes me nervous. So does saying no, or disappointing someone that put their student in my hands. Every call that came in that day, I let go to voicemail. I hated that little red light. What would I say to them? Would it be a mother distraught? A powerful, business-man of a father who would want answers? To make someone pay? I only knew what he told me of his father. He sounded like a very stern man. They never called that day.

The phone rang off the hook for the rest of that afternoon, which was a blur. People were in and out, too, but mostly they called. They only had a few minutes because they were running to a meeting. Most of them knew that I was close with him, so they felt like they were calling with condolences. As his main case worker, I fielded all of the questions about his academic records and his accommodations. I was also called by the Dean of Students, who had called General Counsel, the risk managers, and the Counseling Center first. He wanted my notes and to know if there were any signs that I should have reported. I told you the advisor gets blamed. He filled me in on some other details. Sort of. I could read between the lines.

The hardest part was seeing his friends. By that, I mean the hardest part was holding it together so the ones that knew him well could unload. Sure, grief counseling brings out some rubberneckers, but most of these kids were sincere. What do you say to a person who's just lost someone truly important in their life? When was someone going to say it to me?

When I said we don't have funerals for *these* kids, I didn't mean international students. I also didn't mean students who use a wheelchair, or students secure in their sexual identity. I meant students who have completed suicide. I hate that saying. It sounds so...clinical. The reason that we don't do that is to avoid public voicing of things you hear when sick grandparents die. "At least he's not suffering anymore..." That is music to the ears of someone who is having ideation. A student thinking of attempting is most vulnerable in the few days following a peer's completion. I hate that I know that. We had to manage Min's services with care. But I felt like I owed him something big. He deserved more. I was going to Japan after all, to fulfill his final wishes, and to see to a memorial that someone with a heart that big rightfully deserved.

CHAPTER TWO
NOT JUST A DREAM

It was raining when I left my office. I got fast food on the way home. For once, I didn't mind getting wet walking to the car. It was always nuggets and fries when it was a bad day, and a large coke. I can't have coke after, say, noon. The caffeine keeps me up. Some days more than others, that just doesn't matter.

I've never been a big drinker, and the ride home covered too many miles on the interstate to start any earlier, but it was whiskey when I walked in. I poured it, anyways. The motivation to lift it up and over my lips wasn't quite there. There I stood, all un-tucked and frazzled, waiting for someone to ask.

We had a fight about something earlier. Something small. Small and stupid. She hadn't returned my texts since. This wasn't something I wanted to share by text anyways. I was ready to turn this into another fight.

"What's your problem?" she said.

I don't blame her, and I didn't then. I would have asked her the same question, the same way. We are terribly in love. Sometimes couples fight. That was her first pawn in a match for which I was readying, with practiced openings, through fifty miles of traffic and rain.

What I wanted to do was break down. I'm not a crying man, but this one hit me hard. There's this thing inside me, though, that won't show it, even to her.

"Why do you have to be nasty? I had an awful fucking day, thanks for asking. This isn't what I should have to come home to." And we were right back at it. I wasn't proud of myself for that.

I didn't tell her. Actually, I stormed out. I told her I was "going to the store," and to "eat without me." That's how she knew I was really pissed. Dinner was always sort of sacred. Growing up, my father didn't let us leave the table until everyone had eaten. We couldn't even touch our forks until Mom sat. Everything happened at and around the table. That always sort of stuck, and I've always made a big deal of it. Judging by the sand between my teeth after I slammed the door, though, I must have really been mad. It wasn't her I was mad at.

I walked, in the rain, around the corner and down the hill. There wasn't anything we needed, but I just felt like I had to buy something. I couldn't for the life of me tell you what I bought, but I remember just sort of staring at the hardware section of the local sundries and having the old-timer behind the counter ask if I needed any help.

"More than you know, buddy," I remember saying, under my breath, of course.

"How's that?"

"No, I'm fine, thank you. Just this," I said.

What felt like an hour had only really been about twenty minutes. That was too soon, so I slipped into the Laundromat to watch the machines spin.

When you get to that point where you've brooded long enough, you start to feel bad for yourself, and hungry. That was a good time to grovel back I guess, but the last thing I wanted was any more confrontation.

Whoever says marriage is fifty/fifty is full of shit. On a good day, it's sixty/forty, and we traded off. I needed her to be at about seventy that night. A good marriage is when you don't have to ask. The table was set and dinner was waiting, with her. She could read me like a book.

"Why don't you change." It wasn't really a question. "Do you mind if I make you a dish?" she asked. It smelled awesome, and she could tell on my face, I think, that I was sorry. By then it was well after eight o'clock.

The first half of dinner was quiet, aside from forks and ceramic clanking, and drinks being drunk and refilled.

"Do you wanna talk about it?" she asked. It wasn't pushy or spiteful, or *I'm ending this fight on the high road.* She asked in the way that only this woman could have asked: straight through the bullshit and to the heart of a man she loved. I blinked slowly and gathered a breath.

11

"Do you remember me telling you about that kid from Japan?" I asked, leading, and sullen.

"Oh no!" She said. "The one in the wheelchair? What happened?!" Those exact words that I offered were alone not enough. But when two people have a history, things are repeated. Every other time I lost a student, I prefaced it that same way. And I spoke of him often. She knew I was hurting. "Was it another accident?"

To date, Min was the fifth of my students to have passed on. No educator should have to tell that tale. The first was on the baseball field during his homecoming game. It was "Fall Ball" still, but they had the team scrimmaging alumni. There were even some parents on the field. A line drive hit the kid in chest. They said he was gone before he hit the dirt. They say those things so that parents and teammates don't think they suffer. Actually, in that case, I believe they were probably right. What a nightmare.

Another was a student that I was so proud of. He was almost dismissed academically after his first semester. I helped him figure out an appeal, and we put together a plan for starting the next semester on the right foot. It was the same tutoring and study schedule we'd put together for anyone. This kid took it to heart, though. About a month into the spring term, he came to tell me that he *really* took it to heart and that he was sober for the first time since the seventh grade. *Seventh grade*! Can you believe that? A week and a half later he was home for the weekend to see some buddies that didn't end up going off to college. His buddy was driving. They hit a telephone pole. My student was ejected and his buddy, the driver, blew a one nine. The kid driving walked away without a scratch. The autopsy said that my student was clean. He lost his license the year before, so he didn't want to chance driving.

A third was from a rough neighborhood. He wanted to play football, but he wasn't big enough for the squad. He was stabbed at a party off campus. I don't know all of the details.

The last one, other than Min, also took his own life. He took some cocktail of pills, left a note, and that was it.

I guess you could call a few of them "accidents." Every single one of them was terrible. Every single one of them made me rethink my career. At the end of the day, what kept me going was the feeling that I did alright by these kids, and that maybe I could keep it from happening again. But none of them hurt as much as Min.

"No, it wasn't another accident."

"How do you know?" she asked.

"He left me a note."

"Did you say he left *you* a note?"

I had printed the email. Actually, I only printed his words. The other stuff got cut. I didn't want to remember his words sandwiched in bureaucracy. It was folded, on a piece of printer paper, and it was heavy in my pocket. I folded it with care, but it picked up some wrinkles, particularly at the corners, probably from the keys in my pocket. I couldn't believe I was about to show her. It felt so wrong. Maybe it felt like I was showing some kind of confidential case evidence. We advisors were bred not to share that kind of information. No, that wasn't it, though. At least a part of it was that it was immensely personal, and I wasn't always comfortable sharing the deepest stuff. I had actually given thought to going. It sounded insane. I was vulnerable, and I didn't want her judging me for that.

When I pulled it from my pocket, it was a rash reminder that the day was not just a dream. I unfolded it myself to look one last time. It brought my eyes to mist.

The words didn't fill more than a small section of the page. She flipped it over to see for sure that the rest wasn't on the back.

"How did it happen?" she asked, not wanting to address what she'd read. Actually, it was a bit of a relief. Maybe it was so absurd that there was no way it wasn't just some desperate offer on the table.

"They didn't tell me."

"Any idea why?" She meant why he did it. I just sort of pursed my lips and shook my head. If I could see myself there, staring, I could only describe the look I gave as vacant. She knew. She gave me my space, but not before a familial embrace on her way by. We left the dishes on the table that night.

❖

Midnight passed before I could settle myself to bed. She wasn't awake long; she was getting tired. The sheets were crisp. I must have woken her trying to find the cool side of the pillow. She didn't wake all the way, but just enough to nuzzle up and tell me she was sorry. Her belly was warm. I felt my boy kick, and I could tell that she was smiling. "Daddy, you can't go to Japan," she said, making her voice small, but still heavy with sleep. "Maybe someday," in her own soft voice. "Maybe someday."

I didn't have the heart to tell her.

CHAPTER THREE
A CAMPUS RESPONSE

When I left in the morning, she was still asleep. The ride in was an anxious one. Normally, I would have been calling up my schedule and checking emails on my phone in the backup at the clover leaf, but I couldn't be bothered. Talk radio was humming in the background, but I couldn't get my mind off of Min. I had slept on it, barely, but I really wanted to go. A burning desire about making that trip was eating me alive. It was against every bit of my training, every rule the college had, and not to mention everything going on at home. I couldn't leave her to go there, could I?

I went the long way around, by his res hall. There were remnants of a candle vigil all over the parking spaces in front. The handicapped spot was covered over in chalk. His friends filled it with Totoros and chibis, R's, I's, and P's, rainbows, a few kanji, and other ways they wanted to remember him. Sometimes I was overly aware of the little details, like, wasn't it rude that they colored the handicapped spot? But when I thought it through, that was the one that usually wasn't occupied, so I guess it worked. They meant well. I could tell which ones his close friends drew. They were the most colorful. He would say that he wanted to show me more of his drawings someday, but "School comes first, Mr. Peter." From what I understand, at least from the anime club secretary, he was getting pretty good. Even what I saw early on was impressive. I used to hear about how rich his family must have been. Not because of how well dressed he was, or how many PlayStation games he had, but because he had almost every color Copic.

The Campus Center was quiet. It was still before the first class of the morning. Ron was running the vacuum downstairs. He had his headphones in, but he always made a point to wave. I didn't see Min at the cafe yesterday morning. He was usually there, but not always. At the time, I guess I didn't think anything of it. That morning, it was painful that he wasn't there. The normal lady at the coffee stall was, though. She must have just found out. I tried to wave, and share a sorry glance, but she ran off into the back room in tears. That was the kind of day it was going to be.

The red light was on. It was taunting me. So small, but it was screaming like a siren. The whole room seemed to glow red before I flipped on the overhead incandescents. With a snap of a switch and high little hum, I shed light on a lot of reminders, like the Hokusai, the project piles I couldn't get moved yesterday, my little samurai sword letter opener - a gift from him - and that damned red light.

The last thing I wanted to hear was one of his parents on a voicemail. What would I say to them? Could I even call them back right away with the time difference? I'm not very good at those conversations. I don't ever want to be very good at those conversations. Even though my heart was broken, and pounding, I had to check. I could have crawled inside of myself. I'm not sure why I would have preferred to travel halfway around the world, to a place I've never been, that speaks a language I don't know, to have that conversation in person, but I was terrified for them to call.

The first message was a hang up. Deniability. Second, Donna from the Dean's Office. Freeman's called a meeting and we were to "make every effort to attend." That meant to cancel anything else and be there, though he probably wouldn't. The meeting was scheduled to take place in 20 minutes. There was probably a calendar invite, but I didn't even bother turning on my computer.

"Suzanne, would you please cancel my 8:30 and 9:30 appointments? If I end up taking longer, I'll email you." She wasn't in yet, so I left it on a sticky in the middle of her monitor. If she texted, I would have sent her one, but she turns her computer on before the coffee machine, or that's where I would have posted it. We knew because she told us almost every morning which ones took longer to get going. She's a sweetheart. I wish I could have gotten them to replace her computer.

Seeing everyone move about the quad, coffee in hand, bags slung on one shoulder, like nothing happened was eerie. I knew that the whole world wasn't going to stop, but I wondered if they even knew. And if they did, would he be more to them than the "Asian kid in the wheelchair."

The meeting that morning was about branding a campus response. It should have happened yesterday. Around the table were all of the key players. Except for Freeman. Someone from his office executed the agenda and he would be given minutes. In all honesty, he didn't need to be there, but it would have been a welcome gesture. More than anyone else in that room, I felt that it was my student they were talking about. Sometimes it's hard not to take things personally. For instance, the Bursar was clear that no refund monies would be paid. That was damn near the first order of business. The Dean of Student's Office had already handled outreach to the family and was going to work with whomever was in possession of the body to coordinate shipping him back. That's another saying that didn't sit right. It sounded so mechanical. Who gets into *that* line of work?

Residence Life was in the room. They were supposed to key the shipping company in so his belongings could be packed and sent home. If it was just a drive away, I would have almost felt compelled to offer and take it all myself. Imagine what any one of them would have said if they knew what I was thinking.

Counseling was there for a brief training on how we should be grief counseling. Good thing, because I met with his dozen or so closest classmates and friends already. I wonder who talked to the roommate who found him...

Min was Buddhist. His parents, from what I learned in that meeting, are Christian. Interesting. The Director of Interfaith knew him well. She speculated on a Christian burial back home, for what it was worth to that group, and knew that wouldn't have been what he wanted. She would hold a small prayer meeting. That was all. Her center had special permission to burn candles and incense in a campus building, during certain hours. Those and some flowers would accompany a small picture during one of the coming activities periods. It didn't feel like enough.

Those people were passing around marching orders, tidying up a list of loose ends so that the campus could move forward. It certainly needed to be done. I wanted to scream. We aren't supposed to get attached. Maybe it was the son of my own on the horizon, or maybe he was from a place that intrigued me, or that he was the last person I'd ever expect... Whatever it was, he had me. If I said two words in there, they were "thank you," on the way out. When I left that room, though, I was resolved, and if I gained anything, it was a timeline. I could only speculate on services. Unfortunately, those dates were between the coming registration and final exams.

In the world of advising, as far as time off goes, those are what we call "blackout days." You hold group advising sessions with the flu, review program audits through migraines and bloody noses, proctor exams on your anniversary. You probably won't believe me, but I knew an advisor, once, who was asked to move their wedding date. To think time off for travel would be approved, one would be sorely mistaken. And a "college delegate" wasn't on the Dean's list. That meeting washed our hands of him, but I wasn't ready to let him go alone.

Thankfully I had Suzanne cancel that second meeting, and through a happy accident, my student appointment before lunch called to reschedule. For the rest of my morning, I looked back and forth between airfare and savings, rental cars and credit cards, hotels and due dates. It was going to take either a miracle, a lie, or someone at home that was as crazy as I was feeling, as understanding as the woman I married, and as forgiving as I ever needed her to be.

It was Wednesday. There was an aisle seat on the Saturday flight to San Francisco International Airport with my name on it.

CHAPTER FOUR
HERE I AM

Fast food, again, and I put my hands on as big an iced tea as I could order. I should have been more excited, but I was nervous. Snacks helped. She was going to kill me, and rightfully so. What the hell was I thinking? By then, I was surprised she hadn't called already. She checks the statement, surely she would have noticed that much missing. I should have talked to her about this first. I probably should have talked to my boss about it first, too. What the hell was I thinking?!

There was a Yoshida Brothers disc in the center console; one of their traditional albums; Hishou. I love the fusion stuff, too, but I felt that just their two shamisen were more fitting for where my mind was wondering. If for nothing else, it was calming. I was invested, now, with real money. That was the cresting over the first big arch on the old wooden coaster. The rest of the turns and twists ahead were going to happen, whatever they may have been. To their performance of Japanese standards, I tried to account for them all.

Most importantly, I was going to have to have the conversation at home. That was the first big plunge. I don't like that weightless feeling. This thing was either going to crash at the bottom, or be sent soaring. The uncertainty of which was almost too much to handle after the last clack. Somewhere along the way, things may get looped over and turned upside down at work, there would undoubtedly be the fun, adventurous bit in the middle, leading up to the gut wrenching flat spin to finish things off in the end. One other thing I didn't share about myself: I hate roller coasters.

It was becoming very real. I started to blot in some of the other small details, things by no manner would be easy to make happen. For one, I didn't even have a passport. If I learned anything from the second Karate Kid movie - that one was my favorite one, by the way - it was when Mr. Miyagi was able to get a passport with a next day plane ticket. That meant more money, but the thing I was sweating was the time off to go to wherever it is you got a rush passport. I'd need to get a picture taken, too, unless they did that all there.

Our street was on a sleepy corner of a shady old neighborhood. Most of the houses were two or three family homes, and most were filled with relatives. I would bet that the neighbors three doors down heard the gravel crunch under my tires when I pulled in that evening. She knew I was home. That was a conversation I wasn't looking forward to having. I didn't run right in. It would have been a beautiful night to sit outside, but I just stayed in the car. For how many minutes, I don't remember, but dinner was probably getting cold.

She was a good cook, but mostly a quick one. A lot of meals were *a'la minute*, and they were usually fantastic, but the air was roasted with fatty bits and crispy skin, slow roasted potatoes, and about the finest of things to walk in and smell: gravy. She was apologizing for the fight and the table was set with wine glasses and candles and I felt like a shit. Isn't it always the case, when you walk in on your defenses, thinking you've done wrong, knowing you've spent nursery money to chase a dream, that you're met with an unearned sweetness?

"Hey," she said. "I'm glad you're home. It's almost ready." She was leaned in and basting, or pricking the skin over a fleshy part to take a final temp. My head started hurting. "Do you want to pour wine? How was your day?" Her doctor said that she could have a little wine every now and then. *Everything in moderation*, she'd say. Every time I poured a bit for her, no more than a splash, I remembered that. Moderation. What a way to live...

"Sure, but just a taste for you two," I said, accepting a kiss I didn't feel I had coming to me. "And my day was... Interesting. We need to talk."

We need to talk. Are there four words more clichéd? But I said them. And I meant them. She didn't react. At least not in a way that suggested she knew what I just sank into my flight of fancy. I couldn't have honestly answered if I was going for me or for Min. Not then anyways, though I'm certain about that answer now.

We were having a lot of "we need to talk's," what with the baby coming. For one, day care, at least the place near my office, cost more than rent. We didn't have an extra "more than rent" lying about. If we did, it was only one or two, certainly not monthly. She asked me every week what I thought was going to be best for her schedule. We had family near, and they could help, but I was avoiding having any sort of real and grown up conversations about real and grown up changes we were going to be making in a few weeks' time. For all she knew, I was ready to start those conversations. I suppose I should've been. Maybe this seems like some grand metaphor for running from all of that, but I really did buy the tickets...

I stepped into the ring like I'd seen my father do, with a "head-of-the-household" charge. Not overly bullish, and not underly, like testing new ice with a toe to see if the pond was walkable, but with enough muscle to say *here I am, these are my britches, and they're quite big*. This is what I said: "I needed to spend some money." Like it was my decision to make; the *man's decision*. My voice rang of *and we're not talking lunch for the office*, or even *a set of snow tires*. I put enough punch in there with hopes of not having to justify against such examples. I wore it as comfortably as a wet undershirt.

"How much?" she asked, maneuvering pots to the sink so she could heave the roaster up to the counter. I should have offered to do the lifting, if for nothing more than leverage against the bomb I was dropping. My head wasn't on right, I guess.

She took it better, or maybe it was worse, in hindsight, than I expected. There wasn't any throwing, and that was a good thing. That was the first thing I was worried about. There wasn't shouting, either; there was internalizing. Then there was a very well measured "on what?"

I like to think through these conversations before they happen. One or two of at least eleven different arguments I had in my head on the highway were built on a defense to those two words. In none of them did I backpedal like I did for real. She knew me so well, and I could see she was reading me again. That's where I get myself into trouble.

"Min," I said, sheepishly, almost shaping his name into a question. Who was I to stand behind him like that? I swallowed hard and I went in for a bigger bite. She was waiting. "I told you about what happened. And I told you about his letter," I said, conducting, as best I could. But here comes the lie. "I did a lot of soul searching about this, and I talked to the Dean, well, my Dean, you know the one, she's the one we met in the elevator the last time you came down for lunch... Anyways, she thinks that the college should send a representative. We would do the same for a domestic student. Do you remember I went for Ryan?" He was the one from the car accident.

"Wait, you're not planning on going, are you?" I think that was just rhetoric. After all, I led with how much I already spent. Well, I didn't say *exactly* how much, more implied how much.

"I have to," I said. I really didn't want to shoulder any blame, and pointing to the bosses was a low hanging fruit.

"Can you carve this, please?" She always asked me to carve the bird.

Actually, I take pride in splitting down the breast, keeping the crispy skin on each slice, which is as much a product of good honing as it is good cutting, and sectioning down the wings and legs. This bird was particularly juicy, and the lemons and thyme under the breastbones smelled enough to make my mouth water. We didn't say much else that wasn't chicken related until we sat.

Parsnips were just out at the farmer's market down the street, and they were roasted just perfect, all sticky and browning. She cooked the potatoes nearly as well as her mother did. That's not a slight; I think my mother-in-law is part wizard. The gravy kicked things off. She didn't make that nearly as well as my mother, but hell, with gravy on the table you can't lose. She asked if there was anyone else that could go, and not if I could pass the gravy. I said that there wasn't, and I did anyways.

"Don't they know that we're having a baby? I mean... Japan?! You can't tell me that this is something they just do. They just send advisors overseas? You always say that there aren't enough advisors." I nodded and took it all in.

"Apparently when the family is a major gift giver they do. The family is on board with receiving a rep from the college. Supposedly they were going to ask," I said. Those were lies two and three. The first bit actually was true. They don't give up on donor families just because their kid died.

"And they're paying for this?" she asked. Here comes four.

"Yes. Every penny."

What was I doing? For all I knew, I was going to lose my job for going, and again, rightfully so. I had no business speaking on behalf of the college over there. Stewardship was not my job or forte. They certainly weren't paying for anything.

"So why did you have to spend that kind of money? Couldn't they book it themselves?"

I gave her some bullshit answer about how non-profits operate and reimbursements and so on that really didn't make much sense, but she believed that they would invest in sending someone if there was more money on the line.

"When is this even supposed to happen?" I cleared my throat and then swallowed down some wine. "Saturday."

She gave pause, as expected. The only thing I could hear was flatware and cutlery squealing across china.

"How long?"

"Well I think it's about six hours to California."

"No, I mean how long will you be gone?" I guess I knew what she meant, but I tended to get practical, maybe even a little pedantic, when my head wasn't on right.

"It should be a short trip," I said. "I'm only there for a few days. I'll be gone a week." I tried to make myself sound worldly and well-travelled, but don't forget, I didn't have a passport. She gave an either accepting or slightly defeated sort of nod. I did what I could to bring the food back into the limelight. It really was quite good.

Sometimes couples discuss such things, and sometimes it's left at that. She didn't owe me the satisfaction of her blessing. I knew I wasn't going to get one. I knew she was going to be upset; I leveraged it. It was about as upset as I wanted her to be; as upset as I needed her. There was no way around it, so I shared the blame on a lie, deflected what I could, and tried to just get through a meal. After that, it would be smooth sailing. You learn to not only deal with what you can get away with, but how to live with the way you managed it. It didn't feel great.

Anyway, the rest of dinner was quiet, and then we watched a movie like we normally would, but I spent most of the time online trying to find out what else I needed. I had to ask if she could borrow her father's garment bag for me. Of all people, he was one I didn't want to tell that I was going. We borrowed it when we honeymooned, and it was just the right size. I suppose I could have bought my own, but in some weird way, I convinced myself it was money saving. Spending a few thousand to save two hundred isn't a sound financial platform, especially not with a baby coming.

All I could think of while trying to sleep that night was that I didn't speak a word of Japanese. That, and I still didn't have a passport.

CHAPTER FIVE
THIS LITTLE LIE OF MINE

Had I known of the Boston Passport Authority's 24/7 call line to schedule the appointment, I may have slept a little more soundly. Getting a passport appointment wasn't necessarily all that kept me up, however. I was nervous to call out. Not only was it a really tough day for me schedule-wise, and I hated missing student appointments, but I hated lying. Unfortunately, I've seen them fire people for less, and they didn't much like advisors taking time off. I should've been more upset about lying to my wife. More than anything was that this little lie of mine had the power to kick off something grand and destructive. But don't they all?

It was a nice morning, I could tell. The room was mostly dark. My leg was warm for the width of about a hand or so under the blanket because of the strip of sun peeking across. That bit of brighter-than-normal was a reminder that I forgot to set my alarms. There was usually no need because I never woke later than starting time, even on the weekend, so I could still call in before they started answering phones. It was the kind of morning to otherwise be swallowed whole by blankets that were never more comforting.

The phone said three missed calls before I saw the time. The buzz announced the voicemail that I didn't want to hear or respond to. My heart hit my throat and I jumped up when I saw that it was actually closer to ten.

What is it about calling out that reverts you back to your grade school self? I suppose it was part of the drill back then. There were rules, and you had to follow them if you wanted to stay home sick. It was like getting a day off on a technicality. Here were the big four in my house: fever, pooping, puking, sore throat. If you hit one or more on that list, it was an automatic on-the-couch, "Price is Right" kind of day.

We went to school with the sniffles. The kid from up the street would drop off any homework. He never did his own, so I was always amazed that mine made it back safely. We learn those rules and they stay with us so we know when it's ok to stay down, and then we pass them on to our kids when they're in school, so they'll know.

Those are the rules. They stay with us when we're older, though we change them a bit, and they're on more of an honor system. *I have a tummy ache* doesn't cut it anymore, but it didn't cut it then, either. Mom needed to see you hurl, but as soon as you did...even though we learn in college, when you puke, you feel better. She was the boss then; imagine if the Dean needed to see me puke?

One of the things we learn is how to take those grade school conventions and grow them up a bit; put a tie on them, if you will. Like, *something didn't agree with my stomach* means you have the shits, or *I think it's a bug*, or *I can't keep anything down* means the pukes. Sometimes you could get away with a migraine, maybe even a sinus headache, but not during pre-registration. The Dean got those so she sympathized. Sometimes.

It was the little red light all over again. This time, it was a little red circle in the corner of the phone with the number one inside. I had one message and it was, sure enough, from the Dean's assistant. I didn't need to check to know that. She's an up talker, and she learned a bit about passive aggression working in that office.

"Hi Peter, this is Cheryl from Dean Samson's office in Student Development." Why she introduced herself that way was beyond me. We were far more familiar than that. "When you get in this morning, please call Dean Samson at your earliest convenience. She has a question about when you plan to reschedule your appointments from this morning. We will talk to you soon. Thank you."

There were a few students that they watched carefully. Some were students of concern, some were students of important alumni, and one had his name on the side of my building. None of them were on my calendar that morning. I was a little over an hour late, half when the first call came. It's funny, I was actually offended that she didn't ask how I was feeling, or assume some horrific emergency. It hurt that I could have been the kind of sick that meant not making it to a phone and their worry was some bottom line. That aisle seat was looking more comfortable by the minute.

I had to call right away, but there was some basic prep work to be done. First, you have to twist up some tissue to plug your nose. What I was going to claim had nothing to do with the sinuses, but they're listening for how sick you sound. Next you have to practice your best moany sounds. You don't want to work that one out live. It's all in the throat. Last, and certainly not least, this is like a phone interview; you need to dress the part. In a phone interview, they say to wear a suit and tie so you feel ready and presentable. Picture, if you will, what would be the most appropriate attire, and would afford the easiest access, for when you're shitting your brains out. For me, that's boxers and an old tank top. True story, I have a colleague who swears that he wipes himself raw before he calls, so it "feels right." That is what we call "method." Ferris Bueller, eat your heart out. But the point is, you want to feel low when you call the Dean's office, and you hope that Cheryl picks up.

"Student affairs," she said. "Cheryl speaking." No *how may I help you.*

"Hi Cheryl," I moaned. "This is Peter."

"Oh," she said. "You sound sick."

"I am. I'm sorry, but I'm not going to be able to make it in...today." It came out kind of like I was moving a couch. "I... Something didn't agree with me, I was up all night. And I can't keep anything down."

Yes. Both ends. I went there. This was as unorthodox a move as Schwartz skipping triple dare and going right in for the triple dog in "A Christmas Story." There was a bit of a pause while she deciphered my code. It was the only pleasant way to tell her they didn't want me around in my shitting, puking, moany, stuffed up condition, whatever ailment that may have been. For not too long of a pause she was gone, but it was just enough for a wave to grab the Dean's attention and for her to mouth *it's Peter.*

"You sound awful, dear," she said. "I think there's something going around. Were you going to call Suzanne to reschedule your appointments?" *What nerve*, I thought. *I'm far too sick for that.*

"No," I said. "I will try, though" nearly blubbering. It was one of my finest performances.

"Well we need to get you better," she said. Happily she couldn't see what I was doing at the remedies she rattled off.

"Thank you... Cheryl." I practically coughed her name out. "I think I need to sleep, but I'll talk to you soon." She was saying something about me calling the Dean when I hung up the phone to call Suzanne.

Suzanne seemed to care a hell of a lot more that I sounded so under. I wanted to tell her, I really did, but if I really were to go, they would get it out of her, and I'd hate to see her in any kind of trouble. They elbow people out with the best of them. The admins were busy for sure, but most of them were buffered from the politics of the Deans and VPs. I tried hard to keep it that way for her. I would miss her the most.

The next call, with visions of Miyagi-style same day passports and jet set advising, was over to the passport authority. I explained as best I could what was going on in my head, which felt screwed on righter than it had in some time, at least after hearing what I had to say. They answered every question I had, too. Like, no, they couldn't take a passport pic, and yes, I would have one same day. I didn't mind that my call was being monitored for training purposes, even though I knew I was probably put on some sort of watch list for needing a last minute way out of the country. If they knew my Dean, though, they wouldn't have blamed me.

They were wonderful about scheduling my appointment, only problem was that it was for half past eight. First thing. The *next* morning.

I lived far enough away from campus that I could shop confidently for my trip, knowing I'd not be caught. I tended to be a nervous shopper anyways, and left Target with a whole host of things I didn't actually need, like luggage tags, bag locks, a travel neck pillow, travel-sized toothbrushes, whatever the hell that meant, and so on. The plan was to hit the Hudson news in the terminal for a new book. They had the one I wanted, the new Gaiman book, of course, but I didn't trust myself to save it for the flight. They didn't have the specific power adapter that I needed, though, so I bought the whole set. There was no way I would travel without a phone charger. My father-in-law loved that stuff, so I figured the rest of them could be payment for letting me borrow his bag, which I had to go and pick up.

When I stopped by, he was out on his run, which was just as well, because I was nervous to tell him. He knew that it was a business trip, and he always liked to know where. He usually knew someone who owned a pizza shop, or a friend of a cousin, or some other nice Greek man, but I doubted as much for Japan. He gets anxious; he may have worried too much about who would have driven her if his daughter's water broke. That wouldn't happen, I was sure of it. She was still six weeks out.

She was off again that night, but she'd be working the overnight on Friday, so I wanted to return the favor and cook her something special. Japanese felt about right, and hopefully wouldn't stir the wrong kinds of emotions. There was a great little Japanese market in the center of town. None of this was planned, of course. I just sort of found myself wandering that way.

That was a place where I shopped often enough to know which aisle was for rice and which for candy and Pocky and the like. Something about that day showed me a little slice of where I was hoping to head; it was like seeing through a looking glass.

There wasn't a Japan that existed for me as a walkable, living, breathing place yet. I longed to cement the streets and back alleys in my head. A further off dream was to roam north and south of the cities, to see mountains and ryokans; places preserved by time and tradition. All I knew was filed away in a place I liked to visit, mostly alone. It was filled with ramen and sushi, movies of samurai and monsters, colorful tattoos and painted Shōgun, saké, tea, plum wine, mochi, and the juxtaposed aesthetics of a bold robotic future with a silken and lacquered feudal past. But somewhere behind the Torii gates and neon signs, there was a people, just as juxtaposed, and every bit as beautiful and intriguing. I saw them there buying greens and rice, fresh fruits, steam buns, and bottles of tea. They were comforts from home, the special things that the supermarket couldn't get, and not just novelties. This place tied me to them by bringing us all a little closer to that place.

I knew most of what they were selling, but I spent a little more time, looking closer, trying to find something between the lines. Maybe I thought I was going to learn some secret and illuminating cipher that would let me in on the other end of my flights. While there was hope, there were just bottles and boxes that couldn't be read. I did find a good bottle of mirin, a kind of sweetened cooking saké, which is half of what makes a good teriyaki base. I knew that good mirin mixed with good tamari, a kind of soy sauce, was half of what made a good broth for gyudon, a simmered beef rice bowl, which is one of my wife's favorite Japanese dishes. By attempting to have an immersive shopping epiphany, I, at the very least, had stumbled upon dinner. Dinner is a very good thing to stumble upon.

They had everything else I needed: the shaved beef, though they didn't have wagyu, the onions, though they didn't have Vidalia, rice, of which they had the best of the best, and the fixings for a decent dashi. I'm not sure Vidalia onions would be used in a proper gyudon, but they tended to be my favorite because of the extra bit of sweetness they bring. If I spent ten minutes choosing the soy, it was thirty pouring over the dashi mix. I had seen the Iron Chefs make their dashi, and I'm not talking about the reboot American version, I'm talking the thoroughbreds from the original show. They always shaved their bonito from a block kept in some secret wooden chest that looked like something a sea captain would keep for storing treasure. Their fish shaving blades were honed and papered by heralded blade smiths and passed down through the generations. I like to think that they may have even been used to slice the flakes that fed samurai. It was all quite dramatic, of course, and I couldn't find any of it. They did have prepackaged fish flakes sold in something like tea bags, though. On the back of the package, everything was in Japanese, save for the little sticker that lost most of the instructions in translation. You could only tell the flavor by the little cartoon mushrooms or set of spring onions that danced with the little cartoon fish at the top of the label. I chose what, as far as I could gather, was plain.

I found myself some Pocky, a pack of mango Hi-Chews and some flavored marshmallows, as well as a bag of the little rock candies that Rin - Lin in the Enlish dub - feeds to the soot sprites in Spirited Away. I couldn't resist. While I waited behind a pair of old women who were chatting with the register attendant, probably about my candy selections, I wondered how sacrilegious a tea bag full of dashi mix really was. They had a few packs of the same when they got to emptying their baskets, so at least that made me smile.

Everywhere I looked, I took a mental picture. The way they all bowed slightly and respectfully after they paid, the delicate way the girl waved me forward and handled each of my items like glass, how carefully, and with two graceful hands, neatly folded, she accepted my beat up debit card... There was something there, even if only a glimmer, that made me feel a want to better myself. I felt bad that I was leaving her. The dashi didn't matter. What I would say to the Dean didn't matter. Being there for the ones that were important to me was all I could care to think of. Though I was doing right by Min, it was going to come at a great cost. There needed to be a much better conversation about this trip, and I was ready to be out all that money if it meant doing right at home. Of all the things I bought that day, a little bit of sense came free.

My least favorite, and often least successful part of cooking Japanese food is cooking perfect rice. I never seem to know how much to wash it; the water never runs clear. Every recipe seemed to be wrong about how much water to use, too, even though I had one of the expensive "fuzzy logic" rice cookers. It always ended up too toothsome or gluey, but that night, the stars aligned. I took it as a sign that everything was going to be alright.

She offered to help, but I wasn't hearing any of that. This was my turn. My broth was spot on, we had un-ruined rice, both the beef and onions were tender, and our mouths were watering. I took care to plate them up, and set out some chilled saké, just a taste, and the good chopsticks, the non-splintery, non-disposable ones. The last touch was a fried egg, sunny side up, on top of each bowl. Sweetened beef broth and runny yolk is a gift from the Gods.

Over sips of sake, after bitching about work, I threw down another version of "we need to talk." This one was a little more approachable. I said "can we talk about this thing on Saturday?" If I was going to offer not to go, I needed it to come out on my terms. If she suggested it, I probably would've put up a wall, which wouldn't have been fair for me to do. She had every right to demand I stay. She did nothing of the sort.

"This is more than just some student," she said. "I know that, and I know you know that. I've been thinking about it a lot, and you really need this. Things are going to change very soon. This sucks, and I'm sorry that it happened. It won't be easy, mostly because I'll miss you, but you should go." I read her as closely as I could. As far as I could tell, this wasn't a trap. She was pretty transparent with the pregnancy hormones. This wasn't them making her all motherly and nurturing. This was her stepping back into sixty percent.

"So listen," I said, knowing full well I should've acknowledged her huge gesture. "I was... I don't know what I was saying... this hasn't been easy... Work doesn't know, they're not sending me." You could see it on her face, the way it hit her. It was subtle, but one eyebrow dropped her into a bit of a stare. I spoke again before she could. "I'm thinking about staying. I mean...this is crazy. We're having a baby!"

"What do you mean work doesn't know? They're not sending you? We're paying for this?" I nodded, taking a bite. She wasn't done, but she took a minute to keep eating. "Aren't you gonna be in trouble?" she asked over a mouthful. "That's not like you."

"I suppose so..." I said.

"Do you think you might get fired?"

"Honestly, I really don't know. I'm supposed to go to the passport thing in the morning, but I'm thinking I should go talk to them. What am I supposed to do? I mean, I bought tickets already."

"You probably should say something. You can't just run away."

43

Man. I never thought of it that way. She knew that this job was grinding on me. I was so excited about the baby, but I was nervous. She was right, things were going to change. He was right, too, I wanted to go with everything I had. The budding father inside was sending me mixed messages. Part of him was telling me to stay and hang on to the paycheck. The other was devastated for the family that had to bury their son; especially a son as good as Min. I don't know how, but somehow she knew. She asked, in words that rocked me to my core, how I would feel if someone who knew our boy like I knew Min didn't come. I didn't answer with words, but that was where I would find courage to do what had to be done.

CHAPTER SIX
FREEMAN'S FINAL WORD

Before I knew it, I was in and out of the passport agency. Pictures were turned in, applications were filled out and filed, payment was processed, I passed through security both ways, and my documents were going to be ready to get me on a plane in the morning. I just had to be back by four to pick them up.

I called out to Dean Samson by email at about half past six that morning. No specifics, no dressed up grade school prank, no more lies. I said that Suzanne rescheduled my morning appointments and that I would be in late. I didn't say how late because I didn't know. The temptation to milk it a little was there, but I made no stops.

The commute through the city was, dare I say, almost enjoyable at that hour. It was a little after nine thirty and most of the morning rush had rushed their way to the office. It was fun to wonder where the others sharing the road with me were headed. Were they working gigs that started later? Or going home from one? Did they enjoy their jobs? How do so many people get jobs doing what they have a passion for? Did these people have jobs at all? Maybe they were headed shopping on a well-deserved Friday off? Maybe they were nervous to be going in for a small procedure they've had scheduled for months? Whatever it was, it was anything I could do to keep my mind occupied and keep my gut from getting overly anxious. Then again, what were the odds that any of them were traveling across the world to bury a student? Or heading in to their office to lay it all on the line? This was so unlike me. I was a good little worker bee. One who had taken a lot and said nothing for quite a long time. This wasn't just about Min. She was right. I couldn't just run away.

It wasn't long before back roads and traffic signals pulled me from my storytelling and back to the very real direction in which I was headed. In the same spot, almost every day, past the last neighborhood and by the golf course, my stomach started tumbling. Why anyone went to a job that made them that kind of nervous almost every day was beyond me, but this was a different band of butterflies. I felt my face flush and my stomach hollow. It felt worse to tell the truth about taking time off than it did to lie. Maybe that was because we were always threatened with replacements. "Everyone wants to be an advisor," she'd say. "I have a hundred resumes on my desk..." At lunch we'd repeat those lines, mocking her, especially when it was such a heavy day. They knew we were a good team, and if she had a hundred, they weren't worth a damn next to any from that group, who are all on to bigger and better places now.

The class schedule was ingrained. I was the kind of advisor who knew that on a Friday morning at about twenty after ten, which of those in line at the cafe should have been in Writing and which should have been with their tutor. Whether that was something to be proud of or not, it was what they turned me into. I didn't sign up to police attendance at "High School 2.0." Min was why I signed up. He was the student who gave a shit. He needed help and he knew it, but he didn't brandish his entitlement or forget to check his privilege. Min played his part and he was grateful for what parts others played. He left an echo in that building that too few of the others heard.

I slipped past the morning skippers; they were hoping I didn't notice. The office was as busy as usual, but Suzanne still noticed that I was wearing jeans. The first thing I saw, before I flipped the switch, was a small, burning red bulb. A feeling like he just died and I was expecting messages from his family resurged. That settled down. It was probably just the Dean.

My objective wasn't on my calendar, or waiting for me in the reception area, though I could hear at least three students asking if they could see me. My objective was on my desk and bookcase. This was a soft way out. Kind of like the opposite of easing in before a big grand opening. I had my backpack, and I started filling it with my picture frames and action figures. My diplomas were a little too big to fit in that

47

bag. My alma mater *really* wanted people to know where their graduates came from. That would have been too suspicious anyways. I also had a few small things from my peer tutors that I cherished.

There certainly were things about that place that I would miss, and I knew then that I was going to miss them. Aside from a handful of students, like Min, that made the work worthwhile, and some colleagues that would become friends for life, there were the peer tutors. We charged students for professional tutors. "Fee for service" they called it. They could require the conditional admits to take it, but they couldn't all afford to. Sometimes Admissions would waive half of the fee, and look like the hero, but we all knew that was the strategy to begin with. It's like putting your house on the market: you ask high with hopes of still coming in over what you owe with a counter to the serious buyer's bid. Those of us working to scratch the intrinsic itch wanted services for all. That's where my proposal for peer tutors came from.

This place had a peer tutoring program before. When the fee-based stuff picked up, it took a back burner. When I asked for money to revive it, it was denied, but I was *encouraged* to try anyways, and if it proved viable, they would provide some funding. So I did. And they didn't. I wound up being able to get it on the books for credit for the tutors, which appealed to some. Mostly, I attracted a really solid, albeit small, group of international students. Together we accomplished a fairly respectable offering.

From some of their cultures, gift giving was encouraged. Small tokens, as a gesture of respect, were given to favorite professors, and on occasion, a favorite admin. The first of such gifts that I received was a pair of small masks from a student from Korea. She explained that they were for the Hahoe Mask Dance. I always meant to research that. Regardless, they were truly memorable, and they were coming with me.

Suzanne popped in to check how I was doing, and she caught me packing some things. She had a way of asking me things without actually asking. "Oh," I said. "I'm just redecorating a bit. Did I miss anything important?"

"No, but you don't look so good," she said. What a thing to say to someone faking an illness. She had updates for who got rescheduled to when, but I didn't care. It didn't sound like any major gaskets were blown. Next in the bag were my desk clock and business card holder.

"Ok," she said "what is going on?"

"I'm not sure yet," I said, though I was plenty sure. "There may be some changes, but nothing to worry too much about. I have to go meet with the Dean this..." she cut me off.

"She's been calling. She asked me if you seemed sick on Wednesday and how you sounded on the phone." Of course she would call to gather intel. *Shouldn't she be busier?* I thought. The look I gave her when I shook my head was telling, I suppose.

"Not her," I said. "Freeman." *He'll listen before she does*, I wanted to say.

"Oh," she said, in a guttural sort of way. He had a bit of a reputation, but he had a lot more integrity, and he could pull rank on Samson.

I hired Suzanne. I felt responsible, in a way, for keeping her out of the political stuff. *Always bitch up*, I say. The thing I'd feel the worst about would be leaving her to their mercy, and who knew how closely they'd groom my replacement from their resume surplus. When all was said and done, I was sure to have a chat with her on how to toughen up, and a little dirt on them goes a long way.

On a slower day, I wouldn't have been able to get in and get out without more of an inquisition. She was just too busy to *really* read between the lines. Mid-term grade checks were in, and they had a way of lighting some fires. "I'm headed over there, and I'm still not feeling great so I'm going to head home after my meeting. Thank you," I said." For everything." She was half into answering a call.

"Have a nice weekend," she said, cupping the receiver. "And feel better!"

❖

Freeman's admin, Donna, was far more professional than Cheryl or Suzanne. She was cut from executive cloth, and she didn't make you feel inspected while you were waiting. The clacks on her keys were noticeably faster, too. We didn't, however, know anything about her kids or book club or husband's bowling team. I guess that's the tradeoff.

The Dean's schedule was usually tight, and it was usually held under lock and key. Odd, though, how one could barge in and demand a sit down and find that his afternoon could be moved around so easily. Either there was some fluff, or she was just that good. The latter was more likely. And I didn't so much barge in and demand as I snuck in his door, nearly panicked and left, and told her that I'd like to see if he had just a moment when she asked how she could help. Funny, it didn't seem like she even recognized me.

Dean Freeman was a prick. He was good at what he did, and was someone that, when needed, I was happy to have in my corner. It was certainly clear why the college wanted him as their talking head at open houses and orientations. He was always on point, always at full tilt, and his word was final no matter who else was in the room. Freeman wasn't just clean cut, he was razor cut. More like "could have been a navy pilot" cut. He had two boys, both blonde, a chocolate lab, and a knockout, kindergarten teacher for a wife. He played softball and coached lacrosse. He also taught there as well as online classes at two different Research I institutions, and was the head of more than one professional organization. He had a watch that was worth more than half my year's salary. This was the kind of guy that was on pace to be the youngest college president in the history of higher ed. in New England. Yet somehow, he seemed outside of the normal politics. He drank no one's Kool Aide but his own, and he took no shit from advisors who complained about needing more staff, because really, he probably could have done our jobs with his eyes closed. That made him a prick.

I had very few interactions with Freeman, so this meeting may have come as a surprise. I was not under his direct chain of command, so to speak, other than him being one of the division heads. The last time we spoke, he let me know about Min. It was cold hard math to him, or so it seemed. I had been wondering what it made him feel, and I wanted to see if he let it show. Students die. There has to be campus protocol for that. He didn't have a job description, but all of those sorts of policies were his doing. I needed someone who lived and operated between the bureaucracies at that place, and if that person existed, he would be out in about five minutes.

Five minutes may have never passed so slowly for me in that town. Every second that ticked off the clock slugged like iron. All of the moisture in my mouth sucked away, out through my palms. I searched high and low inside for a reason to get up and go. It wasn't like I was going to ask him for permission. He wasn't the one who punched my time card. He sure as hell wasn't picking up balls I was about to drop. Scary as it was, it felt like the right thing to do.

Screw this, I thought, and I pushed against the arm rests to stand. *I'm outta here.* And at that, four minutes and fifty seven seconds into my sentence, his door clicked and he stepped out precisely by five. "Cahill," he called, like a coach, but with a bit more spit and polish than from the field, "come in." He reached out to shake hands.

There's a lot you can tell from a man's handshake. Now, I didn't grow up in a military home, and I've never called my father "Sir," but that doesn't mean he didn't teach me the right way. You shake firm for one solid pump and you look a person dead in the eyes. Some people, like me, try to match firmness to a person's size, especially if I've never been in said contest with them. I ease up a bit when I meet a student's librarian of a mother, and I turn it way up for his linebacker of a father. You learn, in time, that some men will go for the kill no matter who they're shaking against. This was Freeman, and don't think I forgot. The success or failure of this meeting depended largely on where I met him in that moment. He was slick; he had wiped his hand dry already before he passed his threshold. I made a point of leaving behind as much sweat as I could on the upholstered armrests. Luckily he caught me mid lift, or else I'd have given him something to slip on. Not a chance. Not this time.

"Sit," he said. "Coffee?" He had a Keurig in his office, but it didn't agree with my stomach.

"No, thank you," I said.

"Boy, Cahill, you look like hell." What was it with people saying that? I felt just fine, aside from the belly splitting nerves and the thumping in my temples. "What can I do you for?" he asked. He was in his Friday gear, which still meant a suit, but he didn't have on a tie. His shirt was starched, though, and it surely had his anagram somewhere, maybe on the pocket. Or was it the cuff of his right sleeve? I didn't pause for long, but it was enough for him to ask another question. "How are your students handling it?" He didn't need to say what. "How are you handling it?" he asked again. Freeman wasn't one to sit for long. He was up and about, and he headed to lean on a small sofa that sat in front of his picture window.

"I'm handling it," I said. "And that's why I've come to see you. I need your...advice." He liked that. Always did. "I'm just trying to do the right thing here, and, well, you have more experience with this stuff." The look on his brow and the tilt of his chin offered me an ear to bend, and I accepted.

I went on to tell him everything. There were things said in there I never would have told Samson. He knew about the letter. In fact, you could see him adding notes to that file mentally as I spoke. I looked for his surprise when I explained as best I could what conversations may have led Min to write it, but it wasn't there. He was good. He had me answering questions that he'd clearly formed about whether I crossed any lines with this kid. Freeman oversaw conduct as well as crisis intervention and threat assessment, and he was surely hunting down any possible liabilities. Many of his questions he didn't even have to ask; I was an open book. He almost seemed relieved. I wondered what he was thinking in the first place, but I knew he'd seen it all, and that he was paid to think that way.

I spoke passionately about what Min had to offer and about what he told me about his father. I didn't go so far as to draw connections to what forced his hand, but it was helpful to practice all the things I wanted to say. Still he

54

listened, letting me go. I knew I was giving him things he wanted to hear, but didn't know whether I was incriminating myself somehow. At at least a few details, he smiled.

There was surprise after all, however, at how matter of fact I was about my flight in the morning. I suddenly didn't feel so big in those britches, of which I was immediately and shamefully aware were made of denim. He stopped me right there. "Do your supervisors know about this," he asked, with a phone in his hand and dialed before I could answer.

"Diane," he said, not asked. Diane as in Samson. He got her on the phone. There was only one ring. At best. What a nightmare! I almost threw up in my mouth. "I'm with Peter Cahill and we need five minutes of your time." This wasn't good.

"She'll be right in," he said. There was no fumbling of the receiver. He replaced it like a surgeon when he took back his throne. He put on his conduct officer's crown again and asked if I was actually sick yesterday. This was De Niro in Meet the Parents. I promised myself no more lies, and with confidence, I shook my head the way it ought to be shaken at that question. Mum was the word on whether that would stay between the two of us. He also asked how far along my wife was, and nearly laughed when I said she was due in about six weeks.

Pleasantries for admins weren't her way. What she barked at Freeman's sounded a little like a task, and it didn't sound like she stopped for very long to deliver it before the door burst open. I could feel the eyes rolling out there, but I held mine steady because that's where Freeman was looking.

There were rumors about what has and hasn't been allowed during her "blackout dates." It was convenient because she could deny a request simply because they were against the rules, even if the rules were set by her. Even if the rules weren't exactly...legal. I guess I was about to learn firsthand.

Freeman began by explaining that I called the meeting, not him. Somehow, she was more intimidating sitting by your side and not across a desk. Even more so now that she knew I went over her head. "Peter came to me to offer assistance and discuss closure to the completed suicide case." I didn't like the way that sounded. "As you know," he continued, "there was letter left by the student requesting that Peter attend his funeral and disclose information that is of a sensitive nature to the student's family. I'm not sure that morally, professionally, or legally we can ignore his request." She shifted in her seat and looked to me as if to say *What have you done.* Freeman didn't give her a chance. "It is in the interest of the college to make this a priority." This, however surprising it was to me, was not news to which Samson wouldn't respond.

"No, I'm sorry Michael," that was Freeman's first name, "he's not going anywhere." Not only did she say it around me, but she made it clear whose pawn I was. "We are in the middle of pre-reg, and we need the numbers." Not *we need HIM* or *HE knows HIS students best and they're counting on him.* It was bottom lines. Always. Give them a little time and they'd replace us all. "These are blackout dates. That's not negotiable."

Freeman adjusted his elbow to the arm of his chair, which was well appointed with rich leather and deep set buttons. I loved that look. Budgets were tight, but the Deans' chairs were lavish. "Diane," he said, "this is an important family. If they find out about the letter and learn that..."

"They won't," she snapped, and turned to eye me with a threat. This, from a senior leader in student affairs. She was making my case for me, though. For once I could read Freeman like a book. "They have no need to know of that," she added.

I wasn't going to get a word in edgewise. At least, I hoped I didn't have to say anything. This was working out far better than I thought. They went on about stewardship, group advising, what was fair for the other advisors, whether I could be trusted to deliver the appropriate message, that she should leave that to him, and that this wasn't really "time off." They even argued over details of per diems. She didn't like that he was ready to offer me the rate that she gets. Nearing the five minute mark, which was precisely what he asked for, his word was pretty close to final. It was clear she wasn't accustomed to swallowing a pill of that size. *Only Freeman*, I thought.

"See me before you leave," she said. "It's first thing tomorrow," said Freeman. "And he'll only be gone for...what?" he asked, pointing. I said a week. At some point, I must not have noticed, he unbuttoned and folded back his cuffs. There was the watch. "A week," he repeated, letting his shrug spread apart his hands. And that was Freeman's final word.

"You're expected to be on email," said Samson. "Make sure your notes are up to date. And we *will* call if we need you." She said nothing of safe travels, no words of advice to me or condolences to Min's family. She didn't even ask if I felt better. That hurt. She was slighted and it was going to get ugly. The time off and the trip to Japan on the college's dime was one thing, but the other advisors were more likely to begrudge me her retaliation.

Freeman may have helped, but it wasn't the clean break I was hoping for. Now I was in both of their debts, and I was at Samson's beck and call. I had this grand and romantic idea of quitting in a blaze of glory to do right by my boy Min. Things didn't go according to that plan, but it was a price I was willing to pay to not have to argue for it alone. Besides, from the sounds of things, I could keep my job and not have to worry about collecting or interviews with a newborn in the house. That was money in the bank.

We shook hands again, and I met him with a rock hard grip that said all the thanks I could muster. We saw it in each other's eyes. He spoke first. "Do you know why, Pete? Because of my sons. And because of your son."

"Thank you, sir," I said. "I can't imagine what his family is going through..."

We just about ended on that note. He walked me to his door to open it and see me through. I thanked him again and he smiled. "Did you really plan your child for a semester break?" I pursed my lips and was almost too embarrassed to answer that. "Ha. It's funny, I did that too. You're a good man, Peter Cahill. A good man," he said, and he wished me safe travels and asked Donna to write down his cell number if I needed anything.

"Send me a postcard," he called, as I left his small reception area.

What a prick, huh?

CHAPTER SEVEN
FOR SO LONG AND SO FAR

Things had changed a bit since I filled my bag, but I had half a mind not to return any of it to my office. I was feeling good enough to skip the fast food and head straight home. The hour was still early, and there was no way I was finishing a day like that in the office. Besides, she was working that night and there were only a few more hours that I could see her before being away for a week. What were they going to do? Fire me?

There was no traffic heading out of town, thankfully. I minded my time so that I could get back into the city to pick up my passport. Perhaps the best plan would be to get home, get her, swing back through North Station for four, stop for a nice dinner and have her in for her shift before seven. She liked to nap around that time, so I didn't call. I just drove.

Messages, more than usual, came pouring through my phone, mostly from the other advisors. Plenty of exclamations and cusses were shared on my behalf at the expense of the Dean. Good news travels fast, and I never knew who told them about my meeting with Freeman. At least, I know it wasn't Samson.

There was a bit of a backup at the split, but enough was on my mind not to be bothered. For one, I had only ever been overseas once. Well, twice, but the first one didn't count because we were chaperoned in an English speaking country. The other time was our honeymoon. We went through security, switched airplanes in another country, ran to make a gate, and negotiated cabs and buses to get to our final landing. She spoke the language, though, which helped in ways I took for granted. The logical part of my brain, and whatever it was that made me a homebody, fought to wrestle down this new found sense of adventure.

It was after two thirty when I got home. She was still napping, but my manhandling the mailbox and stomping around the kitchen for snacks was enough. I could have been as quiet as a sneak-thief if I wanted, and sometimes I had been, but I chose the one that would give me an out if she was pissed about being woken up. She wasn't, though, and she was down for whatever I was planning. Actually, in all my running around, I wasn't as clear about the passport stuff with her as I should have been. She wanted to get hers done, too. We both got them in high school and didn't renew after the honeymoon, but she'd been talking about going back to visit her family ever since. Work was always what I blamed for not making that happen sooner. If it wasn't fall or spring blackout days, it was orientation. If it wasn't that, it was not having time during the day to get a picture taken, or get over to the post office to submit the application. It was, all of it, just bullshit. I would have much preferred barbecued octopus and an ice cold set of ouzo shots over a stack of program evaluations and a pre-packaged Caesar wrap.

On a work night, she was quick to change. Whatever scrubs were clean, and something to tie her hair up in a bun was all she really needed. Even the nicest restaurants around the hospital were welcoming to the nurses in that getup. It was hard almost anywhere to get a seat at a bar around shift change, so heading in beforehand would be perfect.

Usually, I was a bit over-anxious watching the time. By three I was antsy; five past I had the doors open; nine past, the car was started; by three eleven, I leaned on the horn. The plan was to park at the hospital with her pass and walk back over. Who knew what the bridge traffic was going to be like. The differences between the two of us could be summed up in the one little way we each approached that afternoon. The passport agency said four o'clock, and I would be dammed if I wasn't there before three fifty nine. She knew, and was banking on the fact that they closed at a quarter to five. It felt like we were always within about an hour of each other.

She hit her seat and I scattered gravel before she could get the buckle done. The little things made me so mad.

Like, when I was half out of the driveway and she asked me to go check that she locked the door, I could've screamed. By then I had at least learned that checking it was quicker. But you can't just check, you have to pantomime that it's really, truly, impossibly locked shut. She was happy, I was happy, we were off. Finally. It was seventeen past.

There's only so much you can weave with a pregnant woman in the passenger seat, at least one who's not contracting. I made it to the backup in record time, and the connector before the Zakim was loaded up already. We always argued over which way was better, but when it came time to decide, neither of us wanted to commit because we didn't want to shoulder any blame. Sometimes we tried getting off and going in through Somerville, but that was usually the worst way of all. I had already passed that exit, though. Ninety three looked fine up to the tunnel, but there was no telling what the roads around Faneuil looked like. We hopped over into the connector backup and I took it on the chin. When she knew I was anxious, she didn't try to mess with the radio. Those were the little things I appreciated so much. My way of acknowledging thanks was to let her pick where we'd eat. That usually never worked out like I planned.

Finally, we were parked at about three after four. I didn't know whether to try to make it back and get my passport or just admit myself right there with chest pains. I asked her to waddle over to Whole Foods and wait for me there. She took the umbrella and I took off running.

We spent so much time in the West End that I knew all the shortcuts behind all the condo buildings. Since we drove through North Station, I had a sense of which lights were the busiest, and those would be the best places to cross. All told, I couldn't say in exactly how many minutes I made it because I was heaving like I hit Heartbreak Hill. I was on her time, now, and I wasn't happy about it, but they weren't closed yet. I hated when she was right.

There must've only been a few minutes to spare by the clock watchers behind the counter when I poured myself inside. I was standing between them and their weekend. In a federal office, I knew that that was a battle I was going to lose, so I needed to be quick. It looked like they were gathering supplies and tucking them away. Everything was riding on this. They weren't open on the weekend, so I could have been screwed out of tomorrow's tickets. I started running through the conversations with the airline in my head. And I supposed the body wouldn't have been back yet, and I *could* fly out on Monday and still try to make it for services. *They're a full day ahead of us*, I thought, and I struggled to figure out if that was in my favor or not. I would at least lose out on catching my bearings, easing off the jet lag, and...seeing a bit of Tokyo. They couldn't do this to me! And she would never hear the end of it...

Luckily the woman who helped me earlier resurfaced after a few minutes and I knew that she could put hands on my passport. She pointed and gave herself a chin scratch like my beard reminded her why I was there. She didn't pause for long, but it was enough to almost pull the pin in my chest with the slightest hint that it may not be ready. And then I saw the light bulb go off. I had to sign some things, and it was a bit less theatrical than Mr. Miyagi's, but she slid it under the window and there was now nothing else standing in my way.

I didn't care how wet I got on the way back. My inside pocket felt about fifty pounds heavier; my step never felt so light. Within hours of one another, both work and travel documents were rectified. It was time to enjoy a nice meal and the last bit of time I could with my family before crossing a country and an ocean to find what I wasn't yet sure I was searching for.

❖

She had chosen burritos. Actually, she had her eyes on a quesadilla, but it was a burrito place that she picked. She called, but I paid such close attention to the one pocket that I didn't feel the other one vibrate.

"Hey," she called, as walked past. She threw her head over as if to say *come on in*, and she headed inside.

Grilled chicken and marinade turned to steam was the first set of smells. My mouth watered before I even stepped inside, where the second welcoming smells were warm and salty tortillas and hint of lime. We went to school nearby, and that was where we met. As many times as I've smelled those smells, and as many as she'd raved about the quesadillas, surprisingly, I'd never been in. *What the hell?*, I thought, enthusiastic to check that box. New things were coming, no need for standbys. Sushi wouldn't have been prudent anyhow.

She hated cilantro. Everyone in the place knew it, too. They even joked with her when she ordered. "Extra cilantro, right?" The woman at the counter said, swiping her card. It was fun to see the little ways that someone else knew her. It was refreshing. It made me forget that I was peeved about being a little later than I wanted. She just about ordered for me. Her order was for chicken, and mine was steak. It was so we could share. Their guac was a bit too...*cilantroy* for her, but I wanted some anyways. And a cerveza. We were too close to the hospital for her to have a sip. They take that shit seriously for their nurses. That's a zero tolerance policy that I could get behind, I guess. I still teased her with the bottle, though.

When the food came out, we had some wonderful quesadillas. I suppose I don't so much remember how good they were as I do the fact that we talked about how good they were for nearly the whole meal. That was something we did quite a bit. It wasn't a feigned closeness or anything, we just really liked food, and we liked remembering where our meals brought us. Those would stick with us as the quesadillas we had before I went on that crazy, whirlwind, unsettling, and not-as-expected trip to Japan.

The walk back in the cold drizzle was a pleasant one. We spent much of it reviewing logistics, trying to figure out that full days' time difference, brushing away the roaming charges, and not believing any of it was real. I wouldn't be seeing her in the morning, but my side of the bed would still be warm. In the grand scheme of things, we still seemed to live between blinks of an eye. She held on for an extra minute when we hugged. I could feel the baby move. She leaned in to whisper that she loved me and that I should be careful. I know what she meant when she said to have a good time, and I also know what she was holding back to not break down before we kissed goodbye.

It didn't really and completely hit me that I was leaving her until I got back in the car. This was our first time apart for so long and so far. If ever I saw a glimmer into the heart and soul of a young and pregnant wife, it was then. *What the hell am I doing?* I thought. I could almost feel what it felt like to stand so tall and tough by my side, but be so scared to be alone. And then I thought about our boy and the words that I exchanged with Freeman. That place had no business wedging itself between us in that moment, but he was right. If it were my son, I would want to know.

My father-in-law's garment bag held everything I needed. Aside from my suit, shirt, tie, and vest, which I decided I would press in the hotel, I packed dress shoes and socks, one pair of jeans, a phone charger, a couple or three t-shirts, a pair of boxers and a tank, a week's supply of undergarments and socks, a nicer watch than my G-Shock - by nicer I mean more funeral appropriate - and my international power adapter. That's all. Toiletries had to go in a clear zip top, but that was only an Old Spice stick and a travel-size toothbrush and paste. In the morning, I planned to wear the other pair of jeans, a tee and a hoodie, and sneakers, so I didn't need to pack any of those. I lined up and trimmed just in case I couldn't find a razor there, which was a silly thought because, as far as I knew, the people of Japan shaved. Who knew whether TSA would let a disposable Bic through? I wasn't about to go online to try and find out. It felt like I was forgetting something, but I ran through the list more than once and it seemed good to go.

With printed passes and a passport ready for stamps, the hardest part of the wait began. That was the night of all nights to sleep early and hearty, though that venture was forlorn. I put in a movie around ten, one of my favorites, too, Yojimbo, but my mind was wondering something fierce and I couldn't focus on the subtitles. The sky was open again. There's no better movie to hunker down with when it rains.

Something about that screening hit me in the chest that night. He's a Ronin. A master-less samurai. His tale has him pitting two competing crime bosses in a small town against one another for his own gains and amusement. This role was the mold, the golden standard, if you will, for the wandering warrior archetype. He's a badass. It's exciting stuff. Eastwood's nameless man was more than just an homage to Mifune's Sanjuro character. This was one of my all-time favorite films, but there was something I saw for the first time.

The name he gives, Kuwabatake Sanjuro, is what grabbed me so. It was a combination of some nonsense about a patch of mulberry, or Kuwabatake, he spied out the window of one of the bosses, which didn't matter, and that he's a young thirty-something, or Sanjuro. I sat back down on the edge of the couch. That was it. He wasn't much more off than I was in age. *How could that be?* I thought. I was transfixed.

His portrayal here was genius; it was never just about his prowess with a sword, his cunning tongue, decisive charisma, or his dizzying range. It was in his eyes. This young thirty something had seen his world from the very top. He knew how to control it. We're lead to believe that he may have been something of a high ranking retainer under some lord, or even Shōgun. The fall didn't end him, it seasoned him; it put him shoulders ahead of everyone else. He owned whatever room he entered. He was a bit wicked in his ways, but you can smell the old code. The honor of a past life left its mark. His was a subtle and nuanced performance. It didn't make me feel that there was much honor in my own day-to-day, but it made me envy what he knew. It made me envy his mettle. Or maybe I just envied that he could carve his own way. To think, I only wanted to watch something Japanese...

Anyway, I started nodding off by the time Nakadai's character appears. The combination of the black and white and reading the subtitles usually made it tough for me to finish a movie like that at night. My own grumbling stomach woke me, though. The quesadilla wound up not being enough to tide me through the night. After a sobering cold glass of water, I found myself standing over the sink eating tuna salad out of a bowl with a fork just sort of staring. I was nervous as all hell. That was something I didn't even like admitting to myself, but I was. That was something that kept me from sleeping until well into the wee hours.

CHAPTER EIGHT
MY FIRST FLIGHT AROUND THE WORLD

F ive alarms, fifteen minutes apart, were usually enough on a work day. By the time the weekend rolled in, I didn't need any to wake up early. What a curse. Even without much sleep, I was up before the first one, clearing the rest, and hanging my legs over the side of the bed. I heard wind and rain through the night but chirping birds and calmer skies sounded to be abound. That helped a bit with the fear of flying. In that moment, I was in my place of Zen. The blankets could have taken me alive, and I had half a mind to let them. The drop from our king-sized pillow top was just high enough to get the blood flowing. I stretched out my shoulders, wiped away the sleep in my eyes, and made ready to shower.

This was the kind of day that called for a celebration. You're not supposed to travel without crossing through a gauntlet of bon-voyagers and weeping well-wishers. It felt weird to walk out the door and lock in a lonely apartment so I could just up and go to Japan. This was about the most grown up thing I'd ever done. I could hear her while I waited for my cab to the airport. She was telling me to make sure the car was locked. She'd have been happy to know that I smiled while I tested both of the driver's side doors.

It seemed like it was a new day; the ground was still wet and the sun was still burning off the haze. The weekend runners and road traffic weren't out yet, so they hadn't had a chance to touch it.

"Coffee?" asked the cabbie. We were coming up on the first of three donut franchises on the way.

"No, thank you. I'm not a coffee drinker," I replied. I always felt obligated to add that. *How often do fares around here refuse a coffee run*, I thought. *Hell, how often do cabbies ask to make a stop?* He did, though.

"You mind if I grab one? Long night..." He said. I don't know if he wanted me to bite on that hook, but I didn't. "I won't run the meter." I didn't want to say no, so I didn't, but I eyed my watch. We were still well on track to arrive at Logan four hours before boarding. I suppose now that I might've stayed so she could have seen me off. This was *my* need to check the doors, I guess.

Every time I get to Logan, I do just fine finding my way around; I don't know why I panic. Every single time, from about ten minutes away, I start to worry that we'll get lost. If I'm not able to read the signs I'll either wind up stuck circling or lost somewhere in Eastie. There's always a trooper on detail, too. If he sees me circling, I know I'll look suspicious. If I look suspicious, he'll pull me over. Usually by the time I get through answering all of his questions in my head, I've arrived safely at my destination terminal, and almost exclusively on the first pass. Now that he's had his coffee, my driver was like a surgeon with his circa turn of the century Crown Vic. Not only was he precise, but his services cost less than I expected. He was nice enough, and he mentioned his two boys, so I gave him a few extra dollars.

The airport was always such a romantic place to me. Not in the gushy, wanna-fall-in-love kind of way. There was always the nostalgia, the sense of adventure. When you're there, it's not all that glamorous. In fact, once you're through security, three hours before boarding, I'll have you know, mostly, it kind of sucks. But people setting off to new and exciting places, or returning to the arms of loved ones with gifts and stories to tell... it's one of the simple wonders we have. Big travel still seems so special.

There was almost no line at the first desk where they check your license and boarding pass. The passport came out quick like from a holster, but they didn't need it for the first leg. From there, security was a bit of blur. I remembered being shy about the x-ray machine that supposedly shows your naughty bits to the monitoring officer, but I forgot about that until I was through. The person after was chosen for a random and then patted down. He didn't seem to enjoy that. Perhaps he wasn't three and a half hours early, like my father always taught me. I grabbed my bag and my belt and I stepped aside to retie my shoes and find a Hudson.

The newsstand was just on the other side of security. They had the book I wanted, and a pack of gum and something to drink. For the next little while, after scoping the rest of the concourse, I switched between thumbing a few pages and watching flights board. I was way too nervous to read. There was this everlasting argument going on in my head about whether I was scared of something happening or not. In all honesty, I was. The other part didn't even like admitting it on the inside. People always say that flying is statistically safer than driving. Car crashes rarely have the same sort of panache for grabbing headlines, unless it's some drunk that's hit a cop. I supposed that the neatly dressed flight officers scurrying about, toting their wheelie bags, who did this for a living didn't get scared. Or maybe they did for every flight. Or maybe they felt safer with certain pilots. I envisioned some sort of secret wink when I boarded so they could let me know that we were with one of the good ones.

I'm a big guy, and I try to be as self-aware of that as possible. The problem with that is that no one offers to say that everything will be ok to the big guy with the beard. Boy I needed to hear that.

Surely she was sleeping by then, but I called her anyways. "Hello?" she asked, quick, in a voice that was half whispered by sleep and half concerned that something horrible had gone wrong.

"Hi. Just me. Everything's fine, I just wanted to say that I'm here. Flight's on time still."

"Okay, honey," she said. The twelves overnight were hard on her, I knew that. That was a huge chunk of why I didn't want to have the conversations about day care. How could I ask her to take on more nights? I wasn't sorry I woke her, though. It was nice to hear her voice. Besides, she was only home for an hour, at best.

"Be careful," she said. As if it was in my hands.

"Should I call you when I get to California?" She paused. She was either drifting or doing the math. I didn't give her time for the latter.

"Its six hours, or so, in the air. We're set for wheels up in a little over three hours." I tried to use official aviation speak whenever I could. It made me feel more confident. I was also telling her, as subtlety as possible, that nine hours was enough time to sleep before I would wake her again in the middle of my first flight around the world. These were hardships that the likes of Magellan never knew. She said ok, and I wished her goodnight. Or was it good morning?

Two hours and about forty eight minutes still remained before we were "wheels up."

The hours and minutes didn't just tick away, they dripped like the basement faucet. If I listened carefully on a quiet enough night, I could hear them grinding my life to slow and bleeding a halt. It was enough to keep me present, but not enough to get me up to do something to stop it. In this case, I couldn't do any more than sit and watch planes come and go in drudgingly slow motion. Man, I need to fix that faucet.

Steadily my section filled with Californians. They had a certain look about 'em that a New Englander could spot a mile away. At least this one group was overheard forcibly pronouncing "chowdah" at Legal's. Some of the others must have also been headed for Tokyo. For one, there was a small group of Japanese businessmen. Each of the six was tall and thin with sharp, black, pristine hair and tailor-fitted suits. Four of them wore glasses. They could've been from just about anywhere en route to the west coast, and damned if I was going to assume, but their passports weren't blue. Now maybe they were from Turkey, or perhaps Norway, given the crimson color, but I felt like I knew Japanese men when I saw them. And Japanese women. There was a group of three: two old, dressed conservatively, and one very attractive young woman, probably a few years younger than myself. I wondered what their story was. There was an old man, who looked to be the rustic sort, and his old wife, perhaps here to visit a grandchild, or the group of six or seven teenagers who filed in later who were visiting colleges. I only made *that* assumption because of my line of work...

Everything is and was tied in some way to higher ed. I wondered if they all had crimson passports, and I made it a point to remember for when we got to San Francisco.

I got to the gate early to get a prime seat. It had to be three things: near the gate, by a window, and within cord's length of a plug. When you arrive early enough, you can have any seat you want. By the time it started getting crowded, I couldn't sit. I was too anxious. Go figure. They called some check-in announcements and welcomes from the airline and then they told us we were waiting for the aircraft to be cleaned, but that we were still on time. It didn't matter, it was nearly show time.

The looks I got when I wandered a bit closer to the booth were wanton. I could see people eyeing me from across the clustered benches. More and more travelers filed in. *Are they just getting through security now?* I thought. Or *Were they at the bar?* Luckily their tab was paid just at the exact right moment when I kicked off the early line-up. Joke was on them, though: I wasn't even in first class. Even if I was, I'd never get *that* reimbursed. Although, I should have asked for a upgrade, but by the looks of things we weren't reaching into the standbys.

Sure enough, when the announcement came across, this flight was sold out. I could have eaten my hat I was so anxious when they started calling seniors, persons with disabilities, and passengers with infants to board, and then first class. Even though we'd wait for nearly forty five minutes before we taxied anywhere, I was in a hurry for the mad dash to get my bag into the overheard. Once that was all done, and it was, in its due time, I was locked and loaded and ready to wait for a bit.

The wait didn't bother me nearly as much as it did the woman next to me. She wasn't terribly unpleasant, though her coffee breath could have smelled a bit less like hotdogs. I even offered gum when I took my two pieces from their blister pack, but she refused. Damn. Overall, she just seemed like she had somewhere important to be. I suppose we all did, but she was fine once we got going, and once she had a few white wines.

I must have read Sky Mall three times and was on to fiddling to get my air jet right before the line in the aisle sorted itself away. I must have also been the only one paying attention to the safety debrief. The seat that I picked was close, but not on the door. In the event of you know what, I wasn't sure I wanted to help, though I probably would have anyways. I felt like she was judging me for my seat choice the entire time she was buckling and unbuckling her stupid little miniature version of the seat belt mechanism. She must have known from my ticket, and that must have been why I didn't get the secret wink about the pilot.

The puke bag always made me chuckle. Most of the times I flew, I took them for a souvenir, but usually just wound up writing phone numbers on them when I couldn't find anything else. The seat cushion sure didn't feel like a flotation device, but I believed the people who were crewing the craft that was about to fly us all across the country.

The taxiing part was always a bit fun. I liked to think of how those things were built to fly, but still needed to be driven. My mind usually wandered somewhere to where there were giant hangers and drafting boards and drivable prototypes of planes. It all must have been very expensive. Perhaps that was what Sky Mall was funding. I was almost willing to bet that the driving part was harder than flying.

There was a big deep breath and at once we all shared an allusive handhold as the thrusters pushed us further into our seats. A few of the passengers were busy with their New York Times, and a few others were with their spreadsheets. Even though they played "too cool for school," I'd like to think they felt it too, the excitement of flying. We rumbled for a triplet of heartbeats at what felt like thousands of miles per hour of break neck speed. And then *whoosh*. Everything smoothed out when the wheels broke free and the cabin tilted its way up. We must've had a navy pilot because, boy, he tilted! I learned that old adage from my Grandfather. The force of the plane pushing away the ground felt like lead in my chest, and the slight bit of weightlessness balanced everything out. I felt like a tethered balloon. As much as I hated rides and roller coasters, the takeoff was always my favorite part of the flight. The whole middle bit was boring, and I was glad to have a good book to read.

One of my favorite faculty colleagues had a saying during the second week of every semester: "And now we are in the air, hoping for little turbulence, free to move about the cabin, as we pray for a smooth landing on the other side." I took the liberty to apply his metaphor to my travels.

❖

I was already out of gum when we landed in San Francisco. Sure, I shared a few pieces, but I couldn't help grinding my teeth. From wherever we de-boarded, I made a B line for the Red Line on the Air Tran to get myself to international and to another newsstand. This was where I would usually worry about my bags, but just having a carry-on was clutch. The officer at the passport counter laughed that I was traveling so light.

"First time?" he asked, eyeing my stamp-less book and light amenities.

"Yup," I said. *No shit, wouldn't have gotten me very* far.

"Are you traveling for business?" he asked, assuming.

"I am," I said. "One of my student's funerals." That bit wasn't necessary, but I was nervous. I didn't expect to be interrogated so soon, or I would have planned through a little more thoroughly in my head.

"I'm sorry to hear," he said, and looked a little closer at my boarding pass. "Japan? Must have been some kid."

"You have no idea..."

The International Terminal at SFO was amazing. It was huge, like some hangar from the future. The way the scaffolding formed the woven ceiling and skylights screamed of big industry. That people built such things was inspiring to

80

me. To step back, it looked like it danced through the terminal like spinning strands of DNA. But the urge to pee won out over any further awe, and I wanted to call my wife.

"Hi honey," she said, before I answered. She called me. I felt bad because she sounded like she hadn't slept. Those days were too long to be flight tracking between shifts.

"Hey babe, I made it."

"I know," she said. "I've been watching. I miss you."

"I miss you too. Did you get any sleep?"

"No," she said. "My back... He's really kicking." I believed her because it was in her voice, but she was being nice.

"Well try to get some rest. I've got about two more hours here before we board, so let me know when you're on your way in."

"OK. Be careful on your flight, please. Call me when you get there, and have a great time. You deserve it."

"Thanks, babe. Have a good night at work. Love ya."

"I love you too," she said.

There was a lot that we both wanted to say. It was in there, somewhere between our words. I don't know why I didn't tell her that I wished she was coming with me, because I did.

Since our honeymoon, I'd only flown a few commuter flights for conference days, and none of those had duty free. The prices were great, especially on the Blue Label. *Maybe I can grab a bottle of single malt for my grandfather on the way back*, I thought. There was no need to carry that to and fro. I tried to remember if we came through duty free on the way in from the Mediterranean. I couldn't for the life of me.

More shops than the local mall were on display there. I had a lot more to do than I did at Logan, which was good for my nerves, because the next leg was over water. I don't know why, but that mattered to my worries.

There was a shop that carried watches. Luminox watches, to be specific. If there was anything out there in catalog form I could've kept under my pillow at night, it was the ad book for their gear. They had a decent price on the one with the titanium bezel and rubber dive strap. It was very tempting. What was a few hundred but a drop in that bucket? But I had no idea what I was in for, and every dollar, I was sure, was spoken for. *Maybe I'll pick one up if they come through on the reimbursements.* I was willing to bet that Dean Samson spent the rest of her Friday trying to find a way to stop my getting paid to go on this thing. With everything else on her plate, like, say, spearheading the retention efforts she was always bitching about, it was nice to see that she had the time to try to screw an honest advisor down. Ok, semi-honest.

Watches and shopping aside, I had to get that place out of my head. For one, I was crossing the Pacific. I'd never even seen the pacific. It didn't feel like I was in California.

Chicago was as far as I'd gone along my manifest destiny. I was always so uptight. Most of my tension, I carried in my shoulders. Part of me wanted to just go sit and have a drink and an app, but I threw down a pre-made sandwich and went to sit by the gate. There was still well over an hour left, but I would be damned to miss a single detail. My phone needed charging, too, so I had to get near an outlet.

It was agony. This leg was worse because Japan was waiting. For some, namely the couple of old women sitting near, and their beautiful companion, it was halfway home. For others, like myself, it was halfway away. We stood like one at this intersecting moment in time, equal, but opposites; one adventure ending, another about to begin. This was where the ripples meet the incoming wave after returning to sea from the shoreline. Thinking back, it burned by, but that hour felt like forever.

Finally, they started calling our boarding instructions. The woman at the desk may have been Japanese. She was beautiful, too. Her hair was almost blue it was so black. Her skin was fair, her eyes were striking, and she wore natural colors on her lashes and lips. She was the kind of almost painted beautiful that I could have pointed out, even, to my wife. Looking helped with the nerves. I wanted to get close enough to the counter so I could see her name tag.

This plane had business class. I always thought that first was finest, but apparently I was wrong. I boarded shortly after the suits in first, and they were all the way to the front of the craft, like any other flight I'd been on. Business class was at the top of the stairs at the back of first. To think, a plane with stairs. I was just behind the curtain, cramped into coach with those two old ladies and a bunch of other schlubs, albeit, we were towards the front. I tried to make a congenial sort of head nod in their direction, but it wasn't well received and it wasn't returned. That was too bad because it wasn't really for them. As much as I considered myself an introvert, sometimes I needed those fleeting, little contacts. I mean, nothing like a flight-long conversation, but a bit of small talk beforehand was all I was asking, or a pleasant "good day," or "safe flight," or something like that. For the nerves.

Waiting on the tarmac that time was almost unbearable. I'd flown once already that day, and this one would bring me to a place I'd long dreamt of going. I suppose the wait wasn't any longer than usual, but it was like getting near home and having to pee. The closer we got, the worse it was to wait. I missed my wife. She was all I could think of; her and my boy. I remember wondering what his little face would look like. We'd only just begun and already I was wishing an end to the trip of a lifetime.

CHAPTER NINE
A KEY TO THE WORLD

For the second time that day I was "wheels up," hoping for little turbulence and a safe landing. By the time we were free to move about the cabin, well above the pacific, I was sitting behind twice as much air since Boston. With every bit of progress on the flight tracker, I adjusted fractions. First, it was a third, then we were two fifths, and a few hours in, I was halfway there. That was a little thing I always did; always looking forward to the next mile or minute or meeting or meal. In the air, it was evident because it was all there was. In fact, it had me so preoccupied that I forgot to read my book.

The Tourist with Johnny Depp and Angelina Jolie was the in-flight movie. I was always a big fan of both of them. It was ok, but I guessed the ending pretty early on. I tried finding common ground with the plight of another bearded man on a traveling adventure, but our stories were quite unlike one another. For one, mine was absent the *James Bond* pizzazz. For another, at least I would like to think, mine was a bit more believable, though a little less sexy. Either way, I made a point to pick up a copy, because I knew it was one my wife would enjoy.

After the movie and a few cocktails, we were three quarters of the way there. I tried sleeping like everyone else, but I was aware of every minute for the rest of that flight. Painfully aware. The prospect of seeing Japan emerge from the clouds was altogether too exciting. Would I be able to see Mount Fuji? Would the lights of Tokyo fill the dimmed cabin? Could we see fields of blood maples? Or the Imperial Palace? Would it live up to my dreams?

There's a sickness associated with Paris. You see, no other city or place on this earth has been more romanticized than that one. I've never been there myself, but there's a Paris in my mind and my heart that comes from places like Woody Allen's *Midnight in*, to *Amelie*, even *Ratatouille* - in which Thomas Keller's food design is stunning - and everything in between. My wife and I have a favorite Bistro in the South End where we celebrated the baby, and will celebrate his birth, that looks like it's from a picture book of the city of light and romance. The sounds; the music; the baguettes and bicycles; the wine; a street side cafe smoking a cigarette… Sure, they are clichéd, but I would want to be a part of it all. That's just it. People have this soft-focus, accordion tracked, celluloid dream of Paris in a perpetual light rain. When finally they make this journey, not all, but some experience a sorrow that it will never fill such lofty spaces in their hearts and souls. It's called Paris Syndrome, and some have to seek therapy to cope. I was hoping with all of my own heart and soul that I wasn't in for the same sort of devastation.

Then there it came, up out of the clouds like a sleeping giant. The seat belt sign sent a shock wave through me. I expected darkness when we arrived, but we flew straight through the night and into tomorrow when it was still only yesterday back home. I didn't see the iconic outline or series of islands on a map, like I expected. At first, it looked like any other place from the sky. But then there was city; massive, sprawling stretches of what must have been Tokyo. Whatever little chunk of island held the airport had no room for anything else. They announced the morning time and weather in English and Japanese, but I was far too excited to care. I was up before everyone else, bag in hand, ready to make my stand in the land of the rising sun.

Passports fascinate me. Mine had my categorical attention, as it still sat like a heavy thing in my pocket. It's a badge of honor, in some ways; a key to the world. Of all the misunderstanding separating all of our borders, that was something we all agreed on at some point, that this little booklet with our pictures and stamps will let us pass through on business or pleasure. I always imagined some secret meeting where world leaders and delegates came together and shared ideas on what to call it, how to set up the terminals, how to divvy up the colors, and decided that the guards would always wear some sort of official looking hat. There's a whisper of humanity in there, somewhere, if you know where to find it. So much can change from port to port, in governance and views of outsiders, not to mention technology, that the whole thing is a wonder. No matter how much divides our states, we still have people that need to fly home, or satisfy a bucket list, or shake hands on a deal. The fact that we have, for the most part, a global standard for letting them, I think, is pretty cool.

"Welcome to Japan," said a man in a hat. I gave a bow to the same slight degree he did when I said "Arigato."

Narita International was huge. It was a lot bigger than the other two. Possibly combined. The flight board was iconic, but I didn't need to look carefully. My flight from SFO was listed as arrived.

All of the signs were spelled out in English. I had seen the terms hiragana and katakana online but knew little of either to tell which script was translating words I could read. There was artwork and pictures of Geisha and "Welcome to Japan" signs where you could stand and take a picture, but I was anxious to find a cab.

Signs in another language, loudspeaker announcements I couldn't understand, Japanese chatter all around, and everyone greeting everyone so politely did surprisingly little to culture shock me. It was quiet before the twin automatic glass sliders opened. They too were quiet, and swift, but a *whoosh* came through and a cold breeze came calling. I immediately felt like I was forgetting something. My palms were sweating. With one simple step, I would enter Japan, and with another, I would be on my way.

Then the shock hit me hard. First it was cars and buses driving on the wrong side of the road that sobered me to where I was. That, more than any of the illusions at my back, set in stone that I was really, finally, standing in another country. Next came crashing back everything I felt for that poor kid. He came through those very doors in his chair, probably dropped off by a driver, just as afraid as I was. Actually, if I were to bet on it, he was undoubtedly less so.

I saw him when he got off the shuttle from Logan. As an advisor to students with disabilities, it was my responsibility to see him as soon as possible so we could situate the door openers for the retrofitted campus center bathrooms. He had about as much luggage as I did. He never came back. I was stepping through that door in his place. My eyes filled and my bottom lip pursed. I couldn't say whether it was for me, for Min, or for his family, but I stood there and I cried. People walked politely past as I tried to compose myself. I backed inside, trying to cover up, in search of a restroom, or somewhere a bit more private. I cried harder than I had in years. I was too tough to cry, so I made myself swallow it down and caught my breath. Through this whole thing, at least as far as Min was concerned, those were the only tears.

❖

The whole way between the airport and the hotel passed like a great wave, blurring my eyes, overwhelming every inch of me that wanted to be out there. I had dreams of driving through Shibuya crossing like Mr. Bob Harris, but it turns out that not all roads lead through there from the airport. Actually, I had no real idea in which direction we drove. I had arranged for a hotel, western style, of course. It was within walking distance of the funeral home, which, with help from the campus database, and some browsing, wasn't far from his parents' apartment tower. They lived in a luxury development whose parking compared to luxury mortgages.

Something small felt out of place. That something I thought I had forgotten was bleary, but there. It was nagging and made me almost forget to enjoy every inch of the speeding panorama. Everything was white and gray-washed and just a touch foggy when I got out of the cab. The moment my first foot hit the curb I nearly shouted that I wished she was with me. That was it. I had forgotten to call and let her know that my flight arrived. I hoped she was feeling better. I couldn't, for the life of me, figure out what time it was back home.

Of all the things that I researched, cabbie tipping customs were not on the list. He fetched my bag and bowed politely. I returned his bow - I hadn't researched whether it was polite for me to do that either, but I assumed that it was

- and stuffed a few hundred yen into his hand. *Hopefully that wasn't an insult*, I thought. Sometimes I wonder if not tipping and hiding behind something aloof and wide-eyed would be better. I erred on giving him a few bucks.

There were cables running above the roads, and bicycles were tied all along, at nearly every pole along the way. I felt better seeing that I was staying in something of a neighborhood. It smelled like food, salty soy, and something fried, which made my stomach grumble. We passed an open air market not more than a half mile back. Across the street, and some unknown number of blocks behind the little strip of eateries, an apartment tower towered. I stood at the foot of a mountain, staggered by what I was up against. *I'd better go check in so I can call*, I thought, turning slowly, keeping his father's castle in view.

Another thing that went into picking that particular hotel was that there were positive reviews about the staff's English. Sure enough, I was greeted well in my familiar tongue by a man dressed in a suit, which was nicer than I expected, given the accommodations. It was nicer, even, than the suit that I had tucked away in my borrowed garment bag. Like he was handing over a fine wine list, he held out a small business card. This, I actually *had* read about.

The business card is very much the essence of one's identity in Japan. It's not like the dick measuring that takes place in American Psycho, but an honored way of presenting one's self. He held with a first finger and thumb on either side, like the cashier from the Japanese market when she accepted and returned my debit card. I knew that I was to read every word of it, and to take a few moments extra to show great interest in understanding who this man was. You also don't put them in your wallet if you keep it in your back pocket. That would be akin to sitting on this man's reputation. I felt funny holding it the way he did, but I read his name, number, and title before I bowed and thanked him. When he turned for me to follow, I slipped it into my jacket pocket.

In our short exchange, I didn't feel like it was his job to greet me and take my bag. I've stayed at a number of hotels in a number of cities, granted, on an advisor's budget. Every time, it's nearly the same story; service for a small fee. This man was bound by some loyalty to serve the patrons of his guest house. He was otherwise quiet, but he anticipated every tread along the journey to my room. His pronunciation of my name wasn't perfect on opening the door, but it was practiced. He had seen my whole exchange with the cab driver from the lobby, so he smiled as such, with a kind and educating eye when he rejected my tip. We understood each other's purpose and he smiled again when I realized that I shouldn't have tipped my driver. His shrug suggested that perhaps the driver shouldn't have accepted, but there we were. He outstretched an arm to introduce me to my room.

My room had all of the amenities that I expected, not just from what I understood a hotel stay to entail, but also as listed on the folio. It was almost laughable. There was everything, right in plain view, as if the small television, fax machine, coffee pot, hair dryer, ironing board, and somewhat ironic rice cooker were called for roll. I dropped my bag on the shorter than average twin bed and dug out my phone. I couldn't wait to tell her how excited I was to get out and explore the city.

I called maybe three times. There was no answer.

My phone had auto-adjusted the time, and when I saw that, I knew I hadn't changed my watch yet. It was well into her shift, so she must have been in a patient's room. Otherwise, with me in the air, she would have picked up.

For the next hour or so, I was pretty excited to get settled. The TV channels were basic. Mostly news with stock tickers, and a few plain Jane talk shows. I don't know what I was expecting, but evidently it's not all MXC or Godzilla movies or the things you see on Reddit. My outlet adapter worked, so I charged my phone for a few, ironed my dress shirt, and waited for her to call.

I had finally made it to Japan, and I was exactly where I would have been at home at that time: sitting inside, waiting by the phone.

CHAPTER TEN
A FISTFUL OF YEN

Y ou have to power through jet lag, or it will kick your ass. I waited for maybe an hour before I put my shoes back on and went. By then it was early afternoon and I hadn't slept at all. The doorman greeted me again by name, again, practiced, and he held the door.

Only then had I arrived.

The air had changed a little, and the fried smell had staled. It wasn't bad, but the dish had been served. I was still hungry, but I couldn't help heading for the tower. Min talked about one of his favorite places "right across the street." He said their bibimbap was better than anything he'd had in Korea. He even said their banchan were better than his Grandma's. I was actually there. It was where he would've wanted me to go. That, and getting a closer look at his parent's palace, albeit with a wisp of morbid curiosity, was compelling enough. With the size of their building, I didn't need to look up directions, but I still checked my phone. No missed calls.

Every step was fascinating, but seeing a six foot, bearded white man was probably more of a spectacle to them. I liked blending in. In Boston, even though I looked different, so did everyone else. There are some neighborhoods back home, though, where things are a lot less diverse, and I'd be just as sore a thumb. Perhaps where I found myself at the time was just their counterpart to that. Actually, that got me thinking. This place was drenched in something; something that I couldn't quite finger; something that was screaming that they were *Japan*. I likened it to my Boston accent when I had to think about whether or not we had whatever this was. My mind raced like Kon Satoshi's Millennium Actress through all of the ages of the Japanese islands. Everyone before me, from restaurateur, to gardener, to market stall shopper, to stoop sweeper, came after another just like him. I saw a living and breathing history, not just in old eyes or beaten brows, but in torches carried on and on. I may have been mistaken by something I put into my own head, but I felt that place in ways I never expected. And then somewhere along the way, I came upon Min's home address.

Their doorman made mine look humble and I resented them for that. But somewhere, up higher than the clouds in their mountain of marble, glass, and steel, they were mourning. In a way, I hoped that was the case. This wasn't a kid that was suffering, at least not in ways I knew, and I knew him well. There was some small piece of me that wanted to go up, but there was a bigger part that wanted to do nothing of the sort. Besides, by then my stomach was roaring.

The front entryway was on the most main drag surrounding the building. Sure enough, straight across, in a sea of light-colored building material, stood bold the wooden wall panels of a Koren barbecue joint. Not only was the lettering on their marquee quite different, and recognizably Korean, but they had constructed a small ramp. It was nothing framed or built up, and it probably wasn't up to ADA code, which doesn't apply in Japan, but boy were those two stair-covering slats touching to see. That, for sure, was where I wanted lunch.

Inside, everything was decorated in more wood, and it was slick; polished and spotless like an Italian Grandmother's curio. Other than the smell, which was drop-to-your knees umami and mouthwatering, decor wasn't the first thing this advisor saw. Their style was unmistakable; I'd seen it so many times. In fact, I was a little upset that I didn't have one of my own. Perhaps one day I would've gotten one. There were three manga style drawings behind the bar, taped carefully to the mirror behind the saké and soju. I'm sure there were others in the neighborhood who drew manga, but it was Min. He had a way with the eyes that was just a bit different from the others. Besides, they were signed "M.P." Min-Ho Park was his full name. From what I understand, it was a common one, but this was an uncommon encounter. He was here. This was the right place.

While I waited for the server to seat me, I took a closer look. Two of them were scenes from anime that he favored. One was from *Bleach*, which he tried to get me into, but I wasn't wild about. Another was from *Nausicaa*, his favorite Ghibli film. Mine is *Spirited Away*, though I'd get a Totoro tattoo in a heartbeat. The third, I didn't recognize; it may have been an original. That was the one I wanted. It was a samurai, stylized, of course, in full O-yoroi - which was their grand battle armor - riding on the back of a great and colorful dragon. The other two were sketchy, but this one was meticulous. The color was explosive. I wondered if they knew. I wondered if I should have told them and explained that I recognized his brush stroke. I decided against it, and to this day, I still don't know if that was the right decision.

Sizzling plates went screaming past us on my way to the table. There were also a few other tables getting started. One group, mostly about my age, was ordering food with a table full of beer. The next was an older couple and they were grilling pork belly at their table. I could smell the sour kimchi that they tossed around with their chopsticks. That wasn't my favorite, but I never thought to griddle it, though I have had kimchi fried rice, which I quite liked.

I ordered up a small carafe of saké while I skimmed the rest of the menu. While we were in Tokyo, we were deep enough into what must have been a suburb for the menus to not have any English. I was wrong to expect it, but I did. At least I could order bibimbap, and point to what was already served and pantomime the kind of stone bowl I wanted.

The banchan came quicker than I expected. I had no clue what most of the little plates consisted of, but they were phenomenal. There were at least a few kimchis and I liked them all, as well as no less than three things that reminded me of radish. The green beans were spicy, and the cucumbers were bathed in sharp vinegar. I was still trying to guess what the other two were when I heard my lunch coming. My wife called it *Korean Fajitas*. I remembered to check my phone. I still had roaming service, but no calls. I snapped a pic and shot her a text of it to remind her that I was over here by myself, and, of course, to spice up her jealousy just a bit.

Bibimbap is one of the culinary wonders of the world. There is rarely a mouth-water that matches a pre-bibimbap mouth-water. The smells and sights and sizzles are irresistible. The key, and the absolute hardest part, is to wait. It's ok to break the yolk, so it doesn't cook right away, and toss it lightly into the rice on top. You have to wait so the rice gets crispy on the sides of the screaming hot stone bowl. And then you scrape. Scrape, scrape, scrape. Then toss. This is the best crispy, caramelized, rich and eggy, toothsome bowl of rice on the planet. With my first bite, I was caught up to where my body was transported and with the saké and every crisp, sexy bite, everything around me danced to dizzying heights. I was halfway through, and the bowl had stopped sizzling, when my phone finally buzzed and skipped across the table.

It wasn't my wife. It was her father. I had a picture of him from one of their infamous Greek Easter lamb roasts when he called. Those were among the happiest times I spent with her family, but his call in the middle of the night from back on the east coast didn't evoke those feelings. I ate my throat and scrambled to answer.

"Hullo," he said. "Ah, Peter. It's your father-in-law." He always sounded like a million bucks.

"What's up, Papou" I said. That's Greek for *Grandfather*. "Is everything ok? Is she alright?"

"Peter, we are here," he said. "She had her water. It's broken." He had some funny ways of saying things, but he spoke them with confidence. Anyways, *That's impossible*, I thought. She was early. Way early.

"Where are you now? Is she there? Is she ok?! Can I talk to her?"

"Don't worry, my man. She is ok. Mama is with her here... We take her to the Mass General." By then I was up and standing outside. They must have thought I was skipping out on my check because the guy came running after me from behind the bar. I gave him the universal hand signs for "hang on, just a sec," and "this call is important."

"Can I talk to her?" I asked again. Sometimes I needed to repeat the important questions.

"Not right now, my man. The doctor is here."

"The baby? Is everything ok?" I asked. "Is he coming now?!" I didn't quite know how to ask my conservative, Greek father-in-law how open his daughter's cervix was or if

99

there was any bleeding or anything else about down there, so I asked again "Is she ok? Is the baby ok?"

"Everyone is ok, my man. Everyone is healthy. Strong," he was giving me a thumb's up. I could almost hear it. That made me smile and calmed my heart rate down a little.

My mind was screaming through what had to happen to get myself back there. I felt small. The funeral was in two days, and my son was coming now, unexpectedly, a day and a half back in the other direction. I would find a way to say I was sorry to Min, and if they didn't understand, I would live with that a lot easier than not being there for my own family.

I hardly heard the rest of what he said, other than something about signatures. We went to a baby class, oh, about two weeks ago? We learned the run down. They were consenting her. She had said all along that she wanted the epidural. *It must be the anesthesiologist*, I thought. I explained that and asked if that was what was going on.

"That's right, my man."

Ok, I thought. *That will comfort her, and may slow things down a bit*. One of my co-workers was six centimeters when her water partially broke, and once they placed the spinal, she was in labor, comfortably, for about twenty hours. It's amazing the kind of detail people are willing to share about such an intimate procedure. However, that long into it after breaking the water, they need to start pushing antibiotics. That would buy me some time, though. "Come back now," he said. "The boy is coming." I said I would. We wrapped our call and professed love all around, and then I paid a fistful of yen for a half-a-bowl of rice and ran the mile-and-a-half back to the hotel.

In the real world, it doesn't happen like it does in the movies. You don't run unbridled up to the ticket window and demand to be on the next flight. At least I didn't. I'm not actually sure that that's even allowed anymore. I had the doorman call me a cab, whose driver I didn't plan on tipping, and I dialed the airline.

After being passed around to a few operators, I finally got through to someone who understood everything and was quite helpful. Evidently, they just started direct flights from Tokyo Narita to Boston Logan a few months back. There weren't any direct flights when I booked, but she explained that was because they were still limited. Lucky for me, there was a seat on a red-eye. It was set for wheels up in about five hours, was in first class, and would only cost me another six hundred some odd dollars. That was easy money to part with.

The hotel had to charge me for one night. Whatever. The doorman understood well enough, though. He knew that this was a once in a lifetime thing for me, and he wished me safe travels and hoped to see me again. I think it was his way of letting me down gently. I really wanted to tip him, but I nodded as best I could when he bowed, and I then was off. I got one last look of the towering apartment building's tallest stretch as I ducked my head into the back seat. *Good*

thing I didn't go up, I thought. I probably wouldn't have
answered my phone.

❖

It wasn't that Narita was less magnificent the second
time I saw it, it's that I wasn't as present. I felt like all of the
checks and security stations just sort of moved around me
and I wound up somewhere far from home, waiting for a
plane. What the hell was I doing there? I was on the wrong
side of a flight of fancy and I was growing up the hard way,
blaming myself for ever thinking that this was a good idea. I
was so certain.

My mind went to the ones that miss this every day. I
didn't like being lumped in with them. Not because of who
they are, or why they were missing the birth of their first,
but because I wanted so badly to be there for her. That was
the part that hurt the most. Some miss it because they don't
want to be there. They probably deserve this feeling, if
they're capable of feeling it at all. Others miss it because of
what the world throws at them, and I'll never take their
stories for granted again. How selfish was I wishing that she
could wait for me?

I looked at people differently that afternoon. Were
there others waiting for this plane to get somewhere soon
because of a phone call? My news wasn't even bad and it
made my stomach wrench. What if someone just found out
their father had a heart attack? What if this wasn't just a trip

to show a family that a college cared about their student? What if this was a big dollar deal to change the face of a multi-national corporation? What kind of business person could live with their decision to stay and see those things done?

And then, as if this was what mattered, I thought about the realities of my own job. Min's family aside - who, if they even knew I was coming, would probably understand my leaving should our paths cross - I was walking away from duties passed down from a Dean. It damn well better be something worth trading it all in for. Without a doubt, it was. But still...it haunted me not to finish a task. As much as I wanted to spit on Samson, for some reason she lit a fire in my guts to prove her wrong. More than that, I wanted for Min. He left me guessing about his father, and he had things he needed them to know, but what? And why would they listen to me? The only thing worse than being bitched out by a Dean, especially over losing the college money, was letting down a student. I should've felt happy. Fuck that place.

Time passed as happily as a kidney stone. I had called as soon as I was settled, but the team wasn't back yet to place the line. That meant she was contracting. That meant she couldn't talk. There was little I could have done, but that wasn't something I wanted her doing alone. Her mother was with her, as was the staff of one of the best hospitals in the world. Somehow that didn't feel like enough.

My parents were scrambled like fighter jets, but by then I couldn't talk for long because my battery was low. The plan was for my father to drive, wait with my mother at the hospital as needed, and be at the airport to pick me up. I didn't even give him any information other than the flight number. He could track a flight like a naval control tower. Besides, I knew that would give him something to do. Beyond that, I was also hoping for a bit more intel with four more boots on the ground. Finding an outlet was paramount, or I wasn't hearing anything until I arrived.

My most selfish thought was an angry one; they would see my son before I did. That was supposed to be the most intimate moment that a couple could share, and it's when mom seals the deal with the baby. I wanted, with all of the fibers of my being, to be there for that. With every moment we got closer to "wheels up," no news was good news.

I found my gate and, of course, I was early enough that the flight two flights before mine was readying to board. I crept and I snuck, taking advantage of passengers too polite to stop me, trying to find a wall plug. When finally I found one, I dropped and opened my bag to find heartache in the front pocket. I left my charger, complete with its international adapter, in the wall at the hotel. In my eager and fragile state, the thought to just buy one wasn't there. There were like chargers charging like phones, so I reached well outside of my normal introversion and I started asking around. I realize now that to them I looked like the guy at the train station bumming smokes. Some hid behind their language, others behind their poise. Some said no. I wondered if they were waiting for the same kind of calls. I sat, sort of defeated, until they boarded.

❖

With what little battery I had, I called again. That time, I called my dad. There weren't any updates, but it sounded tense, like my mother thought she should be in with my laboring wife as well. My dad got it, and he helped to keep the peace. As I suspected, he had zeroed in on my travel arrangements and he spent my battery into single digits reviewing his time table and short cuts to Logan. With my lag, my phone clock, and unadjusted watch, I was lost somewhere in the middle, but I trusted that he would be there. I had to hang up to go and find a solution.

Narita international was well thought out. It was so well thought out, in fact, that things such as travel adapters from North American to Japanese were not readily available in the departures terminal. Between shops and newsstands, I checked the time enough to drain it dry.

Some of the sushi places there towered over the best I could get back in Boston. Again I grabbed something small at the sundry because I was too nervous to sit and eat a meal. In all of the vastness of the culinary empire of that country, I only had half of a Korean lunch and some pre-made, Vietnamese, airport spring rolls. I needed, though, to be ready to ask travelers for their charger. What a pit there was inside of me.

❖

Finally, three long and horrid hours after, my flight was next to get going. The whole pre-plane cycle, from the last plane taxiing away, would last nearly ninety minutes, but that was time to find someone who could help. I sat close to a bank of outlets and I waited, watching the activity outside, but keeping an eye on the foot traffic behind me.

Lucky for me there was a family traveling back to Beantown with a dad who insisted on being early. He was joined with a wife, three teenage girls, a toddler, and a grandfather. Grandpa was wearing a WWII Veteran hat with a first cavalry pin. My grandfather was first cavalry in Korea. My first car was his and I wore his first cavalry plate with pride. I was quick to tell anyone who recognized it that it was his. First, it was to be proud of my Pa. Second, it was to dispel any stolen valor. That had nothing to do with why I kept it. To think...people actually do that... Anyways, I heard my mother, and she was calling it "a sign," even though I didn't believe in that sort of thing. Either way I used it to get my foot in the door. Three teenagers had to have a charger amongst them.

They were good people. Especially their Grandpa. I hoped for those girls that they appreciated him the way I did mine. They did, in fact, have the phone chargers I was looking for. I knew because they all sat tethered to the wall having no interest in what he had to say. I liked to think that they knew all of his old war stories well enough, and assumed that he was just telling his old chestnuts, but I feared that wasn't the case. It was some sixty five years since he set foot in Tokyo last. It was a very different Tokyo. Aside from the obvious - he *was* first cavalry - he said that everything is changed. Everything he saw then was like the things you see in the movies now. I never got to ask him if he found what he was searching for.

We got to talking about why I was there. He was sincere in saying sorry for my loss, and he was thrilled for me that my boy was on the way. He gave me a piece of advice that I'll remember until the day I go. He said,

"Your kids are like a bank account. You'll get out what you put in. With luck, maybe a little extra."

He smiled from somewhere deep and satisfied when he looked at his three granddaughters. For a shimmer, I saw it through his eyes. They were happy; they were together. It was simple. He couldn't have been more content. It was as though the nightmare he brought back was haunting him and he somehow found a way to bring it quietly home to rest. This was not a moment I wanted to upset. He wished me all his best and shook my hand with the strength of an old waist gunner. "Take care of that boy," he said. "They grow up fast."

107

I wasn't upset that I didn't charge my phone. I wasn't upset that my son was being born. That old codger put so much into perspective for me. I hope for those girls that they realized who they had before he was gone. I thanked him again and I started my boarding procedures with first class. This time, it was for real.

CHAPTER ELEVEN
MY BROKEN LITTLE HEART

First class is awesome. There is so much more leg room, and the seats recline all the way like beds. The old man put a strong hand on my shoulder and squeezed as he walked past, holding down the rear behind his three granddaughters, before disappearing through the curtain and into coach. I wanted to switch seats with one of them, but I know he'd be nowhere if it wasn't with his girls.

I was parked next to some douche bag in a suit who was already asking for extra pillows and a dirty martini. I hoped real hard that she put something in it to knock him out, but his monogrammed satin eye shade was a good sign. He might as well have taped a line between the two of us like they do in that old *this is my side* TV trope. This guy looked like he had done this before, and believe it or not, he got his drink while the other dregs fought for overhead space or complained about having to check bags that didn't fit. How is it that someone dressed so well can be so oblivious to the kind of look he got from the attendant? And how could he have possibly seen the safety demonstration from behind his covered eyes? Finally when we started taxiing out, he set some sort of sleep rhythm tracker app on his phone, plugged it in, and turned over. That's right. He plugged it...in! *This* was the way to fly.

So this jerk was asleep by the time we were "wheels up." I must have wrestled with myself for the first hour or so of the flight with whether I should do it or not. It was killing me not knowing what was happening with my wife. I clicked my power button and there was nothing. I had made up my mind.

With hands firmly planted on my arm rests, I held my breath and lowered my seat back down to match his. I couldn't believe I was doing this. His phone was on the opposite side of him, and his charger wasn't long enough to reach me. My heart was pounding. My first move was slow and I tried to contain a creak from my seat cushion. I rolled over onto my side and reached like I was trying to prank a friend on a camping trip. I couldn't reach it. There was nowhere for me to stand, so I turned the rest of the way over and onto my knees. He snorted and reached up to scratch his head. My stomach leapt up and a wave of adrenaline made me shake. What the hell was I doing?

He was back to snoring within moments, and I was back on the prowl. I finally had to rest one knee on my seat and the other across both armrests to reach over and unplug his phone. It made an audible beep, but he wasn't bothered. I held my breath and I lowered like I was doing a *Mission*

Impossible stunt. I had to hold onto my seat with my left hand, which left me my right to palm my device and grab the cord with my first two fingers. It took a little too long for comfort but I finally mated the connector with the port and left my phone on his chair next to him while he slept.

The next twenty to thirty were some of my longest and least proud minutes in recent memory. Finally, my phone grabbed hold of enough charge to make its own beep. I leaned over to look. The little red light was lit in the corner, telling me I had two voice messages. There wasn't enough juice to check them both, so I spent the next twenty to thirty in agony, wondering what I was missing.

I couldn't take it any longer. I returned my seat to the full upright position, stood up, forewent any careful creeping or worry that this fuckwit would wake and I grabbed up my phone. His hit the floor, but before I realized what that sound was, I was halfway to the lavatory.

The most recent message was at the top so it played first. It was my father. He saw that we took off on time and wanted me to know he was watching the flight. The first message, which came in at just a minute and a half before, was from her phone. I could have thrown up. I didn't want to listen to it; I just wanted to call her. They told us not to use our phones. In my mind, they could track who'd done it, and I had visions of being arrested and escorted right off of the plane. Would they have understood? Would it really mess with the instruments? I decided to listen to the message first. I was dying to hear her voice.

It was my father-in-law, again. He introduced himself as such and he explained that his battery was dead. But then he said: "Ah, Peter. The boy. He's here. Mama is ok. Can you come here soon? Ah, the baby has a..." he leaned over to ask my mother-in-law how to say something in English. "Heart. His heart has...how do I say...heart attack?"

I fucking lost it. I nearly dropped the phone, and missed something he said after that. The back of my mouth watered like I was about to vomit. On the rest of the message I could at least hear someone telling him it wasn't a heart attack, but something was wrong. "We'll see you soon, Peter. Everyone is ok. Mama is strong like a bull. Just like her father." I could have killed him. I tried to call, but there was no reception to be had, or something was blocking calls. I sat down on the toilet and I listened to it again. All of a sudden, my biggest concern had nothing to do with who saw him first.

It was just ramblings on the rest of the message. There was no new information. Those words punched me in the chest the second time around and I threw up in the sink. I had no idea what was happening. I was somewhere over Europe and my broken little heart was thousands of miles away.

I couldn't bring myself to leave that little room after cleaning up. It took three people pounding and an attendant threatening to key in. I didn't even bother wiping the strain from my eyes. The attendant saw that something was wrong and she helped me back to my seat. She leaned down and whispered something about flight sickness. If I wanted to say something, I couldn't find the words.

By then, we were only halfway home.

CHAPTER TWELVE
RIGHT WHERE I BELONGED

Keeping calm for the rest of that flight took every stretch and strand of me that wasn't a ball of nerves, and whiskey for those that were. The coast was in view on the flight tracker, with a few hundred miles to go, when my neighbor grumbled himself awake. "What the hell happened here?" he said, looking for his phone and raveling the charging cable up. "Where's my phone?!" He checked his own and the seat pockets and asked himself again. I gave him an *I don't know* shrug and leaned over to look like I was helping. I asked, playing dumb, if maybe it fell. He was up and he was pissed. Luckily when it fell, it didn't go too far; it slipped down against the outside wall. That made it a bit easier for me to deny having heard anything. He was a peach for the rest of the flight.

Approaching home, time moved even slower. We passed over Logan and flew north to turn. It must have been air traffic, or to align with the right landing strip, but it was intolerable. So was the approach, and so was the taxiing. The touchdown was a huge sigh of relief, but then I just wanted to jump off and run. If I had packed any heavier, I would have sincerely considered just leaving my baggage. Any other time I had flown, I was jealous of the first class passengers for being let off first. I was ready to join those ranks. Two words texted to my phone lifted me up and made me want to rush even more. "Out front." I always gave my dad hell for the back roads he insisted on, but he had a talent for getting in and out of there. He was like a Delta Force operator making an extraction. He was my best chance to get into MGH as quickly as possible.

I didn't care who I pushed aside running up the Jetway. Looking back, I probably made some people nervous. I'm lucky I wasn't tackled. He was standing by the car with his trunk open and the hazards going. I yelled "Go!" and jumped right into the shotgun position with my father-in-law's garment bag strapped to my chest. He took a little more time getting in than I would have liked, but at least he didn't buckle; he had a thing about not being told he had to do so.

We were off.

"How was your flight?" he asked. I shook it away.

"What is happening there? I got a message from her dad. Is the baby ok?! I couldn't make out what he was saying..."

"The baby's fine," he said. "Everyone's ok. It was just a long night is all."

"He said something about..." I couldn't even listen to myself say it, it sounded so fake "a heart thing. He said a heart attack? What is going on?"

My dad chuckled and shook his head. "A heart attack?!" he said. "You thought...?" He found it funnier than I did. "Noooo. The baby is going to be ok. They heard a murmur. Just a little murmur. She is in the NICU with him, to be safe, and they are giving him medication. The heart doctors haven't checked yet. They're coming today to run some tests, but the nurse thinks that it's just a small murmur. A PDA, they said." I didn't know what that meant. "They think if they keep him quiet, it'll fix itself with meds in a few days. A few weeks tops. They may need to keep him a bit longer, but he's doing ok. Mom's doing really well too."

"Is she worried?" I asked. If I could only ask one question to tell how bad things were, that was the one.

"She doesn't seem to be," he said.

I knew I wouldn't have made it back onto the highway without knowing a lot more about what was happening, but my mind was so wracked that I was expecting to barge in and search for the doctor like a madman. I couldn't wait to see my son. I felt so much like I let my wife down. But all in all, boy did I feel better than I did on that plane.

"Who does he look like?" I asked, swallowing pride in exchange for a good report on my boy. "Does he have a full head of hair?"

He shrugged and bulged his bottom lip. "I don't know," he said. "Your mother and I are waiting until you see them." A tear came up and I looked over at him. He knew how much I appreciated that. They say at some point you realize that you aren't much different than your old man. For me, it was then. He slapped my knee and said "Let's get you to the hospital, Dad. I have a grandson I need to see."

❖

I ran into my wife's OB at the nursing station after being buzzed onto the floor. We learned about all of that security, and the pink badges, at the baby class. She walked with me to their room.

Patent Ductus Arteriosis, or PDA, is what she called it. When a baby is in the womb, which is filled with amniotic fluid, he (or she) doesn't breathe air. There's a hole in their aorta, sort of like a bypass, because the blood doesn't need to be oxygenated in the lungs. Evidently it can be common for a baby born a little early for that hole not to fully close. From what I understand, he was fairly lucky to be where he was. Sometimes they require surgery. The cardiologists had come, and his probably required surgery. They wanted to wait to monitor the effect of the meds for another day or so. I wondered if they waited for me, but hoped that they would have operated without me there if that's what was needed, as much as it would have pained me. It was awfully deflating to hear all of this, and if my driver had told me that my son was in having open heart surgery, I am not sure how my own heart would have held itself from bursting.

People go through that every day. I could read that much on the doctor loud and clear, so I didn't question any of what she was saying, I just wanted to see my wife. Our son would only have surgery as a last resort, she said, and she asked if she could page back the cardiologist to answer any questions. In every other way, he was textbook healthy. "And what a head of hair," she said. I didn't know what I wanted. It was like gasping for air at the bottom of a deep and unwanted dive. I told her that we would call the nursing station if that was necessary. As best I could, I took a breath before knocking.

❖

She looked beautiful. She looked older, and a bit wiser, having faced a battle and won. That was the first time since the day we got engaged that I was nervous to see my wife.

My Dad reminded me to buy flowers from the gift shop. He even loaned me a few bucks. I only had yen in my pocket. There was plenty on my debit card, but he insisted. When I walked into her room, I nearly dropped them. She welled up. Beside her bed was a bundle of blankets and sweet little sleeping boy. I was expecting a breathing tube, but I was happy to hear his breathing was ok. Everything was quiet except for a few beeps. I welled up, too. He was the most beautiful thing I had ever seen. I started to talk and she shushed me. We kissed, and I stared at him for a good minute before she leaned forward to hand him over, carefully.

"What should we name him?" she whispered. We had made more than one final decision on the matter. My name was on the table at one point, as was her father's, and my father's. We thought to name him something strong, like a conqueror, like Marcus Alexander, or something a little more *everyday* Greek like Andréas or Panagiotis. But what we talked about all along wound up being a perfect fit.

"Nicholas," I said. "He looks like a Nick to me."

"I'm so sorry," she said. "I never meant..." That was my turn to do the shushing. "I'm so happy that you're here."

"I'm so sorry that I went," I said. "If I ever thought..." but there was no rightful way to finish that, no excuse for what I missed. And with the woman I married, there was no need for one.

"Did you get to see anything?" I shook my head, but I never took my eyes off of him.

There's a bit of magic that happens when you see your child for the first time. A face that you've never known becomes something you can't recall having never seen. He was like a clean slate for me to be the best I could, and oddly enough, it was like he'd been with us all along.

We spent some time doing what you do, reveling, strutting a bit, listening, learning, not sleeping a wink, reacting, making mistakes, sharing, loving, worrying. It was all there, and I can still account for every moment of it like it was yesterday.

❖

The Dad jokes must be genetic. They arrive almost as early as mother's milk. I couldn't have been an hour off the plane and I was at it already. Her nurse came in with a student to help boost my wife so she could eat. When she rolled over, I said that "any change that falls out of her pockets is mine, ladies." They chuckled, but they were probably just humoring me. The way I saw it, though, a lame joke must have been ok every now and again for the NICU nurses. They see things day in and day out that can tear a person or a family apart. They do it with a touch of grace and a messy bun tied on top of their heads. They are our finest, and they made me look at my wife in a way I never have before. I wished I could have seen her, been by her side, held her hand last night, but I was right where I belonged, finally.

❖

My Dad drove me home early so I could shower and grab clothes, and then I went right back, in my own car, with little to no sleep in the tank.

You only really know it's nighttime in the hospital because they dim the hall lights, at least on the baby floors.

It's kind of a cruel joke, really, letting you know that you *should* be sleeping. I didn't mind for a minute, though my wife will say that I slept more than she did. If I could've taken some of the prodding, I would have, but that's just another one my privileges, I guess. The one bothersome bit was that they woke the baby every two hours to take vitals and listen to his lungs. It had to be done, but to wake a sleeping baby should be a cardinal sin.

The cardiologists came back at some ungodly hour, shortly after the faculty pediatrician gave a listen. In my mind, when they said the meds weren't working yet, I couldn't fathom why a single day would be enough to know, but they knew. He was breathing well, so it wasn't an emergency, but they were nearly settled. If they didn't see signs of improvement by that same time tomorrow, they would operate.

It was Tuesday morning, which meant it was Wednesday in Japan. This was the day they would bury their son.

❖

That night was as long as any I'll ever remember. I'm not, nor was I then, or in my days to come, a praying man,

121

but I came close. Surgery scared me. It terrified me. He was so small you could practically see the bones and vessels in his chest. To imagine him pierced and cut apart was a trauma I'd never known. To think of what delicate work it was to stitch his murmur made me sick. We're lucky to live in times when so many came before us to sacrifice sons and daughters in search of such fixes. We were hoping to have the fortune to extend our thanks through their unfortunate generations. The words "infant mortality" mean something more with your own son in your arms on the eve of open heart surgery.

Nicholas was quiet for a stretch after dinner, which was later than we were used to. The chair in the room folds down into a bed so that the new moms can have someone stay to help. It wasn't very comfortable, but with my boy laying on my chest, I found peace. He was sleeping and I held him against me, vowing never to let go. My hand must have been warm, and his pulse pumped against my finger. At some point, shortly after eleven, I fell into a cat nap. The med flight coming in overhead woke us both. I thought it was much cooler than he did. Something about that gave me déjà vu. We were right back at the tumult of getting him, and us, through the rest of that night.

Morning stumbled in on the heels of medications and vitals throughout the night. All of the visitors had come and gone, so for those few hours, we were alone. Torment was researching the procedure. Desperation was hoping it wasn't necessary. Agony was not knowing. Helplessness was watching a tired hand administer a final dosage before the decision. Hand-in-hand were a nervous wife and scared husband. Exhaustion was the sum of their fears. We had little worry left to give by the time the pediatrician came calling at first light.

"Good morning," she said. "How is our little man doing today? Did Mommy and Daddy get some sleep?"

"No they did not," I answered. "But, hey, at least they didn't wake me every hour to strip me down and take *my* temperature. Does that cost extra?" I chuckled. She was all business, though.

"Do you mind if I check him," she asked, directly to my wife like I wasn't in the room any longer.

"Please," she answered, and then the two of us were at the edge of our beds.

The first thing was to listen. She huffed hot air, of which I wanted to joke that she was full, to warm the smallest stethoscope I had ever seen. She held it in her first two fingers and made small, soft touches while she looked away. "Hmm," she muttered, before going through the same regimen of listen points. "I don't..." she looked surprised, and somewhat concerned. "I'll be right back. I'm going to page Dr. Macaffee," he was the cardiac guy we'd been seeing. Like that, she was gone through the sliding curtain and out the door into the hallway.

"What the fuck was that?" I said. My wife was visibly nervous and I knew that I wasn't helping, but I couldn't contain myself. "Who does that?" I whipped aside that curtain and stepped into the hall trying to find where she went. I couldn't see her. "That's fucking crazy!" In honesty, that was the scariest reaction, and one we weren't expecting. My wife asked that I stay, which I translated to mean that I shouldn't cause a scene.

Nick was naked and needed comforting. I re-diapered and bundled him and handed him to my wife before I headed to the nurses station. The pedi looked to have found Macaffee in the lounge because they were on their way. Their pace was a bit hurried, but about as much as usual.

"What is going on?" I asked.

"I need Dr. Macaffee to take a listen," she answered.

"My wife is a wreck in there because you ran out." I wasn't making a scene but I was outside of myself to be confronting two doctors walking back to my baby's room to decide whether they were going to cut him open. "Has it gotten worse?!"

"I don't think so. Please, come inside." She opened our door and stepped back, letting me go first.

"What, did she not explain?" said Dr Macaffee. He was charming, with better bedside manner. His smile took the edge away. He also seemed to make more of a show heating up his stethoscope bell. I figured from that that he was more used to working with older kids, and their parents. "Well let's take a listen here. Could I have him Mama? I will have him right back to you. If I hear what Dr. Lewis heard, it should only be a moment."

124

He took him and he listened. But he did more than that. He raised up his eyebrows high and his talked with big expressions to my boy. "Hi there," he said. Nicky pulled and writhed, crying. "Oh that's cold. I'm sorry, big guy. Sounds good, though, kiddo. Almost done..." We breathed for the first time. He touched the same way she did with two fingers on a small listening bell, and then he listened to his back.

"Here he is mama. Hold him, I know that that's uncomfortable." He put his stethoscope back around his neck and pulled a pen from of a pocket that was holding far too many pens. While he was scribbling in the chart, he explained that everything sounded great. We then had his undivided attention.

"Well, someone's looking out for this little guy," he said. That was an interesting sentiment from a man of science. "It's almost all the way clear. Someone's looking out for him indeed. There still sounds like there may be just the slightest murmur, but that should take care of itself in a few days. Mr. and Mrs. Cahill, Nicholas, here, is going to be just fine. I thought we were going to be operating on you, little guy. That little heart is going strong. I am going to recommend he continue the meds and stay for a little longer in observation, but we should have you three out of the NICU in a few days, and home in no time. Your doctor will be in, and I want him to see his pediatrician as soon as he can after he's discharged."

Only then was I finally home.

CHAPTER THIRTEEN
HOGWASH AND HAND—ME—DOWNS

For about ten days in total we stayed. I'll never forget the day we went home. What a two-sided sword. His last few listens were completely clear, as if by some miracle, and the next morning he had his appointment with the pediatrician that caught me on the day I was born. He'd go on to say how old he feels now that he's seeing my kids, and that he saw all of my uncles, too, and tell us what a fine job we're doing.

Nicholas was a big baby for being born five weeks early. He was just under nine pounds, but he looked so small strapped into that bucket carrier. Walking out those front doors with him in tow was the new most adult thing I had ever done, and then so was the slow ride home.

We were getting settled at home when I got the call. Dean Samson. My heart sank to see the number alone, and I nearly had a panic attack when I heard her voice. I never once called since I left early that Friday before my trip, and I didn't answer any emails. Oh she had something vindictive and wicked on her breath, and it was covered over by some righteous *for the good of the order* bullshit.

She spoke in an entrapping sort of snippy way when she asked me who I thought had called to tell her I never showed at Min's funeral. The irony is that she never wanted me to go in the first place. Part of me would have said she'd make a good kindergarten teacher, but now that I was a father, I would have never wished her wretch and foul on my worst enemies' kids.

I explained why I got called back and that we just got out of the hospital with the baby. Not a whiff of a congratulations, and no sign of sympathy. I think she enjoyed this. She said something about how I've let the College down, how I've cost them a potential gift-giver - which I was fine with; that was blood money anyways - and finally, how I've stolen time. I wanted so badly to tell her what I was thinking, but I didn't. She piled on about blackout dates and what's fair and so on, though all I wanted was to go in the other room and see my son.

Anyways, she fired me on the spot. She had balls enough to ask if any part of the trip had been paid by the College because it would need to be paid back. Otherwise, nothing would be refunded. I hung up partway through some threat about higher ed being a small community and I never looked back. Not for a single minute.

When I rejoined my family, she asked if everything was ok. I said that it was like a weight was lifted and I told her that I'd explain later. Nothing was going to spoil those first few moments at home. I had already missed too much.

❖

For the first few hours, we had some visitors, which was fine, but I would've liked a little more time to shower and clean up a bit. People get it, though, when you have a newborn, even if they don't. Our neighbor from across the street was first. She was the sweet Japanese widow of a fine American man who always waved and asked my wife how she was feeling. Before that day I can't remember exchanging many words, but she brought kind tidings, a stuffed Doraemon, and a few small trinkets to bring our boy home into good spirits. She refused coffee, but was happy when we offered green tea. I, of course, was worried that the bags we had were not what she was expecting, but they were fine. A few days later, she would leave us another small parcel of effects, which would include some loose leaf hojicha and an infusing ball. She was very thoughtful.

"How was your travels?" she asked, when we were sitting with steaming cups. I wanted so badly to talk to her about Japan, and I thought she'd never ask. It was almost uncomfortable that you couldn't sneak anything past a nosey neighbor, but I was happy to jump onto some common ground with her.

"It was wonderful," I said. "Actually, I was in Tokyo."
I said it as if to say *you should know the place*. And in fact, she did. Her eyes lit like little firebugs.

"Tokyo?! How wonderful. You should have told me."
She rattled off a list of places, asking if I was able to see what she would see if she returned. I shook my head.

"Sadly, no. It was a very short trip. I was only there for one day. Work related." She was so excited she made me nearly forget that I was newly unemployed.

"One day? For Tokyo? That is very many miles to turn home so soon. Why you not stay for longer?"

"I was supposed to be there for one week. I had to leave early because my wife was having the baby."

"Ah. I understand," she said. "But only one week? When you go back, you need one month." She sat quietly for a few minutes, stirring her tea.

"Daddy and I were planning to return." She called him that to their two kids. I loved their story. Her husband was born and raised in the house that she lives in alone to this day. She tends the garden as he would have liked, and she still lets me help her shovel, but only when there is too much snow. But Henry, who was himself an only child, enlisted to serve his country as a helicopter mechanic in the Vietnam war. He learned the skills tinkering with motorcycles since High School. Sometime during his third tour, within months of one another, he received word that both of his parents passed. Henry always wanted to see

Japan. That's exactly where he went after an honorable discharge and a ticket to a port of his choosing.

The Henry that I knew was an older man, about my height, heavier set, until the end when he lost a ton of weight, with a thickish beard. He always came off as sort of wandering and introspective. When I imagined him during those days, he was the same Henry that I knew, but maybe with a set of *Easy Rider* sideburns. Somehow he fit, in my mind, the form of an old nomad, complete with sandals and walking staff. Far from any path, beaten or paved, he walked, past foothills and hot springs far into the north, attempting to flee from his own sorrows. I never knew him well enough to learn whether he left them behind, but I know he found his next best thing in Suzume. She wasn't an attractive woman. She was, in a word, rustic. But to Henry, she was a cherry blossom in winter.

"When is the last time you saw your family," I asked.

"It's been very long. Very long. Our daughter was only three." Their daughter was my age. Maybe older. Henry passed away nearly a year ago on a surprise trip to see her. That always bothered me. The chemicals that those choppers dumped finally got him. "We write letters often. It's funny," she said. "I was born and I lived in my village all those years, but I would have relied on Daddy to get us back. I will die here, in the house that me and Daddy made." She took a long sip and her eyes looked distant. "I would like to see it one more time. My village."

My wife walked back in from feeding the baby. She couldn't locate her cover, and probably didn't need it in the company of Suzume, but she didn't feel right. "Let me see him," she said. "Oh he is very big." She did not want to hold him, but she was happy to watch him sleep for a few. She looked carefully at my wife, and then deep into my eyes. "He looks like his mother," she said. That was about as honest an assessment as we'd been given so far. "This is a wonderful time. Bless him."

When the bell rang in another few guests, she promptly remembered a load of laundry that needed her attention. She could have stayed. Actually, I would have preferred to talk with her some more. I didn't feel settled about Min. She knew the distance, and I don't just mean miles. She knew the division. She also knew the culture and the etiquette and would have been able to teach me a thing or two about the closure I needed to find. But it was a closure that slipped through my fingers when she walked away from my doorstep.

Our next round of guests were relatives, and the next after that, and they were most gracious. It was weeks before we emptied our freezer of the calzones and pot pies they carried. Actually, it was wonderful seeing them, but it was more wonderful celebrating him with them. We told his story over and over, saying that I had to travel for work. None of them asked where or why I was gone beyond that. Why should they have? I'd have been surprised if half of them really knew what it was I did for work, or used to do, I

131

suppose. Work shouldn't have been on my mind that day, but it was. Only on and off, though. Every time we told it, I was thankful for his little heart more than anything else.

Everyone had their stories to tell, too, while their kids played with the TV or the toys they brought for Nicky. Some of them I had heard a few times, others a dozen, and at least one or two, not at all. I was there for a few, but I saw those in an entirely new light that afternoon. Their stories were like a part of some pledge. It was like we had arrived at adulthood, which was some big happening, but before we could step foot inside the main ballroom, there was a small reception by the coat check. That was where we had to learn the proper ground rules. There were pieces of honest advice intermingled with one-upmanship, amongst a smattering of sentiment, laughter, heritage, hogwash and hand-me-downs. Of course, no one would be there to help us sift through. It was all so wonderfully confusing, and it gave us a glimpse into just how much had changed.

"So what was it you had to tell me earlier?" she whispered. Nicholas was asleep in his bassinet and we were changing, quietly, to at least lay down while we could. I was planning on taking two weeks off, but we hadn't really talked about how to swing my leave on account of his hurried arrival. Part of me was hoping she forgot.

"I don't want us to argue about this, or get into anything," I said. She looked over as she switched off the reading lamp. The streetlight was there to give us light enough to still see one another. "I was let go. Just then. Over the phone. That Dean Samson I've told you about... Bitch." I wasn't entirely distressed over not having to go back, but she would still be painted the villain.

"You were fired? Why? Oh honey, are you ok?" I wasn't sure how she was going to take the news. I was also skeptical of her opening volley. It was a good one, but I knew what questions were coming.

"Before I left, she had it out for me. She never liked the idea of me going. Actually, I don't even think that was it. She didn't like someone breaking her rules. I shouldn't even take it personally. I do a good enough job. It's her loss!" We were still whispering. "She found out that I never made it to the funeral. Those assholes were counting on sealing some kind of deal with this family. Can you imagine?"

"So she found out, but that's why they let you go? I mean, please don't try to make me feel bad about this. I had no control..."

"It's nothing like that. Actually, as much as she sucks, it's my own fault."

"What do you mean, *your* fault?"

"I never called them. I was supposed to be checking emails, and then when I left, I never called. I was in such a hurry that I didn't tell anyone we were in the hospital with the baby. It honestly just never occurred. She said I was *stealing time*. I don't even know if that's what it would be."

"That's ridiculous. Can you fight it?"

"Do I really want to? That place drives me crazy. I mean, I like the other advisors, and the students are great to work with, but I wasn't happy there. And besides, it's too far of a drive."

"What are we going to do for money?" she asked, and I knew it was coming. I just hit savings with a wasted globe trot and our new bottom line would be awake soon, and hungry. She was right to ask it, even though it irked me a little.

"I'll figure something out. I'll start looking right away. I know a lot of people, and I've had my eye on a few openings anyways. I'd like to get back into the city. If I don't find something soon, I'm sure I can collect. We'll figure this out."

Whether she was too tired to go on, or she trusted my words, that was nearly the end of it.

"We always do," she said. "At least now you can help with him at night." She was snoring sooner than I could respond. I always envied her for that.

PART 2

CHAPTER FOURTEEN
MY FOURTH REFERENCE

"W hy did you leave your last job?"

It was already a month. This came from an otherwise uninterested member of my search committee. I feel like sometimes we ask these questions just to ask. It's not always because we have an honest and genuine want to know, but a want to either be the one to ask it, or to punch the ticket because you don't have something authentic to ask. I had anticipated a lot of questions: strengths, weaknesses, five year plans, working with an angry parent, crisis response, hot topics, supervisory experience, ideal supervisor, and so on. I didn't anticipate that one, and some half-yawning sweater vest from Admissions was about to cost me and my family a decent wage. No matter what my words were, I paused. My mind immediately went to salvaging what I could and practicing that answer for the next interview.

Don't talk bad on your previous employer, I thought. I went on in my head for that brief coronary scare of a halt.

Don't do it. Say something. Be politically correct. Politically. Politics! Go with that.

"It was time for me to pursue other aspects of my career path. There was no room for advancement, and the environment was increasingly political." I went on about how I wanted to focus more in a specialized area, which this was, but who knows how much of that they wanted to hear.

I knew better. I've taught better. One of the things I instructed on to my freshman cohort was Career Development. You can never tell if the smirks around the table are for some faux-pas you've just made, or if there's some crazy Dean that they, too, can associate with just a glance. I've been behind both myself. Admissions just scribbled some notes and seemed content to be off the hook to ask anything further. "I hope that answers your question," I said. That's a tell-tale interview tic when your answer wasn't sure-footed.

"Thank you, that was perfect," he said.

For the rest of my half day, I met with members of the division, the head of the division, members of the shop I was hoping to join, and finally the hiring manager. HR was earlier in the day. They laughed off a campus tour because it was my alma matter. This was the second position that I was interviewing for, of four I had lined up. This was the one that I wanted, even though at least one other had a higher salary and a better title. There was something about that place.

In fact, during the tenure of my last role, I had interviewed there twice. Those may well have been my only two sick days. Both of the characters that beat me out were already gone. I kept that in my head all day. There was neither confidence there, nor doubt, but it kept me present.

"Do you have any kids?" the manager asked. She had a picture of a newborn in her arms pinned on a cork board behind her computer. *I didn't think you could ask that?* wondered the career advisor in me, but my face told a different set of stories. "How old?" she asked.

"He's just over five weeks now," I answered. "Nicholas." I leaned back to reach into my pocket for a picture on my phone. I already had just the right picture cued up in case anyone got to talking about their kids. We went through his story a little, at least as far as me being away and his slight health thing that needed monitoring. Maybe I down-played it's telling, but it didn't seem so dramatic now that it was passed. I settled on that being a welcome milestone.

"Oh he's handsome. I wish mine had hair," she said, turning to unpin his picture. Her son was almost one by then, she said. We shared more stories of staying awake than we did about working with students. She told me I looked remarkably well for still getting up throughout the night.

She knew some of the same people I knew, and was familiar with some of my old colleagues, so she never asked why I wasn't working there anymore. She only said that she knew how political it was. Our chat gave me hope. She shared her timeline and we wrapped just about on the hour.

"How did it go," she asked. I called the moment I walked outside. It was freezing. And windy. She was hard to hear, but it was clear that the baby was fussing.

"I think it went well. Shorter than I expected. I don't know, I really hope that I get this one. It's closer than the others. The office was really cool. I just hope I didn't say the wrong thing."

"I'm sure it was fine. We can talk about it later? I have to feed him. Will you be able stop and get wipes?"

"Sure thing," I said. "See you soon."

That meant we were through the supply that we got for his shower. We'd been careful, eating frozen calzones and the like, seeing that we both weren't working. She was pulling in three-quarter pay for the time being, and I didn't begin the process to collect because I ended up having interviews lined up right away. We were in for a few tight weeks, but nothing we didn't know before.

Not a day went by that I didn't think about Min. They asked the right student crisis questions. While I gave another example, he was burning up the front of my mind. Would I even be in this search if it wasn't for what he did? What about if I did make it to his funeral? What would have come of it? Was he right about his parents? Why did he do it, anyways? I guessed and I guessed and I struggled with that fact that I would likely never know.

❖

I took a little longer stopping at the whole sale club for wipes, and I didn't mind the traffic getting out of there during the rush. A lot was on my mind that afternoon, but a phone call made for the first of several turnabouts. I recognized the number, or else I wouldn't have taken the call.

"Yes, is Mr. Peter Cahill available?"

"Speaking," I said, wondering why they ask such a thing knowing it's my mobile. Formality, I suppose.

"Mr. Cahill, this is Nancy calling from Human Resources, we met this afternoon." She didn't say from which University, but we were fairly familiar by the time I left.

"Yes, hi Nancy, it's nice to hear from you." It was.

"I am calling on behalf of the hiring manager and search committee and..." oh great, here it comes. I tried pulling over. She referenced the search committee. I knew I blew that question. "...we would like to move forward with reference checks with your permission." She said something else in the middle that I missed because I was pulling into a liquor store's parking lot. She probably heard the elation in my sigh.

"Yes, that would be fantastic. My references should be on the updated résumé that I provided, but please let me know if you need any additional contacts."

"We have received them, and that is also why I am calling. I see that you have provided three references, but will you be able to provide a reference from a direct supervisor?"

This was a question I *had* anticipated. Submitting the names I had was a gamble anyways. I couldn't call on Samson. I thought about my previous supervisor as well, the one who left six months prior to my departure to pursue consulting. We had a great rapport, but she was still book club friends with that particular Dean. They talked shop too often for me to have even thought about asking her. I could have asked a faculty friend to stretch the truth, but that wasn't the way I wanted it to happen. They wouldn't make me stoop to that. But I thought about her "tight knit community", and that was exactly where I found my fourth reference.

"It sounds like you are away from your files, so if you have a name from your previous institution, we can make an inquiry," she added. I must have sounded like I was searching. The fact that they were eager had me willing to leap.

"That would be fantastic. I would be more than happy to get you his contact information when I am back at my computer, but his name is Dean Michael Freeman. Before I left," I felt like this needed a little explaining, "...I was in an interim position. I reported directly to several Deans while the search was ongoing for my department's Director. I worked with Dean Freeman on student crisis management."

"We will contact Dean Freeman for a reference check this afternoon. You should be hearing from us within the next few days. Thank you, and good luck Mr. Cahill."

141

"Thank you for the call," I said. "And please let me know if you need anything further."

I never called Dean Freeman to ask his permission, and that was the only regret I attached to that place. He came through, as I figured he would. They called me the next morning to offer the position and I was slated to start the following week. We learned something about each other that day in his office, however unspoken. If I had to guess, he was expecting a call on my behalf. More than anything, I wanted to thank him, but we both knew it wasn't necessary. After four years of headache and a few hard weeks of heartache at the end, I was able to close the door on that chapter in a most unexpected way. And to think, I always thought he was a prick…

CHAPTER FIFTEEN
AMERICAN FOLK

Fatherhood was wonderful, and so were my new colleagues. For the first time in my young professional life, I knew what a work-life balance was. What Min started, Nicky finished. In so many ways, I would not have had what I did with my boy so early on if it wasn't for him.

The holidays came, and then were gone just as fast. Baby's first Christmas. We celebrated, as we had much to celebrate. The tables we set were filled from our traditions. There was seafood on the eve, like my father's family used to do, and lamb and all the trimmings after exchanging presents, like my wife's. The week after saw us shooting champagne and then swapping out bottles so we could feed Nicky in the middle of the first night. A lot of happy memories were made, and roots of our own were sewn that year.

It wasn't until a little while after that I thought about what Christmas would have been like in that apartment tower. I suppose good holiday tidings have a way of washing even that clean, in time. I hoped that in time they would have a holiday that would bring happier memories.

❖

I can't remember what work we did before the students came back for their spring classes, or the names of all of those I met with, but I remember how much he changed my thinking. I was probably too quick to take a student over to counseling, but I vowed not to let him happen again. If only there were signs, I could have done more. It's a hard thing, coming to terms with the fact that there was no one to blame.

They didn't learn of his story, from the letter he left, to my overnight trip to Tokyo, until it was necessary for me to tell them, and thankfully my new supervisor was understanding...

One day, around mid-March, I got a call from home.

"Did you order something from...Korea?" Her pause was as though she was fondling the package to read the rest of the labels.

"No," I said. "Where does it say it's from?"

"I can't pronounce it, but it says South Korea."

"Ok, I'll check it out when I get home. Do you need anything if I stop?"

"We're almost out of formula, and if you stop, can you pick up something to eat? I don't feel like cooking."

"Sure thing. See you in a bit. Love you."

"Love you too," she said, and I went about the rest of my day. It was busy since group advising for course registration was right around the corner.

By the time I walked in, a little late, which was to be expected during pre-reg, I had completely forgotten about our call from earlier. She left the package on the counter with the other mail. It was sitting uneven atop credit card flyers, the coupon paper, and take out menus. It was a squat box, longer than it was tall, and probably big enough to hold about a pint. One of the corners was banged in, but it was sealed up well. Clear as day, it was addressed to me. The return label was from someone whose name I had no recollection of ever hearing. I knew the writing on the new "to" label as well as my own; it belonged to Suzanne, from my old office. It must have been received there and then forwarded. Thankfully it didn't go to the Dean's office first.

There was something inside that a shake couldn't identify, but it wasn't overly heavy for its size. I cut through the tape along the tops seams, careful to keep the labels intact, to find out what had arrived.

Red tissue, first, and it was surrounding a small stack that included a framed picture, another picture, separate from the frame, a thickish sealed envelope, and a second sealed envelope, which was addressed to my name. The picture in the frame was hand drawn, and the one that sat alone was an old Polaroid of a small boy without his wheelchair. I wedged in a butter knife and had a slit half torn along the top edge of the letter when I paused to turn the

145

picture over. Some letters, probably his name, were scrawled there. Letters, and a date. The inscription put him at about eight or nine. "South Korea?" I asked. I never needed a letter open quite that fast.

Mr. Peter Cahill,

My name is Yong Lim and I am cousin to Minho Park, who is your student. I am fifteen years old and have attended English school in Korea. My grandmother and Minho's grandmother, Soon-ja Park, is also writing through my pen because she does not speak or write or read in English. We are sad to tell you that Minho has died and he was cremated at his funeral in Tokyo with his father and mother. We were not able to attend because my grandmother says that she is not able to travel from our village. My mother works many hours to support us and my father has also died many years ago, so I must stay and take care of Grandmother. Grandmother spoke on uncle's telephone to Minho's father on the day of the funeral and she has learned that your baby is sick. We are saddened to hear this news. Our village prayed at Jangseung for recovery of his health and for Minho.

My cousin Minho wrote many letters to Grandmother. He wrote to us about you in them, and he also sent to us many drawings and paintings that he made. One that he said was inspired by you is included with our letter.

The small frame. I hadn't looked that closely before, but it was of a samurai, who was wearing a full beard.

He said that "American folk" are very different for him, but that you make him feel comfortable. This is why we are writing to you now. My cousin said that you understand him better than anyone. We need your help and hope that you will agree to help us. Grandmother has fallen sick, and she is also with much worry. She is afraid that she will die, and there is some things about my cousin Minho that we need to know.

Please, Mr. Peter Cahill, will you come? You will find American dollars enough for your travels...

I dropped the pages I was so unsure of what I was reading. Actually, I had a sudden need to recheck the box. Oh I tore at that other envelope without my butter knife. Inside was a stack of thirty seven one hundred dollars bills. They were the older ones, and they were in remarkably good shape. I scurried the pages, scanned lines I had already read, and with the wealth of an entire village from half a world away in my hand, I continued.

You will stay in uncle's house, which has a telephone and shower, and an extra bed. We understand if you are not able to come. If you are unable, please accept this money as a gift to your new son. May he have health and good luck.

He went on to provide a return address, an Uncle's phone number, and he signed the letter in his and his grandmother's names.

"I need to stop getting letters from this kid," I said. And then I turned to call for my wife.

CHAPTER SIXTEEN
A LITTLE CLOSER TO HOME

"No. Are you kidding me? Korea now? And then what? You can't just leave me, and what will you do about work? You just started!"

"I think this place is different. Spring break is coming up and she's already told me that I should think about taking a few days off."

"You should, and you should want to spend them with us. Are you actually thinking you can just leave now? I'll be going back to work soon, and we won't see each other those nights. I need help with him, too. You can't just go."

"I know... I know I can't. All I'm asking is that you just read the letter. And we can't just keep their money. I mean, what am I supposed to do?"

"Just leave it. This isn't something that you should get in the middle of. He's not your..."

"My what?! You know, this hasn't been easy for me. You know that. This isn't about work for me. This is about him now. It's about doing what's right. I can't in good conscience..."

"Don't put our son in the middle of this. It's about you. No. You can't go."

"That's not fair. It's not just your decision to make."

"Well it's not just yours either!"

"Will you at least read the letter? I mean, I don't know what the hell I'm supposed to do..."

"You're supposed to take care of your responsibilities here. Us. This is the real world, you can't just go running off every time someone..."

"I'm not running off. I really think that I should consider this, though. Can your mother stay? I can ask my mother, but she works those days. They have a different week off."

"No! Why are we even arguing about this? It's ridiculous. Why can't they just call you?"

"It's not. And I don't know, but I don't think a call settles any of this. This kid is dead. They need answers as much as I do. I can't just let this go. You get to leave your patients at the end of the day. This is different for me. I feel like I owe them..."

"You don't owe them anything."

"Will you just read the letter?"

"Fine. Where is it?"

"It's here."

❖

"H-how do they know? Who told these people about our son?"

"I have no idea. I would think that they spoke with someone on campus, but I never called them. I never told anyone else. And certainly not soon enough for them to have known on the day of the funeral. We were in the hospital on that day, remember? That was the day..."

"That what?"

"Well, that was when they thought he might need surgery. How could they have known that? How did he just...get better? Aren't you curious?"

"That was months ago. For all you know, she may have died already."

"No. Somehow I don't think so. Look, I don't know exactly what it is that they want from me, but this one isn't sitting right. I don't think I believe in karma, but..."

"Are you listening to yourself? Karma? He just *got better*? I really don't like this."

"Neither do I. But that's why I think I might need to do this."

"Why is this one any different?"

"I don't know, but this one hits a little closer to home. What if something happened to him?"

"Stop throwing that around. Nothing is going to happen to him..."

"That's not what I mean."

151

"What is it that they think you know that's going to let this kid rest?"

"I wish I knew, but it's clearly something that they can't put into a letter. This is the second request this kid's made from the grave. I don't know how I could live with myself if I didn't see at least one of them through."

"I don't have a good feeling about this."

"Neither do I, Threepio. Let me at least call."

"That's not funny. Go ahead, call. You know my feelings. Go, if you have to. I really don't care. It better not be when I'm back to work. And you better not get fired again. We can't live like this."

"I know. I'll call the number, and then we'll talk."

CHAPTER SEVENTEEN
WHO I WAS SUPPOSED TO BE

The first call was placed before dinner. It would have been early the next morning in their village in South Korea. In so many ways, it was a cold call, but someone answered. It was against my every instinct.

He sounded much older than me, and we were far from understanding one another, but I understood him to be the uncle and I think he understood who I was supposed to be. To be sure, I said, and repeated, that the call was for Yong Lim. I don't know what we talked about, and he seemed to say so much more, but the call was longer than necessary.

"So what happened," she asked.

"Nothing. I called. I got his Uncle, I think, but he didn't speak any English. Let's hope he tells his nephew, I guess."

"Let's hope," she said, sarcastically, and luke warm like she'd just lost an argument. "Do you want me to make you a plate?"

My wife cooked that night; *macaronia me kima.* That's Greek for *we don't have anything else in the freezer, so we're having pasta and ground beef.* As much as *chicken scampi* - which is something of a misnomer, because a scampi is a prawn - was my staple growing up, this was hers, and it's nowhere near as bad as that sentiment makes it sound. Actually, when done right, it's as good as it gets. This is rigatoni bolognese with all-spice and cinnamon. It's earthy, aromatic, and it hits the mark for something rustic. With a side of cucumber, tomato, oil, and feta, this is village food at its finest. My heart and my mind were in Greece that evening. That is to say, I was thinking of Min, and the grandmother in my head was not that far off from the one I met on our honeymoon. I wondered on and off about how true that would become.

We weren't ten minutes past clearing plates and my phone rang. The feeling of a cell phone on vibrate can ring a meeting reminder or a message from social media; it can be welcome, or anticipated, or even an annoyance. We communicate so often from our fingertips that it's just sort of there. But sometimes a call can leap your heart into your throat. Some things we take for granted. My face flushed and I was nervous to take the call. There were more numbers than normal when I looked, and I knew who was on the line.

"Hello, this is Peter Cahill," I said. It was half of how I answered at work. I wanted to sound professional, but it wasn't official college business any longer, so I didn't introduce the office. Before I answered, I shut the bedroom door behind me. I never liked being listened in on.

"Mr. Peter Cahill," he said. I saw myself like through a tunnel a mile long and only inches across. He sounded like his cousin. It was uncanny. "Thank you, Professor. Thank you for calling." I wanted to correct him. I used to correct Min for calling me that, but that was beside the point of our conversation. "My uncle is so happy to have spoken with you. He is afraid that you did not understand, and he insists that I tell you that he said bless you. Bless you, professor, for calling."

"Yong Lim?" I assumed, but asked anyways. "It is wonderful to speak with you. Thank you for calling back, and thank you to your uncle. I have received your letter. It came in the mail today."

"Today?! This was sent long time ago. I am sorry that it has taken this time."

"No, I am sorry. I... I'm not sure if it would have been here sooner, but I have started at another University." Hoping they hadn't held it from me for long, I felt like he needed some explaining. I opened my mouth to ask about his grandmother, but the words weren't there.

"My Grandmother is very grateful to know you have received her message." I was happy to hear of her. "Mr. Peter," he called me what Min called me, "will you come?"

"Well, that's why I am calling..."

"Then you will come! When? Uncle will arrange for a ride..."

155

"No, no. I mean..."

"So you will not? Please, can I ask..."

"No, no, no. I am calling to discuss. I would be happy to share what I can with you. Can you tell me a little more?"

"Min was very special to Grandmother," his voice told of how selfless his statement really was. "They spoke many times when Grandmother was able, but now they write many letters because her walking is not very good. He says things in Grandmother's letters that need you to help understand for us."

I was intrigued, and I wanted to help. My mind raced through options like scanning things and emailing, or having him re-read them and ask me questions, but he sounded more desperate than that. I so badly wanted to ask something else about her.

"Grandmother is not well." There it was. "She has prayed for your call. Min has showed her signs that you will come."

"Thank you. Please understand, Min meant very much to me. I am very saddened by this. I haven't stopped thinking about him for... I want to help in any way that I can. This is a very difficult time for me."

"Yes. You have a young baby. Grandmother says that she would never ask something so difficult if it was not necessary. Was the money not enough?"

"More than enough. That is certainly not necessary, and I would never expect..."

"Yes, Professor. It is necessary. We have very much to show you. It is only a small amount next to your help. It would be an honor. This is what Minho wanted."

"I need to discuss this with my wife. Is there anything that I can tell you now?"

"No, Professor. Please tell me very soon. If I do not stay for your return call, you will please forgive me. Uncle will find me to call. We will pray that you come."

He triggered something with those words that probably wasn't intentional, but I had to know.

"Before we go, I need to ask, how did you know... about my son? That he was sick."

"Uncle."

"I don't understand."

"Not this uncle. Other uncle. Minho's father. He was thankful for you to attend Minho's funeral. He came to your hotel to invite you to his home. You had to leave early, and he understands very much that family is the most important. He is so thankful, he spoke with Grandmother to tell her! He insisted to speak with Grandmother. You must understand, he has not spoken with Grandmother in many years. Uncle came to help her to his house for the phone. Together we pray, and Uncle, he pray for your baby and fix his heart. And for Min. We know you also pray for Min. This makes us like family."

For a moment I paused. Those sorts of sentiments made me a little uncomfortable. It was a long enough pause for him to ask if I was still there.

"Yes. I'm here. Let me speak to my wife and see what I am able to do. I will call you back as soon as I can."

"We would be very grateful, Professor. Thank you. Thank you from all of us. Thank you for helping my cousin. Goodbye."

And with that he was gone.

CHAPTER EIGHTEEN
JUST SOME EXISTENTIAL FUNK

Only the sound of cars creeping by filled my space; the whir and rumble of an engine in low gear, and the tires treading heavily on the pavement. Even going slow, I could hear the pitch shift at the exact moment when they passed. But an echo of nothing, of buzzing silence, the extension of the fleeting, final click after he hung the handset drowned it all out. For a few moments longer I bathed in it, getting used to the tingling feeling and remembering to focus my eyes.

I thought back through the words he spoke, and the way that he spoke them. They may well have believed that their praying made a difference here. How could a few villagers saying words half the earth away patch a hole in a pulmonary vessel that small? That's some pretty precise invocation. Clearly, I was a skeptic. In fact, I didn't believe in any of that. I wouldn't. But I had a feeling that she would.

She gave me space, or she didn't assume that I was done yet. I didn't make it easy to monitor my calls. That was a neurosis I gathered from working under people I didn't trust. She also sounded busy with the baby. I wasn't ready to tip my hand to this kid, another neurosis, I guess, but everything he said was compelling, even after repeating the key points a few times. How the hell was I going to convince her of the same?

❖

When I rejoined my family, I puttered around the kitchen like I was still mad about our argument.

"What happened?" she asked.

I kept pacing, putting away dishes and clearing the counter.

"Do what you need to do with him first," I said. She was finishing his bottle, and he was fading. She argued with herself whether to let him fall asleep then or try to hold him a bit longer for the sake of the overnight. He was passed out before the last ounce.

"Well? You were in there for a long time," she said. Nicky went right down. We may have been in for a long night, seeing that it was still only prime time.

"That was...interesting," I said. "I definitely spoke with the uncle earlier. This cousin wasn't much different than Min. It was like talking to him..."

"But what did he say?"

"They said there's things they need to show me. Same shit as in the letter, really. Something that they need my help to understand. Said it was what Min would have

160

wanted. I... They have letters from him, so I'm guessing that's it."

"What was he trying to tell them? Was there something you think they may not have understood?"

"Yeah, that he was gay. Maybe?"

"Maybe he was gay?"

"No, no. Maybe that's what they didn't understand. But why in the hell would they need me to travel around the world for that? It doesn't make any sense."

"How is that sort of thing looked at in Korea?"

"I'd be lucky if I could point it out on a map, how should I know? I mean, no, I'm guessing it's not generally accepted. They sound very traditional. People can't even get married in half of our states. How would it fly in your family's village?"

"Everyone's Orthodox. Not like *liberal* orthodox, *legit* orthodox. I don't think it would go so well. They even deny communion, I think."

"That's got to be it," I said.

"What? Communion?!"

"No. Really? No, maybe there is some last rites thing, and they need to be sure? What did the Chaplain say, again? He's Christian and his family is Buddhist? No, that doesn't sound right. I think it's the other way around. But that probably doesn't mean his Grandmother? I have no idea. Still makes no sense."

"Maybe they want to blame you somehow..."

"No, I doubt that."

161

"I really think that this is crazy that we're even still considering this. I also don't like that they mentioned our baby."

"So I asked about that. Asked him how they knew. Evidently, his father was so touched that I travelled all that way that he went to my hotel. He was going to invite me to his house. For what, I don't know, but I'm guessing that the doorman told him where I went. The father called the village, and I guess that's when they all prayed for him. And get this, they think they fixed his heart..."

She just sort of looked. It was like she was working out an answer, or had a nerve touched. "He said that because we also prayed for Min that it makes us all like family," I continued. "He sounded sincere. You know what I think."

"Yes, I know what you think. You don't believe any of that. But I do. What else did he say?"

"Nothing, really. I mean, he said that his uncle, Min's father, hasn't spoken with them in years. It sounded like his grandmother was hanging on for an answer, but he said they would understand..."

I wanted to go. A big part of me wanted to see this thing through. I don't know if it was a way to test myself, that I wanted to do right by Min, that I wanted to know that I hadn't walked away from my job because I failed, or maybe I wanted to know that I could do right as a new dad. Maybe it was just some existential funk. I had no idea if his grandmother was "hanging on," clinging to life, hopeful that I would come and in some romantic, cinematic way, put her last and dying wishes to bed. Looking at it that way, it sounded a bit trite. Whatever it was, I knew how to lay it on just thick enough.

"This scares me. I don't know why, but I don't like this. But how can I say no? How am I supposed to say no to any of this? It's your call... I don't want to be that wife..."

She was curious. I could see it in her eyes. I knew her too well, she wouldn't have just changed her mind like that. She didn't want to give me the satisfaction. But she did.

"You have to go," she said. "I just..."

"I know," I said, trying not to sound too excited. Truth be told, I was nervous about it too, but I couldn't deny my gut. "Let me talk to my boss tomorrow. I will figure out the best days to take. Spring break is..."

"Next week, I know. I go back the following week. You have to be back by that weekend. It's not an option."

"Do you think I should call him back? Or do you think I should wait until tomorrow?" I said.

"Do whatever, I need to lay down. Don't forget, you're on if he gets up. I'll take the overnight because you need to be up, but until midnight, it's you, babe."

"'Night," I said. I meant to say more. Honestly, I wanted more dialogue on whether I should have called. I wound up not calling then, and I laid for most of the night thinking that I should've. The sensible thing to do was to sleep on it, talk it through with work, see if she still agreed, check flights, and then call at lunch. That was the plan.

❖

I was proud of my boy. He made it six whole hours until he needed to be changed and fed. Two in the morning and I was still awake. "Alright, bud. It's ok," I said. I snuck him a pacifier. That scream, at that time of night, could wake the dead. She was out cold and still snoring, though.

No matter how upset he was, and how awake I was, it still sucked getting out of that bed. My eyes were heavy from the day, and my temples were ringing. The floor was cold, and she seemed to hear when it creaked. Of course, the scream machine didn't wake her. I stopped like I was sneaking around security guards in some old-school art heist, and leaned like an acrobat to create a seal between his blowhole and his pacifier. She nuzzled back down. I scooped him out of his bassinet and took him to the other room.

We had decided that he would stay with us until he was regularly sleeping through 'til morning. His room was all set up, complete with furniture from my Dad's wood shop and the best video monitor we could get. I put hours into painting Disney characters on his wall, just like my Dad did for us. The nursing rocker wasn't all that comfortable for me, so I usually either wound up back in bed, on the couch, or pacing. Sometimes, out of necessity, you learn to rig all kinds of bottle holding contraptions. That night, a series of carefully placed stuffed animals propped up by receiving blankets, on and around the bouncy chair, held a bottle for him while I paced the hallway. I had a call to make that I couldn't let go until the morning. Lunch for me was during the small hours of their morning, and that meant another day's wait. Without confirmation from my wife or my boss, I dialed the last number on my recent calls list.

I was expecting the uncle, and that's exactly who I got. "Hello," I wish I knew his name. "This is Peter Cahill. Yong Lim, please." It came out slower than it should've, and I suppose a bit louder. This conversation was much faster. He repeated something that I found later to mean thanks and a blessing, and he went. He didn't hang up the phone, though. His footsteps were fast. My heart started racing and my mouth went all dry.

This kid already cost me one job. My son, all straddled up and sucking down pumped milk was breaking my heart. He should have had my undivided everything. I could see myself like I was Scrooge looking back, yet I couldn't muster the nerve to let that call drop. This was my new least proud moment.

"Hey buddy," I whispered, wiping a dribble from his chin. By then, his hair was long enough to be in his eyes. I swept that aside as carefully as I could. He was curious of my touch, but he was also nodding. His shallow little breaths made the tiniest snores when he finally fell back asleep. I was proud of each and every breath he made, and at least a part of me, albeit a tired one, felt like I owed it to him to stay on the call. Someday he'd understand. I only hoped that I would, too.

The phone found itself pressed tighter against my ear when I heard the commotion on the other end. With regard for long distance charges, maybe, they ran back. A stack of something, some cookware, or other, took a tumble. He was breathing heavy.

"Hello," he said. "Hello Professor. Thank you, Professor, for calling. I told Uncle to come and get me. I knew that you would call."

"Hello, Yong Lim? How are you?"

"Thank you, Professor. I am very good. Were you talking to your wife?"

"Yes. Yes, I was. We decided that...well, I can come."

He said something to his uncle and there was some praising and semi-celebratory remarks.

"Now I still need to confirm and book my flights. How will I travel to you? Is there anything specific that I will need to do?" I was shooting from the hip. I had hundreds of questions. Did I really just agree to, on faith, fly blindly into Seoul?

"This is wonderful news, Professor. Grandmother will be so honored. Please, if you will tell me when, my Uncle will handle the rest of the details. I will look forward to meeting with you soon. Bless you, and bless your family."

I started to ask another question, and I don't remember what. He cut me off.

"Please, I must go to tell Grandmother, and to make ready. My cousin was right. Thank you again, Professor."

They seem to suck the hardest when you try to take their empty bottle away. There was no clean way to get it out of there and switch it for a pacifier. I had to scoop him again, letting all of his animals scatter. He was quite clear that as long as that wasn't touched, he was staying asleep. So, I carried him in carefully and I laid him down, bottle and all. The trick is to sneak it out just when you lift his head from the crook of your arm. Sometimes you need the pacifier, sometimes you get lucky. I almost wanted him to kick up more of a fuss. I was feeling guilty and wanted to tell her what I'd done. Actually, I wanted to hear myself say it aloud so I could know if it was the right thing to do. When she says to "do whatever," it's usually a trap; one that I still hadn't quite figured my way out of. I would have preferred it to be a vague memory for her in the morning than a surprise. No such luck.

CHAPTER NINETEEN
THAT WAS THAT

Morning came on the heels of about an hour or so worth of sleep. I was up and out before either of those two woke, which was just as well. My wife had one of those bottled Starbucks lattes in the fridge. For some reason, I thought that was going to be a good idea. Coffee gives me the shits. Almost immediately. Thankfully I decided to drive to the station that morning. There's no way a bus is pulling over on the highway to make that happen for you. I screamed into a McDonalds and wound up having to hang out there for about an hour or so. Boy did my morning backfire. There's the second Dad joke. I had to buy something, and fake like I was reading the paper to keep close to the bathroom. Luckily, there are these things called hash browns. If there was a God, this was what they wanted me to eat that morning.

❖

"Nicky had us up all night," I said when I walked in almost two hours late. There was no excuse offered for not emailing, and finally, I worked for an office where none was needed. She understood. Still, I felt like it probably wasn't the best move, barging in late and asking for time off. It was Wednesday, though, which meant we were having a staff meeting. It was just my luck that "vacation time" was on the agenda. It was near the bottom of the agenda, but it was on there.

I trudged my way through a few student meetings. I knew when I was on auto-pilot, and I think I was good enough at it that they didn't. If I could get them out of there with tasks of their own to complete, and with as little added to my plate as possible, it was a good meeting. At least, that was how I used to see things.

Coming in late is the best, if you can get away with it every now and then, because it makes the day go by a lot faster. It was lunch soon enough, and I had no need to call Korea, but home was in need. She picked up after the second ring, and she sounded pretty busy, so we didn't talk for long. When she asked if I knew what day I was leaving, I said "not yet." But she had to go and be with Nicky, and that was fine.

That call reminded me, though. I hadn't researched flights or anything, and had no clue if there was something direct. The money they sent was on my dresser, and I had no intention of waiting until tomorrow to book something. I'd settled on using my credit card and just making the payment later on their dime.

For the rest of lunch, and then most of the afternoon, I blew off stuff that needed to get done and searched for flights. The weekend flights were more, but I couldn't spare the time. Six seats were left in coach on the cheapest one, and then five when I refreshed the page. Something that I didn't have to do just became urgent. I couldn't wait for the meeting to find out, and I wouldn't make them wait much more than they already had.

Hey," I said, knocking on her open door. "Do you have a minute?"

"Sure. What's up?" She was still typing, and half paying attention to what I was up to, but when I asked if I could close the door, she was all ears.

"I was wondering if, well, I know you mentioned about next week..." I was still timid to ask to take time. It wasn't because I was still "the new guy," but because of what I was used to at the "other place."

"Yeah. Are you gonna take some time off?"

"If it's ok, I would like to."

"Of course. What's up?"

"Well, do you remember I mentioned my student from before?" Mentioning it was a tactic; I learned to be good at planting seeds.

"Yes," she said. She knew exactly which.

"I, uh, this is going to sound crazy... I think I might need to make that trip again."

"Really? His much time do you need? You can take the whole week. But is that going to be enough?"

Now, not many of us in the field have bosses like this. She is one in a million. She didn't care for the details, and she wasn't just offering to be the "cool boss." She was sincere.

"So, long story short, I got a call from his family last night."

"Really? How did they find you?"

"Through my last office. Its ok, I'm actually glad they did. It turns out that he wrote to them. Sounds like almost every day. Get this, they sent a stack of cash and want to fly me out. They said they need my help reading his letters, understanding what he was talking about. I thought about this all night. I think they believe that the letters from him explain why. They need to know. I mean, I guess... I would like to know..."

"It's a long way to travel to read some letters."

"I know," I chuckled. "The thing is, they told me that it was at his request. Did I tell you about the letter he left?"

"You did. I've never lost a student. Not like that. I don't know what I'd do, but it's clear that he meant a lot to you. Just keep me posted on when you need to go. Take as much time as you need."

"Thank you. This is not like me to ask. I will make up the work."

"Please. We'll be fine. It should be quiet next week. Go. And you can tell us all about it when you get back. We'll meet in about forty five?"

"Sounds good. Thank you again."

By the time we were through, I was able to grab the last seat on that flight.

❖

During the meeting, I never had to say a thing. When the topic came up, she said "Peter is taking the week. We need to keep the office open, so if you would like to take time, get me your requests, and I will divvy them out. I'm taking Friday, but you two," we were a team of four, "let me know by the end of this week."

That was that. I was going to South Korea, for what God and Min's family only knew, and it was a lot easier than it should have been.

CHAPTER TWENTY
THE FIRST SINCE

At week's end, we decided to go out to a nice meal before my trip. I was packed and ready, about as lightly as I was before, minus the suit. Come to think of it, that was the first time we had the baby out to dinner. I knew what it was like to roll eyes at the couple with the infant, and I felt theirs all on me like daggers. In the end, he did quite well, once he was fed. I got a kick out of how his carrier fit perfectly into an upside down high chair.

Our conversations were where they needed to be. We talked about Nicholas, laughed at the quirks he already had, and we talked about the food and other favorite meals we'd had. Not much time was spent, if any at all, talking about me going away. With any luck, it would seem not longer than her longest work week. We were ok going for a stretch of a few days apart. Finding each other in the middle was easier every time. I learned, as best I could, the truth behind absence and fonder hearts.

She took care of him, and promised to take him through the night so that I could get sleep. She even apologized for the other night, which was crazy. He was ours; we were both responsible. I would have had her sleep every night if I could.

I started reading a primer on traveling in South Korea while she fed him in the nursery. The monitor was on, and I could hear that she was humming to him softly. He was no match for the glider, and was making softer, steadier breaths in no time. There is something that vibrates in our DNA to hear the one we love becoming a parent to our child. It's a bonding beyond love. No words could I have spoken nor touch could I have given to show what she was making me feel. There was something there that was, as best as I could know, and I'm stepping outside of the self I know to say, remarkably spiritual.

After laying him down, she came back from freshening herself. I heard her from where I was still reading. "He's in *his* bed," she said. I knew that voice. I turned, and she was standing at the corner of the hall, half hiding that she was wearing something sheerer than her normal pajamas.

"Yeah?" I asked.

"Mm hmm."

She reached over and flipped the light and called for me to follow.

174

You're supposed to wait at least six weeks after having a baby, and you need clearance from your OBGYN. Longer, if they need to do what they call "repair." Oh how that word made me cringe. It was even past *that* wait period, but as things go, this was it; this would be the first since.

The wait was one of the surprises; part of the list of "things they don't teach in that seventh grade health class." I wondered if our grandparents followed those guidelines, but that was as far as I wanted to wonder about that. It'd been three and a half long months, and the walk to the bedroom seemed longer than ever. She danced ahead, a little shy, but led me by my hand.

Some nights, you are both so intoxicated in each other, and are otherwise swept into a different place. This night, we were very present, and I was almost painfully aware of the physical realities of childbirth. This was something I was desperately wanting, but it felt as staged as it could between a pair of consenting spouses.

It's harder when you focus on the wrong small things. It was too hot under the comforter, too cold without it. The static from the baby monitor was too loud, and the light from the cable box was too bright. She needed to know that the condoms weren't expired. I didn't realize that was a thing. Every sniffle from the boy made us stop to listen. Every wince of discomfort from her made me pull away.

But then there are the good little small things. Like the way she lifts to let you pull them the rest of the way down, or how it feels when she rolls it all the way on you.

There was the brush against the softer parts of her, and the first beads of our sweat mingling. Touching our mouths made everything electric. We fumbled our ways closer, and got familiar again with our touch, and other things not nearly forgotten.

Easing in was like lowering into a lukewarm tub at first, but the water started heating from our bodies. We whispered back and forth, asking and answering that everything was fine. We moved, together at first, and then opposite. It was careful. Our breath still made each other dizzy. We moved until we parched. I could feel that she was raw. When she slipped me out, she reached for the bottle, but the baby made a noise.

"I'm sorry," she said. "I feel so bad." Whether about me or the baby, I didn't bother asking. "I should go check him." Truth is, I was the one feeling bad. I didn't want her rushing if she wasn't ready.

"Go ahead. He'll probably need to be fed soon anyways, so you might as well bring him in here. I'll go get rid of this, do you want water?"

Yes," she said. She reached, and was with a tear at the corner of her eye. "I'm sorry, honey."

"Don't be. Let's go so we can get some sleep."

Nicky ate again around midnight. We both fell asleep with the TV on. One of the late night talk shows was on. The blue and white blur was blinding and the banter wasn't any better. My wife was already awake and mixing. "Can you shut that off?" she said. Happily. The screen made a digital snap and the room glowed for a blink and went dark. "Are you nervous?" she whispered.

"I don't know," I answered, quietly. "I mean, I'm always nervous to fly. But what am I supposed to say to these people?"

"You always know what to say. That's one of the things I admire about you."

"Oh, I talk too much, and you know it."

We chuckled. Nicky was slurping. He hummed with every exhale.

"You'll be ok with him?"

"Of course I will," she said. "My mother will come at least one of the days, and if we need anything, the weather is supposed to be nice, we can walk to the store."

"I don't want to leave you two."

"I know, honey. But you have to. The sooner you go, the sooner you can put this behind you. I know it hasn't been easy. We're so lucky," she said, bouncing Nicholas to show me what she meant. "And they'll be lucky to have you. If anyone can help them find what they're looking for, it's you."

I suppose she was right. I knew Min at the end. But I never really knew what was going on in his head. I had no way of healing what pain they had. My only hope was to give them a glimpse of what he wanted them to know.

"Thanks, babe. Good night." By the time I had fallen asleep, she was still holding him, humming him to sleep. It worked for both of us.

PART 3

CHAPTER TWENTY ONE
A REPEAT OFFENDER

Logan was a breeze. I felt worldly knowing where everything in the terminal was, and I was disappointed boarding into coach. That time, I was at the emergency exit. I agreed to do my part should the inevitable occur.

The clouds were calming. They gave me time to think about what I might say; time to remember as much as I could about him. By training, I thought first in defense of every angle. We were never to admit fault. I made a list of what accommodations we made, everything and anything that could have been a sign, if there was anything different I could have done, what I knew of his friends, the way some people pointed, and those that wouldn't have given him the time of day. Hopefully I was remembering to forget. Somewhere along those lines, I questioned whether I had the guts to look these people in their eyes and say that I let their boy go. Did I even believe that? Would I have to lie or let them know I don't pray? I had to have faith that their intentions were to bury him and not settle some score.

On the other hand, I cared for him over almost any other student I had. Oh sure, there were others who had shared interests, and some who cared as much about their studies, but none with quite the same clumsy charm. He was receptive, too, to what almost anyone else was feeling. That kid would make me work, when all of the others seemed to want to be elsewhere. I wasn't popular when I had to pull a kid in to talk about absences, or call a parent because of some over the top conduct incident. No matter what it was with Min - it was never conduct, or attendance - it was always about my day first, or a conversation he had with the cool History prof, with whom he was on a first name basis, or something that reminded him of home.

We were walking across campus, back from the Dining Center. The semester was three or four days old. "Professor," he said. I had explained that Mr. Peter sounded a little...funny. "Tell me what is your favorite movie."

It came from out of the blue.

"Well," I said. "I've always been a fan of Kurosawa." I almost felt funny talking to the half-Japanese kid about samurai films, like he'd think I was shining him on, or something. I had every one of them; all of the thirty that were released. "I'm partial to *Seven Samurai. Yojimbo* is fantastic, too. *Ikiru. Madadayo.* Oh man, *Dreams.* All of them, really... But my favorite movie is *Red Beard.*"

181

"*Red Beard*. Like your beard," he said, though mine wasn't even a little red. "I have watched *Red Beard*. I think it was too long. The fight scene was my favorite! My favorite is *Nausicaa*. It's from Studio Ghibli."

"I like *Nausicaa*. *Spirited Away* is my favorite, though."

"So is *Red Beard* not your favorite?"

"Well, I meant that *Spirited Away* is my favorite by Studio Ghibli. I also really like *Howl*, and *Mononoke*, and *Totoro*. But *Red Beard* is my favorite."

"Happy as can be!" he sang. "Like from *Totoro*, right Professor? I love Totoro." I knew he loved Totoro.

"How about your favorite restaurant," he said, changing the subject. I was a movie nut, especially for Japanese flicks. I could have gone on. But I was also a foodie.

"That's easy. Elephant Walk. It's a mix of French and Cambodian food..."

"Oh. Mine is Bibimbap Zen." He had already told me about this place, and their bancha that "...are better than my Grandmother's!" He was a story teller like me; a repeat offender. Having eaten there myself, now, made this memory a lot more favorable, and a little more umami. Hopefully, I would get to sample hers.

"What about your favorite *X-Men* character."

"That's easy. Wolverine. You?" I didn't know where he was going with this.

"Professor X. I always liked Professor X," he said. I laughed, and I felt bad when he looked like that was the

182

reaction he usually got when he said Professor X. "Favorite music band?" he asked, quickly.

"Dream Theater."

"Really?!" he said. "They are my favorite band! Do you know that John Myung is from Korea like me?" Actually, I knew that he was from Chicago, and Min was from Japan, but who was I to argue. "We did it, Professor! We did it in four tries. I can't wait to tell Professor Newman."

I knew Dr. Newman well. He was the Intro and Abnormal Psych prof. Calling him Professor sounded a little out of place, but he was still learning the conventions. "Ah. I should have known. The famous *six questions* from Psych 114."

"You know about the six questions?"

"Yes I do. It is one of Dr. Newman's favorite exercises."

Every semester, he challenged the students to meet each other in class on the first day by finding something in common with a peer. He would explain how we were social beings, and that we could usually find something in common with a complete stranger in under six questions.

"Some of the students did it in one or two, but they cheated. They asked question about the Red Sox."

"That sounds hardly fair," I laughed.

"But four, Professor! That must mean we have a lot in common." Actually, he found something we had in common on the first try, and on the second, and third, but he wasn't satisfied until he had a direct match. I asked him what question he had planned for questions five and six. "Your favorite Pokémon," swing and a miss, "and your favorite Nintendo game."

"I never got into Pokémon," I said, cautiously, knowing how rabid and disappointable its fans can be. "But *Donkey Kong Country* for Super Nintendo. Hands down."

"You would love Pokémon!" Again, who was I to beg any different. "I love Donkey Kong, too! Kirby is my favorite… And Yoshi," he got quiet.

From then on, he had a new question every time we met. We weren't ever that far apart on our answers. I never did get to tell him that we had more in common than he thought, because I enjoyed his attempts.

"Chicken salad or Falafel, sir?" asked the attendant. I was somewhere else, but I heard her asking her way up the aisle. The falafel sounded good, and looked better, but I didn't have it in me to order the vegetarian option. Maybe on the return flight. She also gave two cocktail napkins and a small bag of pretzels. My neighbor had the falafel and took a break from her book to open its wrappings.

"Fuck!" I huffed. That made her jump. She was mostly quiet up until then. I felt bad for swearing.

"Are you ok?" she asked. "Did you cut yourself?"

"No," I said, spitting the bite into one of my cocktail napkins. "It's nothing. So sorry about that."

"Are you sure?"

"It's just, I hate celery…" The look she gave me was an interesting one. I really did hate fucking celery. Being from

Boston, you have to go to Maine for a lobster roll without, and it's well worth the drive. I should've asked. I always ask. Why the hell didn't I ask?

"I would trade with you, but I don't eat meat. Let's see if we can call the attendant. I'm sure they have extras." She hit the call button above my head. *That's a bit forward*, I thought. She meant well.

"No, no. It's fine. Thank you very much. I'll be fine." I un-checked the call light on principle of *she shouldn't have hit someone else's call button.* I was stubborn like that, sometimes, and for the rest of my flight, I was stuck eating pretzels. Luckily I had a big breakfast in the terminal, and a few candy bars that I bought with my gum.

CHAPTER TWENTY TWO
YESTERDAY MORNING ALREADY

Flying into Seoul, if I didn't know just a little bit better, could easily have been flying into Tokyo. Tokyo seemed much bigger on the descent, but they both seemed so small on the tracker. Osaka was labeled in the corner after the flight path adjusted. My heart almost exploded when I realized that I was so close to Japan. For some reason, I was more excited by that than by setting foot there a few months ago. The place of my dreams was within reach once more. There was this flash, as sustained as the impulse to blink an eye, that I could change lanes and disappear into that place, that I could become one with a more peaceful life. I remembered why I was in the air, and I remembered my son. A rush came over me, like we landed in the water and I had a sudden need to breathe deep before making for the surface. I felt so far away; I felt so guilty. This had better be worth doing.

❖

When we went to Greece, we were off the plane in Zurich for an hour. Tops. Then we were off the plane in Athens for only twenty minutes. There was nothing else to go through besides baggage, and my wife knew the cab driver. A four hour drive through rocky terrain faced us, and that only got us most of the way into the village. We didn't have a scrap of food until well into the night. I had no idea where I was going other than the fact that it was rural. Actually, I didn't even know how I was getting there, except for an uncle who was "taking care of it," and I didn't know how I was even finding him. But I would be damned if I didn't eat something to make up for that God forsaken sandwich.

There wasn't a lack of eateries. Bibimbap and gimbap aside, I didn't feel comfortable ordering from some of those menu offerings. I wasn't afraid of the food, just afraid of choosing wrong. This was still a special thing for me, and I wanted everything to be just right, while I could still control things. Sometimes, though, I worried too much about making the perfect pick that I ran out of time for anything other than Subway. There was one of those, so I grabbed a combo and sat to eat it as fast as I could. I don't really know why I was in such a hurry. Maybe I was just groomed to be ready for a driver who's perfected the timing.

This time around, I packed a small roll-around. I wouldn't be needing a suit to stay flat, and the garment bag didn't have the extra room for a set of hiking shoes. Min's grandmother lived in a part of the village that wasn't easy to get in or out of, so I assumed I might need them; lucky for me, I brought them.

After hammering two half-foot seafood salads, sans the fucking celery, I made for baggage claim. That wasn't like me to leave my things, but when I don't eat I get faint, and when I get faint I get desperate. A cookie and a bag of chips behind an ice tea helped with the head rush.

Mine must have been the only bag left whirling from the flight in from Boston. It was taken and was being held, but not under suspicion, by someone holding a sign holding my name. Well, my last name, preceded by the word "Professor." In some strange way, his uncle looked much like I expected. He was looking around, across the claim area, probably scanning for "tall, bearded, and out of place." This was my last chance to just go and to let this thing slip away from me, and into an ocean of regrets.

In my right, front pocket, I always kept, from the day they were given, a small chain of beads. These were Greek beads; worry beads. I knew my extended in-laws to be worriers over prayers, so this concept was not altogether foreign when I got them. My wife picked them out. She said they would bring me luck. I forgot them one day. That was the day I was grabbed in a speed trap at the clover leaf for a hundred and fifty dollar fine. "That was a sign," she said. One day I shoveled without them in the pocket of my bomber jacket, and I lost my wedding band. Another sign.

Coincidences, really, but that's what she believed. I kept them more for sentiment. Every time a bead broke, I'd quietly super glue it back together around the chain so it could slide free. I could tap a hand to my thigh in just the right spot to feel that they were there with my thumb while also checking for my wallet. Another neurosis. This day, they were there, and with a folded piece of paper that I'd nearly forgotten I'd had until I checked. It was as weighty as my passport. I needed luck, and a good bit of courage to walk up to an almost total stranger and expect that he take me across country to meet the grandmother of a student I once knew.

It was too late. He spotted me, and was moving my way, grinning from ear to ear, bowing as he walked like he was looking to make certain it was me. He knew, though. He shook his sign and said "Professor," followed by things I couldn't translate. I tried. I really did. But I didn't know where to start. Before we took off back in Boston, I bought a pocket dictionary, and read it during the wait that morning, or was it yesterday morning already? I couldn't remember a single syllable. Actually, I didn't even know what his name was.

"Professor Cahill," I said, acknowledging his sign, pointing at myself. "I'm Peter Cahill. We spoke earlier this week. Is Yong Lim here?"

He smiled and reached with both hands to hold mine, which I wiped clean on my pants. I don't know what he said, but he meant it with his soul. I took him to look older than Min's father, whom I hadn't ever met. The pants

189

he had on were tan and probably canvas and his shoes had Velcro instead of laces. I remember his shirt because I thought that it looked like a light blue picnic blanket, and it was tucked it neatly. He had glasses and a folded up map in his shirt pocket. His jacket may well have been a *Members Only* and he wore the sleeves rolled up like you're supposed to. "I like your hat," I said. He had no idea. "It's missing a few fishing lures." I was nervous.

"Pro...fessor," he said. "Thank... You..." And he kissed my hands. "You... come," he said. He made no mention of Yong Lim, but he treated me like I was a dignitary. He had a slight hitch and a slight hunch from years of working the land that stained and calloused his fingers. I said you could tell a lot about a man from his hand shake. He gave me more with a handful of grit than I had been handed by almost any I ever met.

Our introductions were brief. This man was eager, and under orders, to bring me back home.

CHAPTER TWENTY THREE
TO SHAPE THE MOUNTAINS

Min's Uncle's truck was as old and sturdy as the man himself. Sure, the suspension had softened, and it complained when another person got in, but it was his work horse. The engine was low and throaty, and sounded loose turning over, but fired like a turbine when he gave it some gas. He rattled the shifter on the tree into gear, and we were on our steady way.

Traffic in Seoul was unlike anything I'd seen before. It was ten lanes of fuck in every direction, and the signs and lines were mere suggestions. I was white-knuckled on the door-pull and pushed back into my chair with the other on the dash. Neither of us was belted in because there weren't any, and there was a spring loose under my ass. He didn't ask if I minded that he smoke, or maybe he did, but he did smoke, and I did mind. I wanted to roll down the window, but between not wanting to free a hand, and the lacking crank handle, I sucked it up.

Surprisingly, we weren't long getting out of the vicinity of the airport, and then the surrounding city limits, and finally away from the worst of it on the highway. I loosened my grip for a while and sat my head back, second-hand smoking, wondering if this kid was worth it. For the first, oh, hundred miles, all I could come back with was that, yes, he certainly was.

The terrain was like nothing from where I was from, north of Boston, or even south of the city. It looked nothing like Greece, either. The former was studded more by trees and native lands, while the latter was tan and rocky, mottled with dried green. Greece looked everywhere like Sicily, though I'd never been. This looked like Jersey, with less shipping containers, though they were most likely there, just set further back.

Min made that drive. At some point, he must have. That picture they sent, unless it was mailed to them, must have been taken outside of his grandmother's home. If I could recall, he was outside, so it was hard to tell. I guess it was a gut feeling, not that it mattered much.

We had gone another hundred. Nothing, yet, looked rural, except the chauffeur.

The sun was setting when we pulled off the highway. The road wasn't the final one we would take, but there were fewer lanes, less traffic, grass between the two in lieu of concrete, and there were trees. Not as far as the eye could see, but there were trees, and they were scattered. I'd like to think it was so I could see how far away we were, and have a glimpse where we were going. Mountains were ahead, small ones, probably only hills. But one thing was sure: this wasn't a place he frequented; the sky was too big.

It was then that I realized what I should have all along. Me and my driver had him in common. And now we had that place in common. I wondered what else. *How close were they?* I thought. *When did they last speak?* I wanted to know what he was thinking. Was I some spoiled American? Did he resent that I was closer to his nephew in recent months? Was he thinking about what was going through my mind? I wished I knew how to tell him I was sorry. I guessed, or rather I hoped, that being in his passenger seat was good enough.

Hills first, and then mountains came near and we wove our way through a village that clung to stepped ridges. These were a people with a will to shape the mountains, not a will to master or best the immovable. We would have blown and trucked it away to pave and plant retail or assemble blocks of condo units. *How does one come to owning a mountain?* I wondered. *And when did leveling one become better than this?* I guess it's all a matter of perspective.

Given the thick of the trees, our way was lit mostly by headlamps. The tops of the clay-tiled or thatched-top dwellings were still brushed by the sun. The houses whipped past faster than tree branches. I hoped we were close, but he was moving like a man half home. I tried to gather what I could, like I was an outfitter, surveying a place I'd be expected to know.

Some of the houses were ruined; half of them from the war, the other from a hundred years of vacancy and weather. There were newer and nicer ones mixed among those with walls vented by rifle rounds. I could smell things in fits and starts, ranging from cooked mushrooms to a passing chicken coop to smoking wet pines in a hearth or outdoor pit. Some stretches were open opposite the houses, sheds, barns, or ruin. Other turns were tighter between two rows of built up walls and hung lanterns. The road was bumpy for the whole way, and muddy in some spots.

We had to be coming close. Through a close cropping of trees, we hit a thicketed stretch of field, and then more open road that climbed higher up the hill. We were past the first village.

The second was more of the same, but the road was very much like a mountain road, as it was higher, and houses were only able to sit on one side. Those on the other were on carved ledge below the road. The inlets didn't look safe to drive down in a pickup truck. There were fewer trees in the way with the steeper terrain. By then it was too dark to see back into that valley, and the first village was all but swallowed in the night. What we could see, though, was the great snake that was our rocky way. It was lit just as it was carved, by the spirit of necessity. The utility lines couldn't have been older than two decades and the poles were stripped of bark by hand. The lamps were dusty and gathered bugs. We were headed for the last bend in sight, which wrapped its way around the edge of a thick, tree-covered crest. The last house on my right, which was well enough away from the village proper, was a goat barn. At least I think it was; there was one up on the roof.

Instantly it was nighttime and away with the alley lights went my hopes of stopping. For the first bit of road the drop off into an unseen gulley was pure terror. My poor knuckles needed desperately to meet the lower country. He didn't seem fazed, and he didn't seem to slow down. Except for when the bus came by.

"Ahh," he exclaimed, and he raised up the back of his hand. I knew what *that* meant. We were on the inside, with two wheels on the packed earth at the upward side of the slope. I sucked in and held my breath when he inched by us. It was a small bus, but it was fairly full. I could hear his wheels flaking off gravel from the road and down into the horrible abyss. With daylight, I was sure it wouldn't have seemed so dire, and the slope more gradual, but at that very moment, I imagined them all being sucked away into nothing; down a trench so deep we wouldn't hear the crash. I'd find later that the former were true. They didn't fall anywhere, only tooted once when they were through, and disappeared from my sight in the mirror and back into the second, thinner village.

For how long we drove after that, I couldn't say. Beyond the foot of that hill, where I was a good deal less prone to vomiting, I started nodding off. That was a deep and awful kind of tired that played tricks with the time.

The shocks jolted on my side over a rock in the road. He knew his way well enough to have avoided it, but he didn't. He thought it was funny. Actually, he was in hysterics. Maybe he knew how nervous I was a while back on the higher road and thought he'd have a little fun, or maybe he tried waking me some other way. Whatever it was, it gave him a rise when I damn-near jumped out of my shirt. I must have screamed like he launched us over a bridge because he mocked me, waving his hands and changing his face. According to him, I must have been pretty pathetic, but he meant no insult. Any of my uncles would have done the same.

He was smiling still, and I was too, when he gave me a gentle backhander to the shoulder and pointed just up ahead. There was another, much smaller hill, with nothing mountainous about it, in the way of our road. It stood on one side of the road, or rather, the road was cut around and not through. The edge of another village started peeking around as we neared. Min's Uncle put out his cigarette and started whistling. This was a man who was much closer than halfway home.

CHAPTER TWENTY FOUR
A SHORT BUT SWEET WELCOME

This village felt less hectic, but we weren't driving so fast when we pulled through the border. More people were out and about than we'd seen since the airport; though, on second glance, they were more than just "about." Some of them were following us. Min's uncle waved like a parade float was hitched behind him.

My watch was wrong, I knew that much because I didn't bother resetting it while we drove. I was looking at about eight something the next morning, on Boston time, meaning that it was officially twenty four hours since arriving at Logan for a late morning departure. The clock on my phone said that it was after ten o'clock at night. Those kids following behind us should have been in bed. I felt as young and awake as they were, looking out, trying to see them all. There was no question that they knew who I was and why I was there. The small crowd of three or four grew into almost a dozen by the time the truck lurched into its spot in the widened out belly of the only paved road. He threw the shifter and the truck banged into park. The motor rattled off before the fan stopped whirring. And just like that, he was home.

Half of the dozen scattered when the door on my side creaked open. It was heavy and some rust loosened and sprinkled down. I wonder what I looked like to them, stretching there in the middle of the road they knew so well. Min's uncle had already gotten my bag from his side and was around the rear bumper to show me which way we were headed. I could hear every footstep, and something like a cicada cheeping in the trees. The stars looked like spilt sugar without city lights.

Across the way were homes in no better or worse shape than the villages from earlier. They were sturdy, they were rustic, and they were quite visibly built by hand. Some of the walls were stucco and some were stone. At first notice, the only thing distinguishing those homes from the villages in Greece was their roofing. In pictures, both had an air of whimsy, but these ones in particular had a bit more. Close up and personal, even in the dark of night, they were a coppery kind of red, like the dried clay they were. The eaves were cornered up gracefully, like understated shrines. That likeness spoke to me about the spirit inside.

I understood why his Grandmother wasn't so easily leaving. The stairs were steep and narrow, and the mortar was loose. From the road, just a few steps behind the stone landing, I would have never known it was there. Hidden halfway in a bush, an overgrown railing had loosened as the abutting wall settled. Min's uncle moved fast, while my foot didn't fit squarely on a single tread, besides the one at the turn. Flickering through paper shutters gave light in some spots, but every several steps was into nothing.

We curved under and around the first row of houses and stopped on a dirty road that sloped down further and away. We stepped into the moon and I could see the span of where we were going. This one wasn't as steep as the last, but every few rows of houses stepped down, and there were, for sure, more stone steps. No wonder Min hadn't been back. His uncle took us down one more, and in a ways along a winding foot path to where we stopped and he started knocking.

Every sound was drowned in the drumming of my ears standing before their door. I was caught looking down, brushing dust from my shirt, when the panel slid apart from the wall. Yong Lim was there, and just inside, I could see his grandmother. She was tall and elegant, for what I expected, and craning her neck so she could see me. She smiled like I was familiar. Her son hit my shoulder again and said something short while he pointed at my feet, he slid off his own flats, leaned to pick them up, stepped in, dropped my bag at the door, kissed his mother, and disappeared somewhere out of sight. I could smell sulfur from the match he would use to light his cigarette. "Thank you," I called on his heels as I stood there untying my shoes to be allowed inside.

"Professor!" exclaimed Yong Lim. "Oh thank you, Professor. Thank you for coming," he said. He bowed, as did his grandmother, as did I, standing on their stoop in my stocking feet.

"Please come," he said, nearly pulling me inside. I paused for a moment to stand my bag upright. I didn't so much care about anything spilling, or having my stuff tussled about, but their house, though small, and very rural, was tidy.

"Yong Lim," he said, tapping his fingers and thumb to his chest. He bowed again, very respectfully.

"Peter. Peter Cahill," I said, and I touched my pockets when I bowed. Mine was quicker, though, as I offered him a hand to shake. He smiled and he obliged. I feel like if Dean Freeman were there, we would have shared a glance, but that was one handshake I wouldn't judge against others.

And then there she stood. Her hands were folded neatly in front of well-worn robes; her sleeves and white hair were tied back. At first she didn't seem as old, and she was nowhere near as bed-ridden as I had anticipated. She wasn't nearly my height, but she wasn't nearly petite.

"My Grandmother. Soon-ja Park," he said. He bowed as he presented her. She bowed as well, as best she could, and after, unfolded to reach out for my hands. Her age showed in her movements. She was a porcelain doll, bright and timeless, but fragile and dear. Behind a happy mask I could see a pinch of pain, behind that, the will to hide it away. Under all of it, there was deep loss for the one we all shared. This was not a happy meeting; there was work, here, to be done. Before any of that, and it would nearly kill us all to wait, there were pleasantries to make, and a table to share.

I stepped in to catch her hands. Though they were delicate, they were determined, and they grabbed me hard. In her tongue she spoke; in her eyes, she struggled.

"God brought you to us, she says," said Yong Lim. "As he has taken our son," he continued translating. "We cut first the tree of the straightest grain." I smiled. That was an interesting turn since Min was gay. "What does that say for me?" she smiled, and she pondered. "When I am with him once more, please let me know how to look on him." She turned stoic and stared.

I didn't know what to say so I stood there not saying anything. I looked to her grandson to save me, and he understood. "Please, Professor, you must be very hungry. Grandmother and I..." she said something fast, and louder than she spoke before. "Alright, I did not help that much. Please join us for a meal in your honor."

My face lit like another one of his uncle's matches in the dark room. Dinner, or more specifically, his grandmother's cooking, was one of the few things to which I was so looking forward.

In effect, their home was only one room. Paper partitions blocked off eating and sleeping areas, and behind the former was set a low table for kneeling. The table was square and covered over with small plates filled with color. There wasn't a head, or sides, or places for anyone to sit above the others, except at one spot. At that spot there was a pillow for kneeling that looked to be camel colored silk. Instinctively, I walked to help guide Soon-ja there, but she made it clear that it was for me. I took it more a sign of respect than commentary on the readiness of my knees.

"Are you sure?" I asked. She laughed and was down before her grandson could answer. She answered for herself with a wave. It was an invitation long in the making for her, and she was as thrilled to see me sit at her table as I finally was to be there.

After she spoke, and after Yong said a few words, his uncle poured, saluted, and slammed the first shot of soju. We let the food do the rest of the talking. Chilis exploded in vinegar and long beans swam with dried shrimp and sesame. The zucchini was grilled and the tofu was cold, the soup was spicy and the crab was raw. We had crispy pork and fluffy rice alongside bowl after bowl of soju. And then there was the kimchi.

I don't like kimchi. Never have. Didn't think I ever would. But *this* kimchi, this saucer full of ruined cabbage, rang for me like a singing bowl. The spice was there, but tame, along with the right bit of sour, and a fishiness that was almost buttery. In India, every family has their curry. Here, it's this dish. There was sure to be none like it within a stone's throw, or across the street from an apartment tower in Tokyo, or anywhere back in Boston. I was shy taking extra of everything else, and I waited to try it until they took note, but they didn't run out of anything faster.

Yong laughed at something his uncle grumbled. He had only a little more than a few bites. Soon-ja bickered back at them both. It was the most animated I had seen her so far. Actually, for much of the meal, she was reserved, studying me. She kept fairly composed, but snuck a smile when I ate like I enjoyed something. It seemed otherwise painful, like the work ahead was going to be too much to handle, like it was nearing midnight on the eve of her judgment. When her son insulted her kimchi as being mild enough "for old ladies and invalids," a term I took offense to under Min's roof, he got an earful. Boy was she feisty.

When he goaded, she got mad. When he stepped a bit further, she threw a pickle. I hunched my head down and snorted, and Yong looked embarrassed by the whole exchange. We watched for a response. An uncle that looked shirt-stained and surprised took the pickle, scooped the rest off of his chest pocket and sloughed it onto the table, then took a bite. Soon-ja smiled first and then laughed. He shrugged it off and took another bite. Then she really laughed. Yong laughed too. Chances are, he hadn't seen his Grandmother throwing pickles before.

I looked over, and the uncle wasn't laughing. The more he made faces, the more Soon-ja laughed. He stood forward from his knees and brushed his shirt. Everyone stifled. He made a move towards his mother, and leaned over the near corner of the table. He had to prop a hand down to reach just a little further. Soon-ja reared, not sure of his intention, and spat his name. He seemed angry. He grabbed up the bowl of pickles, rocked himself back, and plopped down to sit cross legged. It was like she'd been keeping them a secret, like they alone made amends for her mild kimchi. He never cracked, but the rest us may have woken a neighbor.

Soon-ja was adamant that I not clear a single plate. That was against my upbringing, and I asked Yong to explain this to her. She nodded when she smiled. He said "You are a good man because you have been made well. Would you have me carry my plate from your table?" She knew by the change in my face that I meant to say no, that I would not. "Please let me attend to you as you would me. As you have done my first grandchild." Her face was proud. Yong was up and clearing before I could bow.

For the time it took the two men to take away the food, we sat in each other's company. There was much we had to discuss, but we said more without words than we could have in any other way. She told of how helpless she felt while he was away and how deep her sorrow ran. I told of how carefully I looked after him and how much he was missed. We shared regret, and we shared reminiscence. Mostly we shared comfort in the fact that the hardest part was over.

For dessert, they brought out a tray of tea, coffee, sweet rice cakes, and strawberries. We took another soju salute, and then one more for good measure and we wound down what ended up being a short but sweet welcome.

204

My head was swimming when I hit the sheets, which didn't have as high a thread count as my hotel in Tokyo; not that I slept there. The hours awake and the wine were a potent combination. I don't remember much about getting back to the uncle's house, except that there were steps, a few feral cats, and a chicken on one of the roads. I think I may have chased it around, which I'm sure was a sight. When I got to my room, I didn't even change my clothes or unpack. The last thing I remember before falling asleep was messaging my wife. I knew she was probably worried. I sent her one word: *Here.*

CHAPTER TWENTY FIVE
THE TRUEST SHADE OF BLUE

"**O**h Jesus Christ!"

I could have killed that rooster with my bare hands. He must have been eager for me to remember him from last night.

Min's uncle was snoring still in the next bed. He was face down with an arm hanging over, and it looked like he didn't change either. He may have given me a tour, but I couldn't remember. I didn't know where I was supposed to brush my teeth or pay back the wine I borrowed, and I didn't feel right poking around.

For a few minutes, I just sat, clearing my throat on the edge of my cot hoping to wake him. He seemed like a man with hard work all over him. I had him pegged for an early riser. Wine does that to the best of us, I guess.

The rooster eventually switched off, but every now and again he made some horrid scratching or errant shout. If he wasn't waking this guy up, I wasn't going to either, but I didn't want to wait much longer to get going.

His house was well enough lit by windows for me to find myself around. The first step off the rug was a shock because the floor was poured cement and it was cold, even through my socks. I found my bag strewn by the door. I must have let him carry it for me. I didn't envy him this headache.

Apart from the one room we were in, which had two cots and a small tube television propped on a folding coffee table, there were four other rooms. One was a small dining area, with a table, and the phone, which was hung on the wall. The other had nothing more than a locked cabinet and some old coats. Opposite that room, there was a kitchenette with two fridges, one was unplugged and used for dry storage, and finally, the bathroom.

One thing I've always taken seriously is bathroom comfort. It's not just anywhere that I'll be able to *really* go. I think that comes from my Dad. When we were younger, he used to leave the campground to drive twenty minutes to a diner. We used to make fun of him for that. I don't anymore.

I had read about these toilets in the floors where you squat instead of sit. You can't flush any paper. I even tried practicing the position in my bedroom before I left. With my knees and thirty eight inch waistline, I was out of breath before I started losing my balance. There was no way in hell.

I saw the shower first, and that there was no stall, only tile and a drain in the floor. There wasn't a sink, either, but there was a mirror on the wall. And then, oh thank heavens, there was a throne. I could have dropped to my knees and kissed it. Using it, before getting changed for the day, was good enough.

For the life of me, I couldn't figure out where to brush my teeth. There wasn't a mirror over the sink in the kitchen, and I'm not even sure the water was running. By the looks of the bathroom plumbing the second time around, a shower may even have been out of the question. He was clean, though, and so was the rest of his place, so he must have washed somewhere. I changed my underwear and shirt, pulled on a button down flannel over that, applied a second layer of deodorant under those, and popped two of the remaining four chiclets of gum from the pack. I zipped my bag loud and dropped it with a purpose, but when I peeked back in, he was up, dressed, sipping coffee, and had both beds made. He offered a cup and I declined. Then he waved me into the bathroom behind him.

There was a small cupboard that was filled with paper. He grabbed off a small piece of no more than two squares and balled it up. He held it to show me and he tossed it in the pail, not the toilet. The message was quite clear. I knew this man for less than a day and that was as intimate an exchange as I could've expected. I was a bit embarrassed to think he'd be sharing the space, in his own house, with anything I left in that barrel. But that's not the bit that really embarrassed me. We all have needs that aren't pretty. What got to me was that I stood so separated in the name of decency that I would have never thought to show him the same if he were in my house. The thing is, he wasn't indecent; not in the least. He was human. It's like we've made communal things more taboo than they have to be. I'm glad he told me, too, because I thought that only applied to the squatters. I thanked him and he smiled.

The pipes rattled behind the wall when he turned on the shower. He had me feel how cold it was, I'm assuming, so I would know that the tank up top, and the switch he flipped, were for hot water. He used two fingers to shave his neck in the small mirror. They were the same two he used to show me that I can brush my teeth in the kitchen sink, and he pointed me to the cups so I could rinse and spit. It was all a little easier after he cracked the seal.

After the tour, we doubled back to the sleeping quarters to flip off the lights. He checked his pockets for his key and glasses. On the way back by the kitchen, he grabbed three tangerines, offered up one, and we were on our way.

We were down somewhere below the main road. His little house had a tile roof and was surrounded by trees. In the alley beside it, there were broken shovels, the rim from an old truck tire, a folded tarp, and some other collectibles of the same sort. When we stepped away from his house and shed, I could see into the valley for the first time.

There were houses like his, mostly slate-roofed and pseudo-sacred looking, though some wore thatching, and a handful had orange tile, and they stretched out for some distance, filling in the space before the mountains. Most of what was ahead of us eventually leveled off, leaving the staggered and stepped terraces behind. The roadways there were tan and mist was rising off of the trees. I felt like I was on the set of a movie; like I had seen this place in black and white. The first stunning splash of color stole my breath away. The sun was hitting just so, and there was a soul squeezing silence like I'd never heard. It was an image, nay, a being, that I wanted ingrained...but he was well ahead and wasn't waiting. His family's business needed attending.

For sure that time I would remember my way back and forth between their two homes. The walk was short, and wound only a little. If in fifty years I could have come back, I would remember the way, and I would remember it as well as the feeling of entering her house again for the first time that morning.

Something about the sun was sobering, and all of my travel was washed away. I was dizzy and wide-eyed just hours before, by the night and by the ride, and it was a passing encounter in a dark place on my way to a bed. I loved every minute and every bit of kimchi I ate, but this, this morning, this knock on her door, was raw. It made my heart hurt for what we had to discuss. It made my red light ring; it made my own child cry. I both wanted to have never gone and to be through with the giving of myself to what they needed. Then something very special stepped my foot through the door.

Soon-ja did not answer the door; it was her grandson, as expected. In a home so small, she was not hidden where she waited. Thinking back, it seemed like part of the whole experience. Even in the hiding light, directed through the shutters, her robes shone the truest shade of blue.

I keep an old tin cologne box in a bedside drawer; have for years. By now, it's dusty and one of the rolled edge corners has a spot of rust. Inside are all of the birthday cards, love notes, ticket stubs, bits, bobs, buttons, hair pins, and a lot of other memories we made after we first married. Damn, I'd nearly forgotten I had something so dear locked away. The box that she had in front of her is what reminded me. Mine was filled with what hers used to hold: happy thoughts.

His grandmother was kneeling at the box, which was positioned on a low table. It was much nicer than mine. With rich brown lacquer, inlaid abalone shell, and a real silk thread lanyard hanging from the key, the vessel itself may well have appraised for more dollars than her house. It was easily an heirloom from deep into her ancestral trees and belonged behind glass. It's worth was exceeded in value by what it contained.

The key sounded hefty clicking open the lock. Yong and I knelt, his uncle hovered. She pulled open the lid and removed a tray of letters and set them on the table. They were cared for meticulously and kept in their original envelopes. Every seal was cut by a razor and there weren't any torn corners or crumpled edges. The air changed around them, and so did her face. It was like the room darkened all around. She knew them and loved them and they were precious to her. There was hesitation, as though she would be opening not only stitches but scars. With heavy hearts, we began.

CHAPTER TWENTY SIX
THROUGH THE EYES OF A CHILD

For hours we would look, from the very beginning, before coming to anything that would concern my being there. There was little rush other than anticipation for answers, but for Soon-ja, much more so than for me or Yong, at least at the onset, this was a trip for remembering. There was also little that I already knew about his past. This was the beginning of her goodbye.

Many of the early letters on the pile had a return address of St. Luke's International Hospital in Tokyo. That put a lump in my throat. There were a few from before, probably from holidays, but those ones were our heading. In fact, they were bundled and tied with a ribbon, like only a few other sections kept intentionally together. The engraving of the logo and return address on the envelopes stood out against writing I could otherwise not read.

Soon-ja laid the top of the pile back into the box, and set aside the earlier few to keep them separate and in order. She pulled the tie and let the lead end unfurl and dangle over the edge of paper. Carefully, she pulled it away, folded it, and set it aside. She took a moment to hold them, firm their edges together, and gather up something to push her forward. Her eyes closed in those moments like she was listening, and her thumbs rubbed the top of the stack. She shifted her hands to hold on the front edge, with the closer side pressed against her. With her eyes barely opened, she counted from the back of the pile and then spilt away the earliest letters and tucked them away. It wasn't anything like shucking the unwanted heel from a day old loaf. Rather, it was like pulling a pressed flower for a final smell.

"Those are from Uncle," whispered Yong, referring to the ones she tucked away. "Not for us." There were four envelopes. "Too much pain," he said. "I have not read them. Grandmother only read them one time."

The first envelope she picked was the size of a greeting card's envelope. Like the rest, the seal was still sealed, and a slit was cut neatly across the top seam. She pulled a piece of folded notebook paper out and smiled at the cover. She handled it like a high end auctioneer, and Yong passed it to me with similar diligence.

On the cover there was a line drawing, in pen, of a window and a Totoro next to vases of flowers and a handful of stuffed cats and bears. The lines were indented like he bore down as best he could to make his mark. The sun outside was shining and streaking rays over the spread of gifts left on his sill, and there were shaded shadows. It looked drawn by a child. Yong read the inside over my shoulder when I turned the cover.

Grandmother,

Thank you for my Totoro. Father said he kept me safe while I was sleeping. I know that he will help me get better, too. I hope you like my picture.

Soon-ja's breathing staggered and her hand leapt up to rid her eye of a tear.

"What does this mean?" I asked, though I thought I knew.

"My cousin was in accident at age twelve years. No seatbelt. Uncle was with him. Uncle's driver was driving. Boys were racing with motorcycle. Very fast. Hit Uncle's car. Driver tried to save, but hit another car. Minho break through window..."

It was signed "M" with a heart. There was a small smudge of brown, dried blood - a sign that he maybe pushed too hard with the hand where they put his IV line.

I didn't hear much of the end of Yong's account. My stomach wasn't handling this so well. By sleeping, Min must have meant that he was in a coma. For how long, I did not ask.

"This was his first day," Yong translated for Soon-ja. "He was very mindless from the medicine. He did not know about his injury."

He never told me about any of this. The Disability Services office had all of his medical documentation, but those were mostly pages with numbers. I didn't even know until after he died that it wasn't from birth. To me, it was always his story to tell. He was going to tell the rest of it now whether I wanted him to or not. I had nothing to add, so I handed back the letter and watched her return and reorder it with care.

She pulled another letter, addressed by a different hand, out of the pile to set aside with the rest. The letter after that wasn't much longer than the first one we read, and it was from him.

> *Grandmother,*
>
> *I made you another picture. There was a helicopter outside of my window last night. Mother says that it is like the one I rode in when I was hurt, but I have never rode in a helicopter. Father says that they are like superheroes. It had a lot of lights. I saw it and wanted to draw you a picture of it. Have you ever rode in a helicopter?*

The helicopter had an *M* drawn on the side and it was wearing a cape off the back of the cockpit. It was something out of a comic book more than a cartoon. Every inch of paper around it was shaded dark by the side edge of his pencil; he used the eraser to reveal the beams of light.

216

That taught me something about how he saw the world. I saw one, too, with Nicky. I knew how that beam tore into the night. By Yong's account, this was Min's third day awake. The next letter was written three or four days later.

Grandmother,

Today I saw a dog! His name was Wasabi and his collar was green. He licked my hand and I laughed. I asked father why he didn't go to every room, and he said that he was very busy with lots of people to cheer up. I hope I get to leave here soon, but I hope he comes back.

There, of course, was a picture of the dog. He was wearing a collar and a vest that had a cross on the side. The name Wasabi was spelled out in marquee letters that were shaded to look like they could light right off of the page.

Grandmother,

It has been one week, so I wanted to say hello. Father and Doctor said it is helping me to draw pictures and write letters to you. I wish you could visit, or we could talk on the telephone. Father says that we cannot. Father has gone back to work now and my friends visit, but they are busy with school work. Mother stays most days and she reads Naruto to me. I hope I can get up soon and go back to school. I miss my kendo classes and my Sensei, too. He will visit with me soon. Mother says that I am hurt. My head is hurting, but I am feeling better every day. I am tired sometimes, but I am getting lots of rest and food to make me strong. I will come to see you when I am better. Here is a picture of me practicing kendo.

His kendogi and hakama were brilliantly colored in blue, not drab like they are in practice, and he drew a multicolored trail coming off of his shinai. It was as if lightning and fire and magic were wielded in its wake. Even at twelve, he had an amazing talent, especially with color. I could tell it was older work because the proportions weren't quite right, and his style wasn't so refined, but it was full of life. Man. I felt bad even letting a criticizing thought slip into my head. Someone brought him colored pencils. Damn. That was a part of his treatment plan.

They looked for me to say something. I made a false start. So far, I wasn't really sure why I'd come. I had nothing for them yet, but Min's and my son's and my own mortality starting nagging. How are you supposed tell a twelve year old what needed saying? How much would I have been able to tell my own son? I'd like to think I knew, but I never wanted to know.

There was only one more letter in that stack that she set aside, and the rest of the hospital letters were from Min, thought Yong. Judging by the pile, though, he was there for some time.

Grandmother,

I am sorry I have not written. I had surgery yesterday. I never had a surgery before. They did the surgery in my back. It did not hurt. Mother was very sad after and Father talked to the doctors in the hallway. They said that my cuts are healing now but I am not getting better. I do not believe them. The doctors will make me better. That is why I am in hospital. I cannot walk on my own yet because I am tired from the surgery, but I will ride my bicycle, and walk to school, and have my kendo practice. They are waiting to tell father and mother if I will have another surgery. They will help me get better.

There was a drawing included of his mother sitting, facing the TV, and his father standing beside the doctor at the end of his bed. At the bottom were his two feet poking up into view. He had striped socks on. I had never seen his father. He looked different than I was expecting. While I don't know how accurate their faces were drawn, one thing was sure: there was gravity. It's hard to believe that this one was drawn by a pre-teen. The mother wasn't watching tv, her head was turned away like she was hiding tears from her son. The father wasn't angry, he was concerned, and possibly a little scared. The doctor was timid to deliver the news. If for a second I thought that he didn't understand what was going on, this picture proved otherwise, whether he knew it or not.

Min's uncle interrupted. I hadn't heard him leave, but he made for the kitchen area to prepare breakfast. I took another look before handing that picture back.

"I didn't know about his injuries," I said. "He never told me any of this." Yong translated. Soon-ja listened. I didn't know what to say. It happened. It was a part of his story now, a part of their grieving, I couldn't change that. I couldn't apologize or offer condolences. This was a bad turn on a road he once traveled. We've all been through worse on his behalf, but they weren't looking for anything yet. They just wanted me to know. "I wish I knew," I said. "I thank you for sharing these."

Soon-ja held the next two for a moment. While I read the first, she occupied herself opening well over a dozen others, all of which were pictures with little notes here or there. She laid them out on the table so we could see them all. Some she had to lean across to place, others she gave to Yong to set. He knew the letters almost by heart, but he kept an eye so his reading wasn't interrupted.

Grandmother,

Mother does not know I am writing and Father is away on business to China. I am scared. I am very upset at what they are telling me. Mother says that I will not

220

walk with my own legs. She is wrong, I just know she is. Do you think she is wrong, too? I am strong like Father. He was hurt too, so I will get better. Doctor talks to me like I am a child, like I do not understand. I do understand. I am not afraid for more surgeries. I am not afraid to show them. They can fix me, I know it. They are superheroes. I will not become one of those people.

There was no drawing with this letter, or with the next one.

Grandmother,

Today I fell down. I tried to stand up from my hospital bed. I could not feel my legs when I pulled them to the side of the bed. I could not feel the floor with my feet. It hurt my head when I fell. Mother yelled when she saw me fall and she called for the doctor. They said that I hurt my back again and there was a lot of blood. I cried. I did not cry because I was hurt, but I cried because I could not feel my legs. I could not move them. I tried my hardest to move them and I could not. The doctors had to carry me to bed. How could they let this happen to me? Why can't they fix me? The Doctors did this to me. Father will be very mad, and he will sue them and they will have to fix me.

I wish I could see you...

I looked at Soon-ja when Yong spoke those words. What must it have felt like to be rendered so helpless by words on a page? Her lips pursed.

"I am so sorry," I said. "I'm so sorry that you all went through this. He was too good." This was a child. A child at his very worst, and here were those feelings for her, preserved. It gave me a pit in my gut. I wanted to say something about it getting better or ending well, but I couldn't, and I would have never been brought if it was only to say such things. My time would come. Soon-ja gave a hand to sit me by her side.

Over the next few weeks, Min sent drawing after drawing, day and night, through rehab and rest, with anger and joy, and at least two more visits from Wasabi. We took our time and looked at all of them. She was very proud, and she held my hand. His notes were mostly short; some were little more than titles. I wonder if they realized that his parents started censoring what he sent.

There wasn't a reason or rhyme to how they were laid on the table. To look, there was a rainbow of color, with dark spots of gray scale sprinkled throughout. He was amassing more supplies too; pastels, charcoal, ink pens, and even crayons. But the ones that grabbed my eye and shouted his name more than anything were the ones done with brush markers and styled after manga.

There are two kinds of manga for someone Min's age, and they follow something like a binary gender system. Shonen are the "young boy" stories and Shojo, "young girl." Think *Dragon Ball Z* and *Sailor Moon*, respectively. He must have been reading lots of both, because he had clear stylings of each in some of his drawings. Shonen are stylized and full of action, and his have him sword fighting, throwing fireballs, running, flying, jumping, and most prominently, posing on strong legs. The Shojo drawings were sugary, like they belonged more in a love story than a fight. He seemed to have much bigger eyes in those. Those were some of the best drawings on the table. Either way, a clear "manga self" was worked out somewhere during his stay. It was his only escape.

Soon-ja had favorites she wanted to show. The ones that brought her peace were the pictures he drew of his family. She liked seeing her son, and she missed seeing her son. Through the eyes of a child, in whatever getup he chose, was the best way to see him. Min seemed to admire his father, at least then. The way he drew him, strong like a hero or wise like a general, was a surprise to what I knew. And his mother was sometimes a beautiful geisha, or sometimes a witch. Not what we know in eastern mythos, like a Salem witch, but with flowing black hair, white robes, and some sort of green crystal. I don't think she was a villain... When he drew them as animals, she was usually a fox.

"May I?" I asked, because there was one I wanted to see a little closer. It was a drawing of the two of them, sketched quickly with charcoal. There were no signs of hospital, or heroes and villains, or fire, cats, swords, or bicycles. She extended her hand in an open invitation.

This was the picture that would have most easily been overlooked. It was minimal in its lines and erratic in its movement. He captured more than a bust of both of his parents standing together. His father stood on the left, half a head higher, and he was holding his wife close, but loose. They were both looking somewhere off the page. She was stifling emotion and he was feigning courage. To look fast was to see a forehead kiss before a flight out on short business. But to study what he saw, the way he saw it, there were two people, raw and exposed, doing what they could do to shelter him from a storm of sorrow. I questioned whether he wasn't just bad at drawing eyebrows, but I truly felt his perception to be beyond naive. I started to worry what his recent letters said about me.

Yong pulled his favorite from the pile. It was drawn as true as Min could have drawn, and it was colored by pencil. It was the same foot-of-the-bed view, with the same striped socks, except his father was holding a small cake. There was a one and a three lit for candles, and just above the bottom edge was Wasabi wearing a party hat.

"He turned my age," said Yong. "I am glad that he had a happy day. Uncle bought him iPhone, first generation. So lucky!" I laughed at his sentiment. How different their thirteens were. "I told all of my friends." And I was sure he did. Actually, it was very sweet.

224

"Wow. That's pretty cool. I didn't even have one until, hm, two years ago?" I said. "Can I help put these away?"

"No, please, Professor. I will clean them..."

Uncle interrupted and called for breakfast, but there was one letter remaining from the St Luke's stack. This one was a greeting card, sent from home, addressed by a different hand than Min's. The same hand penned the note.

Dear Mother,

Today Minho was finally released from the hospital, after eight long months. This has been a very difficult time for our family, and especially for Minho. Thank you for writing and responding to his letters. He was excited every time he received your mail. I don't know how else he would have pulled through. He is very strong, and he is very brave. I feel your spirit within him.

I am better now, and I am getting stronger every day. I hope that I can speak with you soon. Please give our best regards to everyone.

With love,

It was signed with symbols. At the time, I thought it was a mistake that I was able to read one from his father. A photograph accompanied the letter, not a drawing, not a sketch. It was professionally taken, and seemingly setup in their apartment, which looked beautiful. I was only guessing, but seeing how high they were above the city through their picture window, it must have been. Min was holding his Totoro in what would have been his first wheel chair. They were posed, and smiling, and altogether were a beautiful trio, but there was a seed of defeat behind his eyes. Or maybe I was projecting.

❖

The single biggest piece of culture shock found me at the breakfast table that morning. By my phone, at which I snuck a peek, it was right before ten. This was the same meal, identical in almost every way, as what we had the night before. I had no complaints, everything was delicious, and I knew a little better about what I wanted, but it wasn't breakfast. There I was, thinking that Uncle came back with eggs or milk. There wasn't any bacon or sausage or toast. There were oranges, but not juice, pancakes, but stuffed with scallions. There wasn't even cereal. Boy was that fresh batch of kimchi an eye opener. Nothing on the table looked repurposed, though. It was all laid out fresh, and it was a lesson for me in how foods should be pantried.

Nothing exciting like a pickle toss happened, but we bonded. Soon-ja, through Yong's words, asked about my family. I told her about all of my loud and crazy aunts, uncles, and cousins on my father's side, and that my mother's side was a bit spread out geographically. Both stories were familiar to neighbors and relatives she'd had. She was interested to learn that my wife was from Greece and that I saw some similarities in their villages.

"We all come from somewhere," she said. "And everywhere is home to someone. And sometimes even children of the same mother look different. What a world."

She asked me to tell her of my wife. "Is she beautiful?" she asked.

"Oh, she is very beautiful. Here..." I'm almost ashamed of what I did. There I had this one golden chance to tell her why she was so beautiful to me, and I called up a picture on my phone. I was still a little nervous of the language barrier, but that isn't any kind of reason. She wanted me to pass time, to converse, to use her imagination. And there she was, bleeding on her table for me.

"She is a nurse," I said. "She works with people who are very sick. She is very caring, and I am a very lucky man."

"And your baby. Do you have pictures? What is his name?"

A proud papa bear always has pictures of his cub. She was all smiles before I could even produce them. She held her hands around the phone as if she was reaching for the very precious thing himself. "His name is Nicholas," I said. "We call him Nicky for short."

"Neekee," she tried, bowing. She spoke some words that Yong could not keep up with translating. When she finished, she bowed more, and picked more food for her plate. Mostly blander bites.

I recounted the story of flying to Tokyo and having to travel back home, and how I missed his birth. I don't know what compelled me to say so. I didn't want them to think I was searching for apologies. They didn't seem to find my phone charging story as funny as my wife did. Soon-ja seemed mostly concerned with asking why I wasn't able to see her son, like if she asked again it would rewrite that chapter. There was something there that I couldn't yet touch, but her curiosity of him was a little less than nostalgic.

They wouldn't let me help with the plates again. I would have insisted but I had had about as much squatting as a westerner could have taken without blowing out a knee or slipping a disk. I wasn't in any kind of shape to be down for that long. They thought it was funny when I stretched out my legs and back or couldn't stand straight. My technique must have been terrible. I wanted to be ready for the next round of letters and pictures, but we weren't going straight through. Soon-ja had arranged for Yong to show and introduce me around the village. Unless they were in a hurry, for the sake of my orthopedic well-being, a bit of a break was welcome.

CHAPTER TWENTY SEVEN
THE CURIOUS ONE

My legs burned and the sun, at first, was blinding. At that time, there was a little more chatter against the silence and stillness of the morning. Those kids that greeted us were across the road, and there were more this time. Even more came running when one of them yelled something. Yong was a little older, and a whole lot more mature, but it wasn't difficult to place him into that same group a few years prior. In fact, I imagined that group to have always been there, and kids came and went. Min may well have been initiated. The soccer ball that a few of them were passing around made me sad for him.

Yong had little desire to introduce them, but they followed, keeping their distance. I wanted to stop and say "hi" to them, and I offered high fives, to the few that dared sneak close enough. Two of them obliged; the first one, to be the hero, and the second, to steal a little of his thunder. I was like the big man on campus, but I let my guide carry us on. They followed, to see where we were going. This wasn't the first time I felt the curious one.

It seemed like mostly houses and gardens and handmade, dusty walkways with stone stairs on the side of the hill where they lived. As it turned out, though, the village was a good deal bigger than I thought initially, extending as far, as Yong explained, as we could see. To get there, and more specifically, the very western edge of there, if straight ahead was north, we had quite a bit of village to clear first. Yong let me stop, when I asked, at his uncle's house, which wasn't locked. I was happy to have the bathroom in some semblance of privacy. I took the opportunity to don my hiking shoes. *Why bring them,* I thought, *if I'm not going to use them?*

We have old and new in Boston, but this was a brand I wasn't used to. Old here was older than there, and new was man made, and by that, with obtainable means. I distinctly remember a walk to my bus one late spring morning where I watched machine-made building parts brought up by a hoist. All I could think was that *we* figured out how to do this. We got so good at building things that we started stacking units on top of blasted out quarries and industrially frozen marshland, whatever the hell that was. Network wires are mapped in before floors are poured and there's track lighting and granite for the counters is cut to minimize waste. It's down to, well, a science. Seeing the way this place was built, and fixed, science seemed a little soul-less and humanity-sucking. There was an old woman spooning rice and kimchi for a handful of neighbors patching her roof tile. Every minute I spent I was reminded that we were more than just half a world away.

I said "ann yeong haseyo" as best I could. You'd think it would get better every time, but I'm dreadful with languages. Just a simple *hello*, and I can bungle it up by overthinking and practicing in my head. At least they seemed to smile and appreciate the attempt, or they were the most polite people I'd ever met. I felt like Lieutenant Aldo Raine in that one scene at the movie premier. But I was thankful for Yong introducing me to hands that I know Min touched. They were old hands; weathered and seasoned, but welcoming none the less. In fact, everyone I met was young or old. *Where are the parents?* I wondered.

It didn't matter much, I was a spectacle. When they knew who I knew, though, their story changed. How do you tell someone you've lost that they made such an impact on the people they left behind? I felt guilty accepting their graces, but their graces gave me courage. I remember some conversations with Min about how he wanted to come back. I could see why. I wasn't even gone, and I wanted to come back.

We walked and we were greeted for well over an hour. The return wouldn't be so long since most of the greetings were accomplished up front. The houses thinned

231

and then ended before a final farm and an open stretch of field at the last turn.

Our view opened wide to the backside of the mountain. If any breath was left at the top of the rising road, it was taken. The sun was hitting its highest stride and the peaks all glistened. They must have timed my view for midday. There were hundreds of peaks and they were carved all the way around, and the mountain was layered with tier upon tier of raised tea hedges. The earth was green and bright and the mist rising was silver and sparkling. They had striped the mountain along the curves that nature provided. Almost every row had pluckers at work, and they were sweeping from west to east plucking leaflings along the way. They dressed in tan robes with rolled pants, a pointed hat, and, I'm assuming, straw sandals. My back hurt just watching.

"It's like a dragon's back," said Yong. I had heard of *that* place. It's the famous, and perhaps the world's most captivating, tiered rice paddy in Longji, China. This one was much smaller, and less winding, and not so iconic, but before my eyes, it was without a doubt one of the most majestic images I've yet to see. "That's what we call it," he said. "When cousin learned of the real dragon's back, he argue with Sensei that the real one was here, with Grandmother. He was punished for it."

"Punished?"

"Yes, yes. It is bad to speak against Sensei, Professor. Are your students not punished?"

"Well, yes, but...punished how?"

"With bamboo stick. Sensei feel bad for cousin, so he punish the top of his legs because he knows it doesn't hurt cousin very much. He wrote to Grandmother about this."

Against a beautiful and peaceful backdrop of planting rice, I was ready to be sick. He was so matter of fact.

"Was your cousin punished a lot in school?" I wondered what other drawings and letters of it were waiting for us. I didn't really want to read those.

"Yes. I think so. He was not a very good student like me," he laughed.

"Yong, was Min punished a lot...at home? Did your uncle punish him?"

"Oh no. Uncle work very late, and many days. Especially after hospital. In Japan, mostly Sensei make punishment. Minho's mother punish him with taking PlayStation 3 or iPhone. Grandmother wants to know if you punished Minho at University."

And there was the rub. He said something else, but I stared at him through a tunnel, not hearing another word. My guts knotted and all I remember is the worry I had for whether he saw my face change when the first surge hit my chest. My face got hot and I felt pins and needles down my shoulders. It hit me three times more between my lungs and my knees weakened. He didn't seem to notice. He continued speaking, pointing out over the workers. Each time it struck, I heard a ring in my ears. And then I went dizzy, and cold, all over. He laughed about something, and I thought it was me. I gave a dumb smile, and tried to find something to lean

233

against to gather bearings. I was so worried that I would drop right there at his feet. My mind ran to how far we were from a hospital, to my stuff that needed collecting at his uncle's house, to the phone in my pocket, to my wife's voice and the smell of baby shampoo on Nicky's hair. My left thigh was throbbing.

I didn't drop. As far as I could tell at the time, I wasn't having a cardiac episode. My pulse wasn't racing, and after what must have only been moments, I felt the most amazing, relieving, nurturing feeling I ever remember feeling. His laugh came back to my ears, as did the humming tea pickers, and I felt a cool breeze brushing against my forehead and over my ears.

"Are you ok, Professor?"

I wasn't. He asked only because I failed to answer something else just before. I took a moment to check. I clenched fists full of sweat and rubbed them dry. I was too embarrassed to tell.

"Yes. Of course. I'm fine. It's just so beautiful here, is all. Min must have loved it. Thank you. For sharing. Should we be getting back?" Their house wasn't home to me, but my instinct was to retreat there. I spoke quickly, wanting him to move us along.

We set back and for some reason, one which I would never fully understand, I remember feeling guilty that I wasn't working as hard as they were.

CHAPTER TWENTY EIGHT
NOT MY FAULT

"I'll be right in," I said. "I just need to make a quick call."

I didn't consider the time until the hinge in her voice reminded me. It was after ten o'clock, last night, which meant bottle time, and she was pissed. It's not my fault she left her ringer on.

"Do you have a minute," I asked.

"..." Nicky was screaming. "Can I call you back," she said. It wasn't a question, and she ended the conversation.

I didn't want to go inside, I knew she'd call, even if she had to just situate him.

The appeal of me seemed to wear off some. The kids were kicking the ball against the back side of an old stone building behind a rusted out Renault Alliance. That was the first time I was alone in a few days. Of all things, I started wondering where their church was. I didn't want to go, and I hadn't some sudden desire to worship, but I wondered where they prayed for my son. Was it even in a church? To have our names spoken in such ways in such buildings this far hit me in a romantic, and as best as I could know, spiritual kind of way. It would have been the farthest reaching ripple of my small existence.

"Hello?" I answered in one ring. I was lost pondering, not realizing if it was minutes or hours that passed.

"What's going on?" she asked. "I'm sorry, it's just, he had just fallen asleep. Is everything ok?"

"I...don't know, really. I mean..."

"What? What's up?" She was trying to listen, but was distracted by him, which she should have been.

"It's nothing really. I'm just finding out an awful lot."

"Is it beautiful there?"

"Oh my God, yeah, it's amazing. I wish you two were here."

"Why did you call, you sound like something's up."

I didn't want to say. I found myself picking at stucco.

"Well did you find out what they wanted?"

"I think so. They haven't exactly said so, and...I think it sounds crazy, but I think they think I had something to do with it, maybe..."

"What?! That's ridiculous!" We had already gone over this, and we agreed that that was ridiculous. I don't know why my gut was feeling defensive. "Why do you say that?"

"Well, his cousin took me out to show me around. Just now. And his Grandmother has been showing me some of the old letters. He was in a pretty bad car accident, by the way. That's why he was in the chair. I never knew that."

"What does that have to do with you?"

"Well, evidently, he may not have been a great student. And when a student is defiant over here, they get hit. I'm guessing with rulers?"

"That happens in a lot of places."

"They've been calling me Professor. He called me Professor. I don't know. I have a feeling they think I was hitting this kid."

"No. This is insane. We don't need this shit. I don't need this shit. I need you here, helping me with the baby. Go in there and tell that this is bullshit and just come home."

"You know I can't do that. Not now. I need to see the rest of these letters."

"And what is that going to solve?"

"I really think there's going to be something else in there. Now I really need to know what he was telling them. Babe, if there is someone that's responsible, I need to know. If this kid was bullied in any way... I mean, what if this was a hate crime?" The very words made my skin crawl. I hadn't considered it before. "Get some sleep, I'll try to call you again in the morning."

"Should I be worried?"

"No. Don't be crazy..."

"You called me."

"I know. Is not like that. Actually, I think it's going ok. No need to worry."

"Well why did you call?"

"I don't know, he said the thing about his Grandmother wanting to know if I punished this kid, and I don't know, I think I had an anxiety attack. It just scared me is all. I needed to hear your voice."

"Oh my God, are you ok?! Peter, get home. I don't even know where you are if something happens."

"What could possibly happen? Get some sleep. I love you, and I'll call you in the morning."

"I really don't like this, and *don't* call me Threepio!"

"I know. I'll let you know what happens. I love you. Now get some sleep. Threepio."

"I hate you."

"Goodnight, babe. I miss you. Kiss him for me please."

"Be careful. I love you too. Call me in the morning."

CHAPTER TWENTY NINE
SOMETHING WORTH FIGHTING FOR

It was a little after lunch, which I learned we weren't eating, when I rejoined them. They were waiting at the table in front of another stack of letters. In fact, there were several stacks laid out, and more on the floor, and more in boxes. She asked if I wanted something, but by the manners I was raised on, I wouldn't impose until at least the third ask. I was starving. I was only asked once.

It probably took Soon-ja the better part of the two hours we were away to get the others back into their envelopes and put in order. That was a job she would task to no other.

Of the stacks she set out, half had artwork on top, some complete, some only sketched in the margins, and most were handwritten, but a handful were typed. I assumed those ones were written from home, maybe from his father's office. I scanned for something of an answer, trying to find out whether his story really needed us trudging through all of the earlier chapters from school to summer to day trips to vacations to a sprouting little samurai self he imagined over many pages. There was something specific there for me to put my finger on, and finding it probably wasn't going to be easy. And, if for a moment I thought that Yong wasn't receptive to my reaction, I was wrong. We were in the room with a white elephant, and I felt stared at more than by the team of little soccer players that followed us around.

"Why do you think you are here, Professor?" I could hear authority in his Grandmother's words, even if some of it was lost in his cousin's translating. My eyes moved around the table but hers were fixed. "How we teach our children is very different," she knew that I took her question as hypothetical. "You are not here for me to find blame. Minho's actions were his own. He was always headstrong," whether she believed that or not, it was not an insult. "I asked you here because he respected you and he cared for you very much. He wrote to me about the things he wanted me to know. I want to know more. I want to understand. Please forgive, Professor, but I never went to University. There are years of my Minho here," she said as she tapped stacks and fanned pages. "And my grandson was not happy." She slid a separate box toward her from under the table. There wasn't any, but she brushed away dust from the cover. This was a selection kept very safe, almost sacred.

"Yong has helped me to change these words, but he does not understand them. He is still very young." That led to a brisk exchange, which I am certain she won. "These all came before going to University. Minho's father is a very proud man," she dropped the letters and they slapped against the table. "His son, Minho the artist, was going to be a businessman. But Minho did not want to be a businessman. Look at the beauty in his artwork. The letters in this pile are every reason why Minho did not belong at your University." She took a moment to compose and to allow for the rest of the translation.

With all the fingers of her right hand she spun the pile and then slid it over. "This was not his father's business." The top page was another self-portrait. It was colorful, but not styled after a manga. There was another boy next to Min and they were holding hands. A colorful rainbow was drawn behind them, and there were small things all around that they must have had in common. It was clear that Yong hadn't seen those letters in a long time. He asked something that got him a cuff on the back of his head. She knew, and she was supporting him with vigor. What a relief. "Please," she said.

There may have been other letters leading up to that one, with hints along the way, but that was *the* one. I wondered if and how Min ever came out to his parents. *He must have*, I thought. Did he ever tell them that he didn't want to go? They said he was defiant in school, but I never saw it. I was guessing that his head was foggy after the accident and maybe he was behind. The Min I knew wasn't a fighter. There was love on that page, in the eyes of both boys. That's not so easily faked, not that I didn't believe him, but

241

my heart broke a little that day. That was something worth fighting for.

"Who is this?" I asked. Yong must have added his own spin to earn another cuff behind the ear.

"His name is Yoshi," said a defeated translator, rubbing the back of his head.

Like the dinosaur? I thought. *Like Min's favorite Mario character*, I realized. I wondered if it was a first name, abbreviated last name, a nickname, or some kind of pet name. It didn't really matter, because that wasn't exactly what I was asking, but she wasn't done explaining. He looked like a Yoshi, though.

"They were friends together from an early grade. They share many interests. Minho loved him very much. Minho was very mad that his father did not send him to same art school as Yoshi..."

His uncle paced in the background, griping his disapproval. He had clearly known, and was harboring something, but Yong had lots of questions. The three of them rolled embers and picked at old wounds. Soon-ja seemed to be defending Min, and the other two changed their tunes from challenging to mocking. It made me uncomfortable for the Min I knew. She ended that quickly.

"Did Minho ever speak of this with you?"

I thought long and carefully on whether I could truthfully deny what she was asking. I could. He never mentioned it.

"To be honest," I said, "No. I mean, he did seem to resent his family. Do you know this word?" I was asking Yong. Soon-ja responded that she did know my meaning. "I never understood why. In fact," I laughed a little, "I was almost afraid to speak to his parents because he made them seem like monsters. Seeing his pictures, now I'm not so sure."

"There are many more pictures. You would not lick the skin of a melon to taste it, do not judge my family the same way. They are not monsters, but sometimes we do things we do not mean to the people we most care for. Minho was very young, and he was in love. He saw the world in rainbows and cartoon dragons. All he saw was a father trying to separate him from Yoshi, and not his father's true intentions. I want to know that there was some joy in my sweet grandchild's final days. Please tell me about the Minho that you knew."

"I... Well... Min was a great kid. He was always polite. To everyone. He always seemed to have a big imagination, you know. A sense of wonder. He seemed to be doing well in his classes, and was interested in what his professors were teaching." It all sounded very generic to me, but she hung on every word.

"Did he make any friends?" she asked.

"Now, see that's what is so interesting to me. He did. He seemed to make very close friends, especially with the other international students. He didn't..."

"International students?" She asked.

"Yes. Students from other countries."

243

"I understand, Professor. But, please excuse, but I find your system quite interesting. Do you mean to say that the students are separated like this? Students from America, students from China, students from Africa, and so?"

"No, no not at all. International students have a different path. They have to jump through more hoops, and in many ways have the hardest transition, but they can be some of our best students."

"Like Minho?"

"Yes. Some even smarter." I don't know, it sort of slipped out. I didn't mean to offend them. Luckily they weren't offended. They either didn't think he was as bright as I did, or they were impressed with how smart the others must have been. I couldn't quite tell. I still had the floor. "Where was I? Yeah, it's common for international students to make friends together. Have you travelled? Been to the bus station or airport?" She nodded, but I wasn't sure to which. "And would you rather have sat there with other people from your home country, or would you sit and speak with strangers? I know that I would be more comfortable..."

I could tell by her brow that I was insulting her intelligence. I really didn't mean to. Sometimes I do that and it's only because it helps me to make sense of something. "I'm sorry. I just mean that, yes, Min made some friends very quickly. He joined many clubs. He even wanted to start his own drawing club. He was at all of the school events, except for the athletics." I was spinning. There wasn't much else I could think to say without answering to something specific.

"Would you read his letters he sent from University?" she asked.

"Absolutely. That's why we're here," I said.

"We will leave you. She asked me to bring you iced tea and crackers. Grandmother will rest now. Uncle will leave us as well, and I will shop for dinner. Please feel free to make this your home, but please, she asks, handle them delicately."

CHAPTER THIRTY
ALONE WITH MIN

Yong brought a tray, not long into my sifting of the pile, carrying a sweating glass of boricha and a dish of twisted, pink puffs. The tea was made from barley and the crackers from shrimp. A little honey helped the flavors of both, but reminded that there were bees buzzing nearby, and I didn't much like knowing that. By the time I wiped the condensation off of my fingers so as not to pucker any pages, I was alone with Min.

There must have been two or three years' worth of writing, and it was almost all sent during his first and only semester with us, with some sent the summer before. I fanned through the first few, skimming the drawings to try to date them by big events accordingly. The first one that grabbed my eye, naturally, was a picture of the school's mascot. We wore him emblazoned on polo shirts at open house events and orientations, and the like. The very sight of him nearly triggered another panic in me, which should be an indication of how happy I was to be working elsewhere.

The date on that letter was nearly a full year ago. April. It *was* at an open house. Funny, I didn't remember him attending one, and I certainly would have. Usually, international students didn't make the trip for open houses; they trusted their college counselors. That's not why, though. We were trained to keep an eye out for students who had the kinds of disabilities that would cost the school money. Min would have at least meant electric door openers, and maybe some specially ordered Res Hall furniture, and God knows the shower stalls and science labs weren't accessible. Sometimes they tried to encourage those kids to go elsewhere because they didn't want to shoulder any costs. They always tried to make the advisors do it. I can at least say, proudly, that I never put any of *that* blood on my hands.

That particular drawing caught my eye. Not because it was of the school's symbol, but because it was of the costume version of the school's symbol that, sure enough, some sophomore work-study student was wearing. This wasn't a mean looking wolf like you'd see in a highlight reel, dunking off a trampoline through a flaming hoop. They paid the lowest bidder and wound up with a silly old cross-eyed wolf that you only get to see when you go to campus. The President insisted he be the open house ambassador, and we all just sort of laughed when he came around. I scanned through Min's note, though, and he seemed to like him. It looked like it may have even inspired his next Con costume.

>...*He's a white wolf! I don't know how to make such a costume, but I've always wanted to dress as San. I can make the mask from papier mâché, and a white fur cape. Yoshi can dress as Ashitaka! I asked to take my picture with him on my iPhone. Maybe Yoshi can make a wolf like him. He is very good at cosplay.*

I was willing to put money on Soon-ja not knowing what Princess Mononoke was, let alone the two main characters. I smiled. If Min needed someone to explain his references to his Grandmother, he picked the right person. But knowing San and Ashitaka was far from why I was sitting in South Korea. So I read on.

>*Father introduced me to the Dean of the business school. They seemed to be like business partners.*

Knowing what I knew, Min's father's name was probably on a to-do list for the day; a donor to cultivate, if you will.

>*He said he would love to have me in his Young Entrepreneur's Club. I want to join the anime club, too! And there is an Asian Student Union and they have Chinese New Year, and they said I could help!*

There was another drawing at the end of the second page. He drew a dragon, like the costume dragons that dance at a Chinese festival. Only this dragon had a set of wheels holding up the boy holding up the tip of his tail. I used to love that program, and I especially loved the dumplings they would make. I would have loved to see him there.

The campus is small and the sky is big...

He used to say that.

Everyone is nice to me, and they hold the doors. I will study business, but they even have art class and computer class too, which father said I can take as elective classes. I think that I fit in here. I hope that I can be happy. We can have guests stay, and maybe Yoshi will visit, and maybe my cousin Yong can come too. Father and I will go to see Boston for a few days and to see the Red Sox. We will see Daisuke Matsuzaka! Father is very excited.

Behind every student, there are stories and conversations, and there are sacrifices. I thought about Soon-ja's question, about why international students are so different. Aside from this kid's father cutting a check, I suppose I never considered the sacrifices. His letter wasn't so different from the conversations that any other student would have. Only, he was leaving everything even further

249

behind. If I read this a year ago, I probably would have just brushed it off.

A few of the letters that followed dealt with school things, and the mundane. There was something about construction in their building, and a business trip his father took. I looked for drawings of Fenway or Duck Boats, or China Town. I tried to imagine how hard the cobble stones at Faneuil Hall would have been for him to walk but there weren't any follow-ups from Boston. The next one that grabbed my attention, though, must have come shortly after their return. On the cover page, there was a sketch in black ink, filled with watercolor red, of San's mask. Even though I didn't have her sides to any of these conversations, it looked like Soon-ja asked who San and Ashitaka were. I wish I knew how to tell her myself the way that that touched me.

Father said we can go to Comiket this summer! He will take holiday and stay at the hotel with us. He said if Yoshi has to go, then I should dress up as Super Mario.

Low hanging fruit, even for a Dad joke, I thought, but I probably would've made the same. It made me chuckle, anyways.

This is a picture of San's mask. I already started making it out of papier mâché, and I'll paint it with acrylic. San is the warrior princess who attacks the evil Lady Eboshi for destroying her forest. Ashitaka comes

250

*to save her, and together they help to heal the forest
spirits from their sickness. They love each other very
much, but San decides to stay and protect the forest
when Ashitaka goes to be with his people. They will be
apart, but I think that one day they will meet again.*

Maybe it was just the coincidence of the wolf.
Maybe not. Maybe young love wants to find itself in stories
and fairy tales, and maybe that helps to ease the pain of
impending separation. From what I understand, Tokyo's
ComicCon is world class, and this kid was going to have the
time of his life. So far, so good.

*Now that school is finished, I will spend the rest of
summer preparing...*

I checked the date again. Middle of April. *Huh, did I
miss his graduation?*, I thought. I flipped back to the
beginning to look through again. Lo and behold, I had missed
it. There wasn't a drawing or a picture with that one for
some reason. It turns out, high school graduation in Japan
takes place in March. I didn't know that. I used to think that
some of the students that made it to the April open houses
just...had April vacation. Boy was I wrong.

There wasn't much in that letter besides thanks. She
must have sent a gift. He didn't really explain much about
the ceremony, only that he found it boring. The dinner
seemed fairly uneventful, but he enjoyed the company. He
said they went for *American* food, with a wink face,
whatever that meant. There weren't any mentions of Yoshi. I

251

would suppose that some families, like back home, were more "traditional" than others, or whatever term that's synonymous with "un-accepting." They probably didn't celebrate together, and that's a little sad.

There were a whole lot of letters from the summer, and he wasn't kidding. He detailed every step, but here, he didn't draw pictures, he took them. He was proud of his work, as he should have been.

> *...The first step was to make a cast of my face. I wanted the mask to fit perfectly. Yoshi and I learned this in one of our art classes. The strips of plaster felt so slimy!"*

He had on a smock and his hair was held back with a headband.

> *But then it got very itchy. Yoshi made his face as well. We had to breathe through straws while it dried...*

I flipped through the stack of photos. There were a few pictures of them sitting shoulder to shoulder. Some female friends were helping, and in that particular picture, the one with the straws, they were laughing. From the casts, they made a few plaster faces each and painted them and attached hangers on the back. I never saw the inside of his res hall, but I was willing to bet that one of them was hung on his wall. In the remaining shots, they helped Min paint his face with the accents that Sen wore. He looked...convincing. It made me smile.

The next letter was dated for about a week later. He took photos to document the whole process. For the body of the mask, he used a Styrofoam ball - like the one that would be Jupiter in a third grade solar system - split in half. He used old reading lamp shades to make the eye and mouth collars, then he glued a thin foam noodle down to make the ridges. After papier mâchéing front and back, sanding it smooth, and priming, he painted and lacquered the surface red, white, and gold. His finished work was amazing; it looked professional. I wondered how long it took to complete, because to me, there was no way he did it all in a week.

Next, he worked on the earrings, which looked like wide, flat, white stones, and necklace, which looked like tiger's teeth. Both were done in polymer clay, which was baked and sanded. The hair piece looked like it was cut from a shaggy white bathmat. I don't know how he made the knife and spear, but they looked good, too. The last letter about the costume was dated mid-May.

❖

Grandmother.

I am writing from our family vacation in Okinawa.
Father is here partly on business. He will meet with a
delegation in a few days to discuss opening a new
office. They are interested in tax incentives. He said it
would be good for me to learn this for when I go to
business school. Mother says that I had to come
because they did not want me to be home alone. She
thinks that I would have invited Yoshi to stay.

Okinawa has many beautiful beaches. I do not like the
beach, I cannot go. I used to like going to the beach. I
hope that we can go to Okinawa Churaumi Aquarium.
I want to paint a picture of the whale sharks. I have
not seen whale sharks before. I wish that we could
come to see you for vacation. I miss you very much.
Will you come to visit me again one day?

M

Grandmother.

Today we went to the aquarium. It was amazing!
There are many things to see, and we spent the day.
The sea tank was as big as the ocean! I got to see the
whale sharks!

There was a post card size sketch included.

*When we were in Boston, we saw the New England
Aquarium. They have boats that take people into the
ocean to see the whales, but in Okinawa, they have the
whales inside! I wish for Yong to see this, and Uncle
because he loves fishing. We will be leaving Okinawa
tomorrow. I will be happy to be home.*

M

His sketch of the whale was backed in mostly blue,
like he dipped the card in glowing, electric ink. It was a trick
of the color. The black fish spread nearly from edge to edge,
and in the lower left corner sat a small silhouette of a boy in
a chair, dwarfed by the dancing giant. There was scale and
there was awe, like seeing a satellite watching the planets
form. There weren't any words that I would've known to
explain how powerful that experience must have been.

Grandmother,

*I am sorry I have not written. I asked Father if I could
see you before I move away to University. He said that
this is not possible. Because of my injury, I cannot
come to your house in the village very easily. He also
says that you are too old to travel to Japan anymore. I
wish that you could have Internet so we can see you...*

For the first time in my life, I was in that place. Never had I ever been handed that stack of letters, or known of their existence. For some reason, though, in some other place, at some other time, it felt as though I'd read those words before. Aside from those being the words of my late student, and a boy who missed a distant Grandmother, they weren't otherwise compelling. But still, there was a strange déjà-vu about that one. At the very least, it felt like I was closing in on something.

The rest of that letter had little to do with me, or Yoshi, or College, or Korea. The next one, though, came from Comiket. This letter was a peacock in a crowd of pigeons. Every free inch of paper was sketched and doodled in Technicolor from everything they saw, but first, was their photo.

Yoshi's red hood covered most of his face except his eyes. His blue robes and brown pants were hand stitched, and spot on. He wore the cape, too, which looked like he may have thatched by hand.

And then there was Min. Beaming from ear to ear, and he earned it. Aside from the mask, which was propped up on his pulled-back hair, and the makeup, robes, spear and knife, he had his wolf. With two wooden cutouts painted like the white wolf Moro and attached on either side like a carousel sleigh, they decorated his chair. My eyes shot over to the letter

Grandmother,

*We won an award for our cosplay! We had to go on
the stage. I was very nervous. Everyone applauded and
Yoshi held my hand. For the whole con, people wanted
to take my picture. The picture I am sending was
posted on the official blog!*

Sure enough, they were wearing their medals.

*Yoshi and I had fun playing games and meeting
friends. I never saw so many people in my whole life.
They said nearly half of a million attended! So many
people slept outside, but father would not allow it. He
stayed inside the hotel making business calls. The
people were all very kind, and we met some of our
favorite artists. Also, people did not care that we were
together. For the first time, we were able to be
ourselves. I had the best day in my whole life...*

In his whole life. We've all said so before. I've said
about a burger or a bowl of ramen that it was the best I've
ever had. I know which movie and which rock album
inspires the want to rank things as my favorite. My best day,
having my son. But have I ever gotten to experience who I
really was? I didn't know. Not like Min did on that day. His
words were no match for his page decorations, and his love
for Yoshi was screaming loud and clear. I believed him. But it

hit me hard in the chest, that word *whole*. By my handling of his letter, he'd already lived his whole. This peacock of a page was perhaps the best day he ever had. It was an honor to hold that day in my hand. It made me want to find one of my very own. It made me want to hug my wife and son.

He went on in there about stuff they ate and pictures they purchased, but for some reason, it was of little interest to me. I wanted to chase him through his next chapter. Comiket was August, and it would be his last letter before sending one with my name attached.

The feeling inside for that next letter was of nerves and face flush, of nostalgia and heart ache. It was as desperate to be reading his words as it was watching through Ikiru. The ending is so clear, so very visceral. Hell, Kurosawa tells you Watanabe's fate in the opening credits: his stomach cancer will end his life. Every step towards the close is a heart wrench tightening around a very certain thing. I could read on, and hope to find him well at the end of this pile, but that wasn't going to happen. Now, the question remained. *Will I find out why he did it?*

Grandmother,

We moved into my dorm on Monday. My roommate is named Matt and he is a lacrosse player. I do not know if we will be friends. He told his friends that he is happy to have a Chinese roommate to help with math homework. He has been to practice for many hours in the day and then out with his friends until very late. I don't mind when he is away.

It was very busy with International students moving in. Many students have come from China and Hong Kong. There were a few students from Japan, and one girl from Korea that I met so far. They are very nice to me, and we ate together in the Dining Center. One boy is very good at drawing and one of our Orientation Leaders said that he is the treasurer of the anime club and he would like us to join.

My room is on the first floor because there is no elevator. They gave me a button with Velcro to my chair so that I can push to open the doors. Father keeps asking about snow. He will be flying home soon. Yesterday I met my Advisor, Mr. Peter Cahill. He was very busy, but he helped me make my schedule. He thought it was very funny when I called him Mr. Peter. I did not get all of the classes that I wanted, but he said that he would help me if something else became open. He was very happy to know that I am from Japan. He smiled when he said that he always wanted to go to Japan. I told him that I am from Japan because I heard him say that to another Japanese student. I did not tell him that I am really from Korea...

This part was a bit like hearing my own voice on a recording. I knew what I said, and I remembered having such little programmed responses, but felt a little outside of myself hearing them back. I'm not sure what response I would have rattled if he had said where he really was from because my understanding of that had all been changed so much in present company.

I have had orientation for two days, and will have two more days. They are teaching me about American University classes. My Professors will give me points for speaking in class, even if I speak wrong. In Japan, I used to get in trouble for speaking, and for being wrong, so I think that I will do very well here :) I wish that I could have classes with Yushi. I miss him very much. I don't think that my roommate will like it if he visits me, but I will find a way.

There are activities to do during the weekend, and the rest of the students will return on Monday and Tuesday. Classes will begin on Wednesday. I am excited for that.

Minho

Just words. No pictures, no drawings. To me, they felt a little lonely. Had I only known then…

"Hello," said Yong. He was helping Soon-ja shuffle back into the room. "Please excuse," he said. "Grandmother needs to make a bathroom." She looked very curious as to my progress, but they were quickly through. It was just enough to break my rhythm, but something uncomfortable stayed with me.

There were volumes remaining, and the letters were longer. Some were several pages thick. He must have written more than once a week; he must have spent a small fortune on post. There were a hundred pages at least; probably more. But there was a bottom to the stack, which was a grim bit of reminder of when he died. A parenthetical piece of time I held, and the last remaining days and sentiments of a quirky, charming, hopelessly in love, and seemingly lonesome young man. I am not the reader who typically flips to the last page of a book to turn back and work towards a known conclusion, but with that cat out of the bag, I couldn't help dropping the weight in the middle.

His last letter was dated just one day prior to his death.

Grandmother,

My greatest pleasure has been writing to you and reading your letters. I wish that I could have seen you and that I could have told you more, but know that I will be in a better place when you are reading this. You have supported me and loved me for who I am.

261

Please do not be sad for me. I am not afraid. I am not a coward.

I will do my best to send you someone very special. Mr. Peter always made me feel better when I was feeling sad, and he will do the same for you. I told him one time about our village, and our dragon, and it made him happy to hear. He knows how special it is to me. He told me to do whatever it takes to return home someday. I will return home.

When I return, please let me be with Grandfather.

Until we meet,

Minho

CHAPTER THIRTY ONE
SOMETIMES STUDENTS DIE

Fuck. The walls started closing and my lungs slammed shut. I read the last words through pinhole eyes and had to read them again carefully because they were deceived. Sweat poured all over and my hands quaked. I dropped away the letter like it hurt to hold, like it was an admission of guilt for a crime I didn't remember committing. I was inside of a nightmare and there wasn't any waking to make it go away. It was my fault. I did this, and I owed these people far more than an apology. Before I could even know what I just read, and before the paper fluttered down and thumped on the table I was up. With bloody thumbs I dialed, and then staggered my way to find fresh air to relieve the choking.

❖

She didn't answer the first or second call. "...What's going on?" she asked. "It's 2:30 in the morning. Is everything ok?!"

"No. No, I fucked up. I don't... It's my fault. This kid's dead, and it's my fault. What am I going to do? What am I..."

"What?! What happened?"

"He sent a suicide note. It's my fault. I did this."

"Calm down..."

"I can't. I... I shouldn't have come here..."

"Hold on." I heard the floor creek and the door swing shut. She walked out into the hallway so she could talk without waking the baby. "Tell me what happened."

"He wrote all these letters. In the last one, he said that I told him to do whatever it takes to get back here. I never meant...this! I... I actually remember the conversation. Like it was yesterday. It was, I don't know, two weeks before, maybe three. I don't know how it came up, but we started talking about villages. Maybe he asked about the picture of your village. I think he said that and it reminded him of home. He said that there were too many stairs. And there are... I didn't know. I was trying to be encouraging, you know. I thought it was harmless. It was a fucking throwaway line. Now I'm racing. What the hell else did I say to this kid? I..."

"What do you mean?"

"I told him to do whatever it takes to get back here. That it will be worth it."

"So what? That's all? It's not your fault, honey. You didn't do anything wrong."

"Well, what if he took it to mean... I don't know, it sounds silly, but...dead or alive?"

"That's ridiculous."

"He said that when he returns, he wants to be with his Grandfather."

"Where is his Grandfather?"

"Buried, I think... He said that he would try to send me here to cheer them up, or something, because I always made him feel better when he was sad. I had no idea. Look, if he was having any kind of ideation, I didn't know about it. Maybe he had depression? He never said anything to me! But if he somehow heard me say that getting back here was a way out, it's my fault. This is *my* fault. What the hell am I going to tell them?"

"You don't have to tell them anything. It's not your fault. Will you come home?"

"I can't. I have to go talk to them. They're waiting. I... I'm so sorry."

"Why are you apologizing?" It was rhetorical.

"I don't know. I...can't even make this right. I don't know how I can go in there and face them."

"They don't blame you. You said it yourself. You made him feel better. They see that..."

"I hate this. I'm going to be sick."

"What else did he say?"

265

"I don't know, I didn't read everything. One minute, everything seemed fine. He was at comic con, and then moving in, and then this. That's it. He's gone, and there's no one else to blame but me. I have to go talk to them. I'll call you when I can. I'm so sorry."

"Don't apologize. Call me back, ok?"

"Ok. I love you. I...never meant for this. I shouldn't have left you."

"I love you too. Call me back."

I paced for a while, wringing my hands and shaking my head. Everything about that place brought me pain that maybe I robbed him of seeing it again. I didn't know what I would say. Before I could decide, Yong was out the door and calling my name.

The room wasn't moving like the way I left it. Soon-ja was collecting the pages. Her face was still. That letter was on top of the pile; she knew that it was read. Yong didn't need to translate, but he asked her question. "What can you tell us?"

My breath was deep, but I bit my lip and shook my head. All I could do was rifle through lines I'd learned in brown bag luncheons, or from brochures at the Counseling Center. *Bad Things Happen To Good People, Too!* or *Sometimes Students Die,* or *...We May Never Know Why.* They didn't want to hear that stuff. I couldn't just game my way out of what they had to know. The teacher was calling on me, though, and I hadn't done the homework, so I deflected. "What would you like to know?"

"Do you know why?"

"I am so sorry. I do not." She waited for more. It had to be honest. "The Min that I knew would have never... If I ever thought..." I had to think carefully over every moment I shared with him. Maybe some secret was buried between the lines, or deep within those pages. Maybe we really would never know. "You said that your Grandson was in pain. He never mentioned that to me." I had to tread lightly so I didn't blame the victim. "I should have known. Maybe I could have helped. I remember that conversation...the one that he mentioned in the..." She tapped the page. She was following with little help from Yong. "He was so happy to speak of this place. He spoke so fondly of you, of your village. He was very proud to be from here." Her head raised a touch, re-animating that pride. "We reminisced. That helps sometimes...when students are homesick... I also... He seemed to be doing everything right. He was involved. I mean, he had his anime club, he was part of the Asian Student Union, he was with friends. He seemed, for the most part...normal." That wasn't the right word. It made me cringe.

"I am so sorry. I really hope that I did not say something that..."

"There is no one to blame, Professor. A hundred hands touch a tea leaf before it is plucked. Knowing what you know now, if my Grandson came to you homesick again, would you speak differently with him? Would you not wish for him to be home?"

I was not prepared for her to ask this of me. I had to think carefully. My eyes met hers and then darted to the letters. I looked at Yong, and to his uncle. And then something over in the corner caught my eye.

She had small table set with a Buddha and a picture of her late husband. Two sticks of incense freshly lit. I could smell the beech wood. Beside those sat a framed picture of Minho in his graduation attire, which consisted of a formal black button down jacket, sitting next to…Soon-ja! She made the trip to see him walk across the stage. It was clearly a huge surprise.

"No," I said, reveling in what appeared pure, familiar, even, and the happiness in his eyes, and the laughter on their faces. "I would never take that from him. In fact, I think, maybe I didn't push him hard enough... There's so much that I would do or say differently if I had him in front of me..." I pointed. "There. There is the Min that I knew. I had seen that look, or at least something like it. Not every day, but often enough. That's why I have no words for what happened."

It helped me immensely to see that photo of him. There was a thing in his face that only revealed itself with a certain smile. The way his eyes creased in the corners and one cheek dimpled. That was a thing that couldn't be faked. That was how I would decide to remember him.

"That is what I wanted to know," she said. "Nothing will bring my Minho back, but if I know that there was light inside of the dark, then I may someday find peace."

"I can tell you of the times he smiled like this, and I can tell you of the Min that I knew."

"I would hear your every word."

"But, if I may, can I ask you a question?"

"Yes, please, Professor."

"Where is Minho's Grandfather buried?"

She knew what I was driving at; those eyebrows couldn't lie. She may have been expecting me to ask.

"Minho's Grandfather. He was a silly man. He loved his grandchildren very much. He was a fisherman, but more than anything, he loved his tea. Sometimes he would pour it with soju. He is not buried, Professor. His wish was to have his ashes released over the tea fields..."

"On the dragon's back."

"Yes. It's not usual to do this, you see. But he wanted to be reborn as a cup of tea!"

The dragon's back, I thought. Like an arrow between the eyes, and with unrelenting clarity, it hit me. "When I return..."

She nodded like it took me long enough to figure it out. "Minho wanted to have his ashes released with his Grandfather."

"This is his home. Do his parents know this?"

"No. Minho's father does not know this. He will not allow it, I'm afraid. He is a very proud man. To Minho's father, a family belongs together."

"It seems to me that he has family here, as well."

Her only response was a half-smile before she bowed.

"Will you please excuse me? For just a moment?"

❖

"Babe, it's me," *who else would it have been?* I wondered.

"What happened?"

"We talked. I think everything is ok with them. Like I said, they don't blame me."

"I told you..."

"Well, it doesn't make me feel any better. But listen, I understand what he wanted. I don't know what the hell happened, and I'm not sure we ever will, but I might be able to help them make peace. I have to go. Back to Japan. I have to talk to his father."

"What?! What are you talking about?"

"I have to go and at least try to talk to him. His Grandfather wasn't buried. His ashes were spread here. That's what he wanted."

"No. No, this is none of your business. You have no business. This is a very personal matter for this family. This has gone too far. You need to come home."

"And I will. I feel like I need to see this thing through now. It's what he wanted. It's what his Grandmother wants. I at least owe it to them to ask."

"Why doesn't she ask? It's her own damn family."

"It doesn't seem to be possible. There is something going on here between those two. Maybe that's what Min wanted me here for..."

"Are you listening to yourself? You sound..."

"Crazy. I know. It sounds crazy. But I feel like I might just need to do something crazy to do right by this kid."

"..."

"I love you. I am going to see if his uncle will give me a ride back to the airport. I will call you if I get a flight. I can only imagine that I would want to fulfill my son's final wish."

"...You're a good man. A good father."

"I love you."

"Just hurry up and get home."

CHAPTER THIRTY TWO
GOOD KARMA

For the whole ride back to Seoul I tried to decipher Soon-ja's concession. We drove for hours in that rickety truck. I couldn't imagine that this was her plan all along, but maybe deep down, she was desperate, or ready at least, for me to offer. I didn't so easily put this kind of foresight past Min, either. As crazy as it sounded to me at the time, on some level, maybe I believed that it was good karma for a prayer they once made on my behalf. Something taken, something owed; a son for a son.

No matter what transpired to put me back on the road away from their village, they insisted that I take the cash I tried to return. I nearly hated myself for not having the money, or the willingness to take it from my own household, but I knew that was a fight I wasn't winning. That was a lesson I learned from my father-in-law. If for nothing else, it made us square; we were partners in this endeavor.

❖

There was a flight that had openings in standby. It wasn't definite, but it was something. That wait was terrible. Not more than five minutes into it, I started doubting my rash decision. There I was, with the hopes of that woman behind me and the wishes of that boy weighing on my shoulders. I couldn't read, I couldn't eat, I couldn't sit, I couldn't focus on the news, so I quickly found myself pacing. It probably made some people nervous. None more than myself. But I was nothing if I wasn't true to my word.

By about half past six, for a quarter past seven flight time, they started making the call. That wait was worse. All of the salarymen loaded into business class, and then the rich folk and upgrades went into first. They let on elderly and pregnant passengers, and a few parents with young children, and then began boarding by section. The line was too long to tell. The worst of it came when I was standing alone with all my worldly belongings waiting for the tally. It was a good sign that no one else was standing by, but all the looks and head nods were making me crazy.

After a good, solid, agonizing seven minutes, the agent reached for the microphone. A cruel trick if he was just going to wave me forward. He didn't. He called a final boarding call for all of the sections numbered back to the rudder. *Oh come on,* I thought. But it was looking like there was a chance.

They returned to their tally. I sweat bullets for another four minutes. *What am I going to do if I can't get on this plane? Do I try again tomorrow? Should I just go home?* I didn't want to sleep in the terminal, and I had no way of contacting Min's family. I felt like my journey was about to end.

They moved again for the microphone. They must have been toying with me. But this time, they called three names and gave them a final board warning. The second agent checked the computer screen, while the first read names from the sheets. A third one checked her watch.

And then, the most incredible thing happened. After nearly all of the punishment I was willing to handle, I heard my name! Even if it was mispronounced, it belonged to me. They called for a "Mr. Peter Kahil" to the boarding desk. Evidently, the flight was oversold by two. There was one seat waiting, with my name all over it, so long as this other guy didn't show. I didn't care where it was, or if it cost me extra, or that I was practically going to be rushed down the Jetway when he didn't show, I was on my way back to Japan.

Like the second time, and not entirely unlike the first, I was excited by the idea of where I was going. Part of me didn't want Japan this way, but the rest of me wanted to be there no matter what.

Port to port, we were a little over two hours, with about ninety minutes in the air. That would have been plenty of time to plan out what I was going to say, but I couldn't bring my head around. All I could do was pour over how many small things like that I've said. I thought that most must have taken them as intended: harmless pleasantries. I honestly thought that one was more than mundane, but somewhere near the bottom of my search, I couldn't help thinking it was a little...empty. Sure, with some romantic ideal, I wanted him to return to his village and see his family. In delivering that line, though, I gave no mind to helping him over the things in the way. What I wouldn't have given to re-have that conversation.

Not long after nine thirty, I was checking in to the hotel, the one with the doorman, only it was a different man on duty. I dropped my bag at the front desk and took off towards their apartment tower. I had little intention of checking in, and I hadn't planned far enough in advance to even consider where or whether I'd spend the night. The other thing I didn't consider so carefully, walking the streets well after dark, was the extra invasion of the hour. They were most likely nearing bed time. While this was important, it wasn't an emergency. Thinking of the picture of Soon-ja and her Minho, and putting my mother and son into that frame helped me past the pacing at the foot of the tower.

His castle was bigger to me than it was last time. The ceilings in the lobby were too high, and the walls too sheik to hang a chandelier, but behind the concierge there was a water wall. Everything smelled pleasant and clean as a whisper of warm air from a vacuum and a spritz of perfume on a casino floor. At least, that's what the carpet reminded me of. The lights were set to where they were plenty bright for conducting business, but would be remembered a little dim.

Their doorman was cut from the same cloth as the one in the hotel down the road. His suit and handshake were both impeccable. His command of excellence in the absence of incentive was remarkable. Maybe I was wrong about the tipping, though, because there were more dollars in the IWC on his wrist than there were on four wheels in my driveway back home. His tie probably out-valued everything I had with me. He wore it all with an air of intellect.

When Yuto - that was his name - picked up the handset, there was no turning away. It was answered on the first ring. The conversation was quick and contained my name. In no less time than it took him to hang up, the elevator was open and he instructed me to take a left on floor number thirty two.

At least one surprise was that the numbers in the elevator went above thirty two. I thought for sure that they would have owned the whole penthouse and roof deck. Somehow it made me feel a little better that they didn't.

To say this man has been portrayed favorably so far would be wrong. Min made him out to be hard, and even his own mother used the word monster in breath with his name. Thinking what kind of man could send his sweet son to where he didn't want to go made me defensive. That call I avoided, the one that never came, would have been the chance to break through ice as thick as an ocean.

I never had the chance to knock.

"Mr. Cahill, please, please." He was holding my hand sooner than I could respond, his head held low like at a funeral. How very appropriate. "So very honored to meet you. This is quite a surprise. Douzo. Please come inside." We drank each other in as I passed him to step into his foyer. "Oh no please, Professor. Not necessary to remove your shoes." He was wearing a white hotel robe over a blue satin pajama set and black leather slip-on house shoes. His hair was mussed, like it had already hit a pillow. "Please, make yourself at home. Can I get you anything?"

"Oh, no. Thank you," I said. The view was astounding. At night, the lights were lit, and the cityscape was immense. "I am so sorry for disturbing you at this hour." The lights in that room were a touch dimmer than the lobby. It smelled of air freshener, like a teenager trying to avoid getting caught smoking. A blue light and nondescript sounds from a television came from a room down the hallway. Their house, though smartly appointed and free from clutter, felt a bit empty, like a playground in the middle of winter.

"It is not a disturbance, Professor. Only a surprise. It is an honor to have someone who knew my son standing here with me. I want to thank you," he held a choke in his throat, "for everything that you have done for my Minho." This was unexpected, and quite disarming.

Min's mother wasn't anywhere in sight, or within earshot. I scanned for a mantle, or someplace where an urn may have been displayed, but did not see one. I don't know whether I grew accustomed, or the volume was lowered, but I didn't hear the TV anymore. Nervous did not begin to describe what I was feeling, and I knew I was wearing my tensions out loud.

"In fact, Professor, I received a call from my brother yesterday. He said that you were with him and my mother?" I knew they were brothers, but my mind didn't make much of it until then. They looked alike. Even Min's drawing, which was remarkably, and in a charming way, accurate, didn't make me notice any sooner. The difference was that this man had more sorrow behind softer eyes. Actually, I didn't see a General or a cut throat at all. "I was so happy that our prayers were answered." I didn't know what to say. "To what do I owe the honor, Professor?" He was anxious is all; he wasn't pushing. I was too nervous to realize that he had to.

"Mr. Park..."

"Please, Professor, call me Ken."

"Thank you," I said, not sure I could oblige. "Please call me Peter. It is a pleasure to finally meet you. It has also been an honor for me to be with your family."

"My home is very beautiful." He meant where his roots were buried, I assume, but my current surroundings also fit that descriptor. "Please, sit. Are you sure I cannot offer you a drink?"

278

"I am sure. Thank you." The couch was plush, white, and leather. Ken sat on the edge of a separate one that faced mine over a glass and gunmetal coffee table. He was less rigid than I had imagined, but he was hanging on my every breath. "I am so sorry... For your loss." He nodded in acknowledgement.

"He was too young. Too young..."

"I was able to spend some time with his Grandmother. Do you know about the letters that he wrote?"

"Yes, of course." I nearly forgot about *his* letter. The photo it accompanied was taken behind me, at the picture window. "When my mother invited you, I told her that I did not think that it was a very good idea, but she is stubborn. Did you find what you were looking for?"

"I... Well, to be honest, no, I don't think so. I don't know if we'll ever know why." I wanted, and didn't, to sugar coat those words, but there before me was a sincere man that insisted otherwise.

"Know why? Isn't it obvious, Professor?"

I didn't answer but with confusion in my eyes. It wasn't obvious from I had known, or read, or could gather from any of this piecemeal detective work.

"I thought for sure my mother would have told you this. That boy Yoshi ended his life only three days before my son. He left a note. Addressed to me. It says that life without my son was unbearable. He says that he will wait for Min." He broke his fragile mask, or he would have seen mine

279

crumbling. "Professor... I... It broke my heart to have to tell him... We received Yoshi's parents. They came straight away after his...body...was recovered. He was found in Aokigahara..."

So there it was.

I had heard of this place. The "Suicide Forest." It's a hiking trail near the base of Mount Fuji. To the north, I think. The story goes that people hang themselves there along the trail so they are easily found. My mind was racing, and my heart hurt. This would have all played out very different if I stayed for his funeral. I supposed then that Yoshi was a Buddhist, too. Min was. Only after cremation could they enter their afterlife. Our old Interfaith Director said so at that "damage control" meeting after it happened. That's where he would *wait*. That's why I was there. I realized that I wasn't listening. He realized that I was devastated.

"I had no idea. I...didn't know about Yoshi until only this week."

"That surprises me," he said. "My son trusted you very much. He spoke of you very highly." Somehow this didn't make me feel any better; only guilty.

"I am so sorry, Mr. Park. I feel like somehow this is my fault. That is why I have come to speak with you."

"Nonsense. I know where the blames lies here, Professor. You cannot speak words to convince me otherwise."

"I told Min to do what it takes to travel back home. To your Mother's village."

"Mr. Cahill, please." He brushed me off. "I have had many regrets in my life. One of them was not sending my son to your school. I am more convinced now of my decision. You have seen my mother's home. There are no elevators or lifts. He would not have been able to bathe or use the bathroom. You know how difficult it would have been, but only now after seeing for yourself. You feel bad about what you said, but what you said to my son was not wrong. This is my fault. And it is my fault that he could not return to our village."

"I'm not sure I understand."

"I was driving the car. We were at a fundraiser for my firm and I was drinking. Surely you read my letters, too."

"No. I mean, there was one…"

"I used to be an alcoholic, Professor. I had only had a few whiskeys that night, and I thought I could drive. I walked away from the accident untouched. I thought that my son was dead. I have not forgotten for a second. I did not have any since." His eyes were hollow and his words were haunted. Yong must not have known, and Soon-ja must not have wanted to volunteer that side of the story.

"But my biggest regret is calling to tell him about Yoshi."

"You did the right thing by calling, Mr. Park." I tried to think of what Freeman would have said - something about what we could have done if we were informed. He didn't need to hear that. Surely, he knew.

"Yes, I did. But for everything I have in this world, including my life, I wish I could speak to him differently that night. Minho was angry that I would not let him come home. Final exams would be approaching. I wanted him to stay focused. I told him that Yoshi...was a coward..."

My face dropped. Suddenly and violently, I understood.

"...And now my son is gone. I understand that you have a young son. I pray that you may never know..."

"Mr. Park, I am so sorry. I... I wish I had known..." He was giving his all not to be in pieces. I noticed the bottle of Nikka on the table, which had some missing.

"Mr. Cahill, what brings you to my home at this hour on a commuter flight from South Korea? What is it that you wish to ask me?"

There was no hiding behind any cards now that his were all on the table. He went all in, and I was called. He was so exposed that the bravery to ask was no longer my concern.

"Do you know of the last letter that Min sent to your mother? Have you seen it?"

"No, I have not," He thought very carefully before proceeding. "She told me that I would have to come to her to read them. And that's a problem, Mr. Cahill. I have not been on speaking terms with my mother since the accident." He paused to collect, and something dawned. "So she's used you to come here and tell me."

"No, I don't think it's like that, Mr. Park."

"It is very much like that, Mr. Cahill. I would have half a mind not to hear it, if I had half as much pride as my mother. But I will not deny you to fulfill this journey. On behalf of my son, what did it say?"

"His letter was addressed to your mother. He told her not to be sad for him. He told her that he is not a coward." It was a knife between his ribs. I wasn't sure that sharing that part was necessary. "He said that when he returns, he would ask to be with his Grandfather. His Grandmother explained what that means, that his..."

"You've come to ask me for his ashes. It is late, Professor. I suggest that you be going." He stood to show me out. From somewhere behind his foggy facade came the face of stone that Min would have had me know. I thanked him for his time, apologized for my intrusion, and welcomed his invitation.

There were many words that I wished I had spoken. They came crashing down on the lonely elevator ride, and the dark walk back to my hotel. I was in for a long and sleepless night.

CHAPTER THIRTY THREE
WHERE I'M FLYING NEXT

Restless, indeed, was the rest of my night. At first I was mad, but I had about as much right for that as I did to march in and demand he hand over his son's remains. Then I got litigious. I wouldn't have even known where to look to find out whether his request in that letter was somehow binding. I even went so far as to wonder if what he told his son was criminal. At the end of the day, no matter what I thought, I was an intrusion, and I couldn't make my next decision alone.

"Hey. Is he sleeping?" She answered on the first ring. It was about time for Nicky to be down for his morning nap.

"I just put him down. I waited all night and never heard back. Is everything ok?"

"I don't know. His father just, sort of, threw me out."

"What? Why?"

"I'm actually not all that surprised. He told me everything. Evidently he was the one driving in the accident that put Min in a wheelchair."

"Oh God… I don't know if I would be able to live with myself."

"Well, I'll tell you, he seemed to be barely holding himself together. The other thing is that evidently Min was seeing this kid from here. From Tokyo. They went to school together. He was out as long as I knew him, but I didn't know about Yoshi."

"Wait, like that Mario dinosaur?"

"That's what I said! Apparently they were friends from an early age. Min was mad that his father sent him to Boston because Yoshi stayed in Japan. I wish I asked him more about the whole school thing. Maybe Min applied and didn't get in? I don't know. Anyways, there was a lot about Yoshi in these letters, but I can't imagine why his Grandmother didn't tell me…"

"Tell you what?"

"Yoshi hung himself three days before Min."

"You didn't tell me that Min hung himself."

"Honestly, I don't know how he did it, but I don't think it was that. All I know is that his roommate found a lot of blood, so I don't think it was that. Anyways, evidently his father had to call and tell him. He was pretty broken up about it. He wouldn't let Min come home."

"That's awful. Was there a funeral?"

285

"I don't know. Probably something quiet, at least. That's not even the worst part, though. He told Min to be strong, and that Yoshi was a coward."

"Oh..." it was guttural.

"That's a dare in my book," I said. "And Min said that he wasn't a coward in the note he sent to Soon-ja."

"Oh God. That's just awful. Who is Soon Jah?"

"I know. Soon-ja is the Grandmother. So he tells me all this, and then asks why I've come. So I asked him."

"Just like that? You asked if you could take his son's ashes? Peter Cahill. Of all the anti-confrontational people that I know, *you* travelled around the world to ask this man..."

"What do you mean?"

"No, actually, I'm impressed. I think that it's sweet. I mean, I would have thrown you out, too, but I think it's noble. You're a better man than most."

"Well, thanks. Except now I don't know what the hell to do. And he thinks that this was his mother's plan all along. Supposedly they haven't spoken since the accident and she saw me as a way to get to him. What do you think I should do? I mean, do I go back? Tell them it isn't happening, and then come home? That's it? Do I just leave? Come home now? I might still have the Uncle's number in my phone. Maybe I'll try to call them in the morning."

"Do you think you should call tonight?" I was surprised. She was playing ball.

"I don't know... I mean, I just feel so bad about this whole thing. I guess they should know. It would help to know where I'm flying next, I suppose..."

"Don't let them take advantage of you. You've already given them too much."

"I still feel like I owe them some sort of...closure, you know?"

"I understand. I think. Peter, I have to go back to work in a few days..."

"I know, I'll be there."

"Well, it's not just that."

"What's up?"

"I was hoping that we could do something... Spend some time together. Just us, you know? Before I go back. I miss you. And I feel selfish even asking, but..."

"What's up?"

"Peter, I work overnight. I need to sleep before I go back. You can't keep running back and forth like this. I need you here. He misses you, too."

"I know, I'll do what... Hang on, my phone is ringing. Oh. Hey, this is them. Let me call you back, ok?"

"Call me back, please."

❖

"Peter Cahill?" I said. They knew who it was.

"Professor. This is Yong Lim speaking." I knew who it was going to be, too. "Uncle just finished speaking with

Min's father. He was very upset with Grandmother. Grandmother says that she is very sorry to have caused you this great inconvenience." Yong paused to speak with his Uncle. "Grandmother would like to see you one more time. To thank you in person. And to apologize. However, we understand that you may need to be home with your family."

I didn't want to commit one way or another. I was tired. Emotionally and physically, I was drained. It was a long way. I wanted to just be home playing with my boy and waiting on take-out, but my mind wandered back to being at work, comfortable, delivering lines. These folks were without their Minho. That meant something deep down to me now. And all I could think of was that the whole time his story was unfolding, another family was going through the same for their son. How much further would I need to go to feel somehow satisfied? Was that in and of itself selfish of me? What would I have wanted for my son?

"Professor?"

"Yes, I'm here. I'm sorry, Yong. I am trying to sort some things out. Is it ok if I tell you in the morning?" I didn't want to lead anyone on any further, and I had no idea if I had any further business with them, but I honestly didn't have another answer.

Something heated was exchanged between the two on the other end of the line. I felt, for a moment, like they were starting to take my willingness for granted.

"Yes, Professor. Thank you for your understanding. I will sleep here at Uncle's house and Uncle will stay with

Grandmother so that I can answer your call. Thank you, Professor."

"Thank you, Yong. Please wish your Grandmother a good night."

❖

"Everything alright? What was that about?"

"Well, that wasn't very helpful. They said they'd be happy to have me back, to thank me in person, but they'd understand if I needed to leave."

"So come home. What did you tell them?"

"I told them the same thing I'm going to tell you, I guess... That I'll have to let you know in the morning."

"That's not fair. This whole thing is getting ridiculous. Please just come home."

"Babe, I really love you, and I'm really tired. I need to sleep. I'll be home soon. And I promise, you will be the first to know my plan. I just... I really don't..."

"Do what you need to do. I have to go, he's crying."

I didn't hear anything, but she sounded pretty upset.

"I love you. Good night."

"You too."

❖

After showering in that small stall, and wishing I had that bottle of whiskey to polish off, I picked myself up and packed myself to bed. It was hot and miserable and uncomfortable and sleep felt like it was at least a thousand miles away.

If for nothing else, I thought that I'd like to go back and read the rest of his letters. At least that way, I'd have more to remember him by. The guilt of not knowing about Yoshi sooner was eating at my insides. Maybe he said something. Maybe they would have hidden *those* letters from me, too. I felt manipulated. So far, they've told me more about *their* son so, in a way, I failed at what Min asked me to do.

That brought some deep, dark curiosity, that maybe I said something else. I couldn't handle not knowing what else was attached to my name. Then I worried how I was taught to worry. What if Mr. Park demanded those letters? What if he had them subpoenaed?! The extent of his reach still escaped me. He could deny ever having his conversation if there wasn't any record that it happened. Had I pushed him too far?

Then there was my own family. I missed them terribly, but I was ok without the screaming in the middle of the night. Nothing ever prepares you for that, and it's as hard as they say, but you never *really* know until you've lived it. I felt horrible leaving her to it all alone. If I wanted to be grown up enough to be a father, I knew I had better start taking all of the responsibilities that come in tow more seriously. What the hell was I doing, lying there under scratchy sheets in Tokyo? If anything, she should have been there with me. I didn't know how I would ever make this up to her.

What if there *was* something else I said to him? Could I put them through who I'd become if I didn't find out? Could I put them through the nightmare of my being pursued legally? I didn't work for that place anymore, so the chances of them washing their hands of it were probably staggering.

The storm was perfect for my mind to wander into unwanted places, whether they were rational or not. That didn't keep them from coming or me from worrying myself sick over them. But there I was, in the middle of a battle on foreign ground, in enemy territory, alone, trying to decide between my family and my dignity. There was no winning that war.

Choosing to put my family first should never make me feel the way it did. However, at some ungodly hour, I purchased a ticket for a direct flight back to Boston. I chose to run, to live with not knowing, to let him lie against his will; at odds between a family divided.

I've already established that I'm not a praying man, but I spoke to him that night, and I asked him to forgive me for leaving. My only hope was that he was finally with the one he loved.

CHAPTER THIRTY FOUR

TWENTY FOUR MORE HOURS

Morning came with a call from the front desk before my alarms went off. I set four because I was afraid I wouldn't get up for the first three.

"Mr. Cahill," it sounded urgent, and it sounded like a familiar doorman from my previous stay.

"Yes," I said, shaking off the sleep. "Speaking."

"Mr. Cahill, there is a Mr. Park to see you. Should I send him, or would you like me to have him wait in the lounge?"

Oh shit.

I needed to get up anyways. I was already showered from the night before, which was only a handful of hours ago. The only thing that was still unpacked was my phone charger. I was up and halfway dressed before I could answer.

"I'll be right down. Thank you."

I slipped on my shoes, rubbed on some deodorant, grabbed my garment bag, smelled my breath, and slapped my pockets to check that I had everything before staggering to the elevator. My head was pounding like I was hungover.

❖

I didn't see him at the front desk, and the lounge was empty. Maybe there was another lounge?

"Mr. Cahill, good morning." It *was* the same doorman. He seemed to recognize me.

"It's good to see you again," I said. "Good morning."

"Mr. Park is waiting for you just outside. Let me take your bag, please."

Sure enough, there he was. He was dressed in a three piece suit. I didn't remember if he had on glasses the night before, but these were horn-rimmed and black with rectangular lenses and made him look at lot more official. He was talking on his phone beside a black Infiniti, whose driver was waiting behind the wheel. The concierge held the door while the doorman showed me out. He loaded my bag into the trunk without even asking.

"Professor. It is good to see you again. I apologize for the intrusion, and I am sorry to have to wake you like this."

"Good morning, Mr. Park. What's going on? Is everything ok?"

"Yes, Professor. Of course. Minho's mother and I had a very long conversation last night. I want to apologize for the way our conversation ended. I have reconsidered your request. It would be my honor for you to accompany me back to my village. It is what my son would have wanted."

"I'm honored, Mr. Park. Thank you. I'm sorry again if I caused any problems by coming here. But I'm afraid it's not possible. I've already purchased my ticket back to Boston. I'm supposed to leave in about," I looked at my watch, "three hours."

"I will see that your airfare is refunded. It would mean a lot to my family, and to me, if you would reconsider." He looked like an Emperor bowing before a peasant. It must have been something to see.

"I will have to check with my wife. This is sudden. She will be expecting me. She's returning to work after her maternity leave, and I need to be back myself. I am so sorry, but I really should be going."

"I will personally see that you are on a plane home before this time tomorrow. Do you have twenty four more hours?"

My bag was locked away. He wasn't going to take no for an answer, so asking was a formality. How very Japanese.

"Let me call my wife."

"Yes, please, Professor. Our flight leaves at seven thirty five." That was a little over seventy five minutes away, which put my wife at a little after dinner, and me wondering how we were ever going to make it on time.

I strolled a little so that my conversation would be private before dialing. Again she answered fast.

"Hey," I said. "I didn't realize you were having company."

"Oh, it's nothing. My Mother is here to help me with him. I'm exhausted."

"I'm sorry, babe. It's good that you two can spend some time."

"Yeah. Are you coming home?"

"So listen..."

"That doesn't sound good."

"I don't know. His father showed up at my hotel this morning. He's waiting with a driver. He said he's reconsidered and he wants me to return with him."

"Why does he need you for this?"

"I don't know, but at this point, I kind of want to see this thing through. He said he'll have me on a plane home by this time tomorrow. I told him I already bought my ticket, but he is insisting, which is kind of a big deal, I think."

"Did you already buy your ticket?"

"Yeah, last night."

"Why didn't you tell me?"

"It was late."

"It would have been early for me. I was up. But I guess it doesn't matter now. What are you going to do about the money?" She never missed a step

"He said he'll take care of it. I can try to get a refund, if we have time."

"What do you mean?"

"We're in a hurry. The plane leaves in about an hour. So, I guess I should be going. I'll call you if I can."

"You owe me, you know."

"I know. I will make this up to you, I promise."

"Be safe."

"Will do."

"Alright," I said, and whether this next part was true or not, "I'm ready."

CHAPTER THIRTY FIVE
MEMORIES WE CHASED

Mr. Park had arranged for a flight on a private jet. The driver may well have been part of the deal because we drove right up to the aircraft. I felt important; I felt like Tony Stark. I couldn't help looking over my shoulder to the glassed-in concourse to see who was noticing. One little girl pointed and waved, which made me feel even cooler. My wife would have probably been terrified, so I decided to wait to tell her about this one.

The jet was a Gulfstream, and the roar and whine of the engines warming was magnificent. I almost couldn't hear their Japanese over the rushing wind. My dad would have thought this was way cooler than the models in the terminal. I wanted to refrain from taking a picture to play it cool, but when Ken offered to have the driver snap a shot of us with the pilot, I couldn't say no. He took a few before fetching my bag and clearing the car off the Tarmac.

What I felt was almost Presidential when we stepped up the Airstair. The cockpit was open and the other pilot was making ready. "Pick any seat you would like," said Mr. Park. There weren't too many, and they were all on a window and an aisle. It was well-appointed, and damn well better than any craft I've ever boarded, but it wasn't lined with wood and gold like you see in the movies. But how could I complain. I certainly couldn't hide my excitement.

"Called in a favor," he said, with a wink. "My CEO. He was very fond of my son. He has a young daughter. They may be interested in looking at *your* University, now." I was relatively sure he remembered where I worked. That was a whole other conversation worth having, but the driver came back, and my attention belonged entirely to him.

On board came the urn of a boy I once knew. It was carried to the seat behind me and belted for safe travels. "I would have him fly home no other way," said a sad father, eager to let him rest. "I am going to check how long," he said, before making the few steps up to the cockpit. He needed a moment, but I like to think that he wanted me to have one, too.

The vessel itself was sleek and not ornate. Brushed under a clear lacquer coat sat a simple painted sumi-e style dragonfly. This was a common symbol for such an uncommon son, but in so many ways, it was most fitting. Long has the dragonfly stood as a pillar of spirit for Japan. I know of the story of the dragonfly from the mythos of the Samurai. He is peace and he is harmony. He brings joy and luck. His ability to fly is a dance of beauty. Unlike even his closest kin, he can change direction, and with little effort he avoids obstacles and evades barriers. He is boundless and elegant. Always transforming and ever adaptive, he stands for progress. Though his path may be changing, he flies ever on. And on the field of battle, his adept stood for certain victory. I could think of no better guide to escort him on his way.

The other side to my musing was the absolute finality, in my own beliefs, of the container of his remains. Since the beginning of this journey, he was made mostly of memories we chased, not flesh or bone. Now, those bones were dust. A hope somewhere inside of me lingered on the thought that he wasn't gone; that somewhere at the end we would find him. It was a cold reminder that we failed him. There he was, with a final flourish of dignity, encapsulating all that could have been.

My time with Min was brief, but the impact he had, and the life he lived after his death would stay with me for the rest of my own time. With him sat a power to both affirm and destroy the faith I had in myself to continue on my path. Could I truly continue to look at this as a job, with all I've taken for granted, or could I find a calling in the lessons I've learned?

"We'll begin departing in a moment," said Mr. Park. "I cannot thank you enough for joining me."

"The pleasure is all mine," I said, and truly, it was.

CHAPTER THIRTY SIX
RELUCTANT AND READY

We landed in Seoul a few minutes after nine. There was another car waiting on the Tarmac. For the whole drive, just as our time in the air, we traded stories. I learned so much about Min and his family and I shared stories about my brothers and parents and in-laws. We talked about traditions and the quirks of our cultures. We talked food and celebration, and how we honor our dead. We went on about our respective careers, and what path led us to take them. I learned that he was an investment banker, and he was surprised that I didn't pursue engineering. We arrived back near the village sometime after noon.

Mr. Park asked me to tell him about his son, and I shared a few things that I thought were authentic. It's not easy when you've only known someone for a short time to know what kind of person, or student, or son he really was. It's become blatant that you don't always know what's affecting a person, either. There were a lot of little things that gave me insight into how wide open his eyes were, and that meant a lot more to me than grades on a midterm. His father wanted more, though. He wanted to know what made his academic mind tick and that his drive was head on into some business venture. He wanted to know where his money went.

That didn't sit right with me. My student was gone, but so was his son. I was trying to make sense of what I needed to do differently. While his father wanted to hear of his excellence, his Grandmother only wanted to know that he was happy. Maybe that's the answer. We are all something different to everyone around us, and maybe it wasn't right for me to be upset about what his father wanted to hear. I could tell him, in so many words, of the student I saw, who was eager to learn, and of the path he was on, which would have put him in a prouder place in his Father's eyes. I couldn't tell him how to feel. He didn't need to know that Min resented his major, although I'd be surprised if he didn't already, or that he never made it to a single meeting of the Entrepreneurship Club.

When we pulled off the highway and onto that stretch of country road, it felt vaguely like home. I suppose that had to do with familiarity and feeling welcome. I wondered how long it had been for Mr. Park. He gave instructions to the driver like it was his own back yard. His eyes were wide. It gave me butterflies to ascend the first

301

foothill and pass through that first village. He was at the window like a puppy.

"Stop here, please," he said. "Stop, stop, stop," though he wasn't driving as fast as Min's Uncle was earlier in the week. The driver had a Korean name, and he spoke Korean to Mr. Park, but he understood him well enough to stop. I think he spoke English for my benefit. When he got out, he walked back to the small farm table that our driver passed. He took longer than just completing the transaction. It sounded like they knew one another, or were at least being very friendly.

"Ah, thank you," he said getting back in. "For my mother. Her favorite. Would you like to try?" He was holding a brown paper bag full of ripe, red cherries.

"Oh, they look delicious. No, thank you, though." This was not my appetite talking; he knew I hadn't had any breakfast. It also wasn't my want for Soon-ja to have the first bite. This was purely that thing where I was uncomfortable saying yes to food on the first ask.

"These are the best that there are," he said. He ate one while looking out the window, measuring what he felt to be home. "Best in the world. No question." Given the circumstances, I certainly believed him.

My insides were churning when we got to the back end of his boyhood mountain. "Isn't it beautiful," he said. "Have you seen the tea fields?"

"Yes. Yong took me. It's beautiful."

"Oh we used to go there when we were in school. We would steal my father's soju and go up there to sneak a drink. He used to blame my mother. *No son of mine* he'd say, but I think he knew. Where do you think we got the idea? He used to do the same when he was young, and his father said the same thing to his mother. Ah, so many memories. This over here," there was a small pond, actually, more of a big, permanent puddle "is where I caught my first fish. It's where I taught Minho. He," he said laughing, "was so sad that he made me throw it back! I guess it wasn't a big surprise..." I assume he meant that Min was gay? "I had too much pride to tell him that his fish was bigger than mine! Ji-hwan still eats fish from there." That must have been the uncle's name. I was kind of embarrassed that I hadn't asked earlier.

He put his hand on my arm when we pulled up to the top of the old stone stairwell. There wasn't a welcoming party. I assumed that there shouldn't have been, that what we were doing was a surprise. With two packages to carry, there was still one thing to decide before we wound our way back down to Soon-ja.

"Will you please do the honor?" he asked.

He, of course, was asking whether I would be the bearer of Minho's urn.

"These are from me to my mother. I do not want her to think they are from you," he added with a wink.

"Are you sure? I wouldn't feel right..."

"Nonsense. It was very thoughtful of you to come all this way. My son thought very highly to ask that you do so. It would be my honor. Besides, these cherries are heavy."

I obliged.

Physically, they were heavier than I was expecting. The burden was heavy beyond the weight of its insides, though.

The vessel itself felt like fine China, smooth and thick to the touch, and cool from the car. I did my best to carry it well, not to let it shift from side to side. The stairs worried me. It also made me nervous to know that we would be opening it and emptying him out. I tread carefully where my feet didn't fall squarely on a step.

I remembered the way myself, but I wasn't going to rob him of the opportunity to be my guide. He had little stories for every alley way and every shed brought back memories. I was happy to hear them all. He waved to everyone that paid him any attention. A few seemed to respond politely, but I could tell that this was a big deal. Mr. Park's return would be the buzz about that village for months to come. If Soon-ja had a telephone, they would surely have ruined our big entrance.

"Welcome home, Minho," he said softly. "It hasn't changed. Oh Mama. This has been too long." He took a moment to adjust himself and compose. "Douzo," he said, and he waved me forward so that I would knock.

My mouth parched. I could feel my heart beating fast past lumps in my throat. I caught him adjusting his tie with a quick look back over my shoulder. And then I knocked.

At first, nothing happened. Then, from inside, someone shouted and shuffled, and footsteps that were less than quiet came rushing to answer. I had almost forgot, Yong was staying, waiting for me to call.

Nothing was slow about the way he slide the door open. His face lit when he saw me, and then Mr. Park stopped him in his tracks. It was as if he'd seen a ghost.

"Kyung-Joon," he said. "Kyung-Joon!" He turned. "Eomeoni. Eomeoni!" he shouted before disappearing.

Mr. Park stood stoic. He would wait to find out if he was welcome. I understood that it was my place to stand aside.

Soon-ja came to the door with the assistance of her son. She saw me first, and she saw that I had the urn. And then she saw her son.

"Kyung-joon..." She held out her hand. "Nae adeul." Her eyes glistened. "Nae adeul."

Mr. Park handed me the cherries after all. "Eomeoni," he said. His eyes did not contain the tears as well as hers.

Her other son guided me by the elbow inside. The letters had all been cleared, and morning tea was getting cold. He helped me put down the urn and carried the cherries into the kitchen. He said "Yong" when he motioned for me to stay.

"No, it's ok. You stay here. I'll go. I remember the way." He understood when I insisted to push myself passed him.

Mr. Park and his mother were reconnecting quietly, speaking words I did not know, sharing emotions that were not possible to misunderstand. They would have a lot of reading, and much to discuss, but in those moments, there wasn't anything else that could have mattered. I don't think they noticed when I walked by.

❖

"Professor? You are here! I waited for you to call. How?"

"I'm so sorry. Your uncle asked me not to. He's here. He's with your Grandmother now. Come with me."

"Uncle Ken is here?! I am excited to meet him!"

He was off at a healthy pace, and I walked hard to keep up.

"Wait, you haven't met your uncle?"

"No. Well, yes, I have, but it was long ago. Ten years ago. I was young and do not remember, but we have pictures. Oh, please excuse," he said. "Wait for me." Yong turned like he had forgotten something. When he came running back, he ran right by and said "Ok, let's go!" He was carrying his uncle's old camera case.

❖

Everyone was inside and sitting to fresh tea when the two of us barged in. "My nephew!" called Mr. Park.

"Uncle Ken!" They were much more boisterous than the others. He had a hug around his uncle halfway before he was off of his knees. "Thank you for being with us today," he said.

"My dear nephew, this is where we belong. But do not thank me. I believe that thanks is in order for our friend, Mr. Cahill."

Soon-ja gave me a smile. It was sincere, and cut through the little bit of schmooze in the air. I don't know if in a dozen other lifetimes I would have repeated the steps to bring me to that exact moment, but so long as I was there, I wanted to make sure that it wasn't wasted.

"It was nothing, really," but it was. I left my family far behind when they needed me most. I've changed jobs, racked debts to travel, borrowed from people with less to give, put my own family last, nearly ruined Tokyo for myself, and selfishly tried to shoulder some of the blame. But at the end the day…

"I'm just happy he's home."

I thought I felt sentiment from Soon-ja, in her hand gestures, in her words. Yong leaned in to whisper, though, and I was wrong. "She wants to know what we're waiting for. She says *let's not make him wait any more*." I, of course, couldn't help wondering what this bloody country had against lunch.

Both Mr. Park and his brother tried arguing with her, but she would hear none of it. At her age, I believed with all my heart that she could have held her own against the two of them physically. I figured what they were fighting about when she reached an arm out to each son. She wasn't out of the house in years. I remembered something her grandson told me when I learned he was Buddhist. He talked about how she became a Christian, and that she was baptized in her home because she couldn't leave. I've walked that way to the tea fields. I needed my hiking boots; this wasn't a good idea.

"What's going on?" I asked. Soon-ja snapped some very pointed sentiments. Mr. Park translated, sort of.

"My mother is stubborn, is all. Mr. Cahill, would you...do the honor," he pointed to the urn over his shoulder. "...again, please. It appears that we are going now."

There's not much you can say at a time like that. You walk at the pace set for you, you carry what you've been asked to bear, and you do your best to be out of everyone's way.

Word of Mr. Park's return travelled. That brought the initial gawkers. The real spectacle, though, and one that brought a whole village to attention, was Mrs. Park. Her sons did her waving. Her eyes and her focus were forward. For once the dragonfly flew to the lead of another.

I thought I was big news with a small pack of ball kickers behind us. We walked, Yong and me behind the three in front, ahead of a throng that grew and grew. They walked eight or twelve or more abreast; as wide as the roadway would allow. When we turned the first corner at the foot of the valley, I could no longer see their end.

She stepped mostly under her own power. Not once did she stop, and not once did her eyes wander away from her purpose. The hardest way was upon her, and a thousand helping hands behind, but what we would all witness was an act of sheer will, and one of undying love.

Soon-ja freed herself from the hold of her son's and fell to her knees. Silence fell on the heels of a gasp. Helping hands were pushed away, but then she held them again, and guided her boys to join her. Yong took the vase from my hands, laid down a lens cloth from the camera case, and set it on the ground. He had me join him.

One by one, in sweeping procession, those that were able joined us. The tea farmers, even, dropped their tools and lifted their hats to behold the horizon. For once, in more years than I would care to gather, they came away from their work.

Soon-ja leaned forward to bow on her hands. In place of prayer, she offered one simple kiss to the ground she'd shared and the tea she'd drunk and the place where her spirit may finally rest. She stood alone and turned herself around.

With her eyes opened wide, she swallowed them whole. Praying hands came up to meet the middle of a streaming pair of tears. "Gomapda," she whispered. "Gomapda." She was frail and triumphant, heart-broken and fulfilled, reluctant and ready.

She gave them one final look, and one last blessing, and she called her son to join her. Mr. Park asked me for the urn. Together, walking one behind the other, they began their slow ascent.

The crowd tightened behind me, craning to keep them in eye sight. They were humming in suspense. It was something to be a part of, I only wished I knew their words.

The two of them travelled carefully, and slow, climbing, sometimes, with all fours. They walked and they climbed until they were small to our eyes. The tea planters were back at their work before they reached the ridge around the topside of the old dragon's back, but they watched. Soon-ja remained determined, and her silhouette against the sun pressed on. On the summit, they finally stopped. It appeared that they were speaking. Her hair and the unbuttoned flaps of his jacket blew in the wind. With fortune, it was coming up from the southern crest, opposite the tea fields. It was a good wind that would carry him well into the valley.

The crowd around me grew excited. Soon-ja and her son weren't stopping, though. They continued along the ridge until they were out of our view. I wanted to be up there with them, but it wasn't my place. So we waited.

For some time we waited, wondering if we would see a cloud rising. We waited for it to be finished. We waited, as it turned out, until they emerged again, heading west along the rim and further into the valley. They were smaller still, and almost an hour into their voyage. When they turned the far peak, they were gone and outside of any hope we had of playing a part. This was going to be as it should; this was going to be for his family.

❖

"Yong," I said. "Do you know why Min's mother may not have come?"

"Cousin's parents divorce."

"What?! When?"

"Soon after Minho die."

"Oh that's terrible," I said. I didn't know if it really was terrible. When it settled on me, I didn't really know if I was surprised. I made no attempt at wondering why. The *when* was telling enough. All I could wonder was what else this poor family would have to endure.

"I'm sorry," I said. "I didn't know. Thank you for telling me."

"It's ok, Professor. I did not meet her, too."

"Well that's good, I guess. What about you? How is school?"

"I stopped going. In South Korea, not everyone can go to High School."

"No? Why?"

"It is not mandatory. Also, it is very many hours and I am needing to help care for Grandmother. Father died when I was very young. Mother is working. She send money for Grandmother. She works many hours, and I need to stay and help."

"Did you like studying?"

"Oh yes. I was a good student, not like my cousin, and I enjoy my studies very much."

"What was your favorite class?"

"I enjoy my business economics classes. I wished to become success with business like Uncle."

"What you are doing is very respectable, Yong. Will you make a promise to me?"

"Yes, Professor."

"When you are able, I want you to promise me that you will go back to school."

"It's not possible, I'm afraid."

"Promise me that you will try."

His little gears started turning. I couldn't stop myself.

"It's never too late. And school is so important. You're a smart kid, I think you will do very well. Will you stay in touch with me? Will you let me know?"

"I can write to you?!"

"Absolutely! And I want to hear everything."

"Thank you, Professor. I will like that very much."

"Hey, they've been gone an awfully long time, haven't they?"

"Yes. I think they will be finishing soon. Where Grandfather rests is very far."

❖

I was nerve-racked and on edge waiting, and I wasn't alone. They weren't going to sit back much longer. Soon-ja and her son were clearly too far for us to see anything scatter or blow in the wind. That's what they really wanted, after all.

The furthest farmer stood first. She heard something. She tapped her ear and called for a stop to the singing. A few of the others walked to her side to help listen. We could see, in relay, every noise they could hear. Ji-hwan was back to his feet. One of the farmers finally understood who was calling and turned to run. She was waving us forward, calling "Doum! Doum!"

"She is saying *Help*," said Yong.

Before he could repeat himself, I was gone.

I ran straight through, clean across the first field, to where they were waiting. I could hear Mr. Park's voice carrying on the wind. He was just over the ridge, just out of sight.

"Mr. Park!" My voice echoed.

"Professor!" he called. "Water! Hurry!"

There were buckets. They were near. Most were filled with tools. The tea hedges were aligned in rows, with alternating paths to walk and work. I cut across, and I trampled some plants. The farmers didn't understand. "Yong!

313

Tell them I'm sorry," I shouted. He was still running to catch up.

I threw their tools and ran to one of the standing irrigation pipes.

"How do I turn this on?!" I yelled.

Yong had made it to the workers. They weren't pleased, but he tried explaining.

"A little help, please!"

Yong made his point, and someone from the group scrambled. She shouted across to who must have been a foreman, and he scrambled at the controls. The spouts creaked before they started spouting a rainbow of mist. More shouting came from the farmers, and they rushed to cover over the hedges with bags and blankets. The tea must not have needed watering. I may well have flooded the whole crop.

The bucket filled quickly. "Alright!" I shouted. "Shut it off!"

Yong yelled the command. I sloshed through the puddled pathway and made straight for the ridge. The climb wasn't easy. It was everything I could do not to spill the whole bucket. Some was lost. The bucket was easier to carry, but I had no idea what I was going to find up there.

When I disappeared over the peak, the crowd behind me grew quiet. Under different circumstances, it would have been peaceful. Mr. Park was close, and his mother was on the ground by his side. He was hunched, trying to talk to her, trying to keep her awake. The urn was sitting upright less than three steps away. Gripping the bucket with both hands in front of me, I ran to their side.

"What's going on," I said. "Is...is she ok?"

"I think so," he said, breathing heavy. "She collapsed. She pushed herself too far. She needs water."

"Here," I said. "Soon-ja, can you hear us?"

"She can hear you," he said. Her head was heavy, and her eyes were rolling, but she was awake. He spoke to her while he set the bucket by her legs. His hands plunked into the water and he cupped some to her mouth. Her eyes scrunched tight, and she lifted her head a little to lean forward. She took a drink. Mr. Park soaked his pocket square and wet her neck. He soaked it again and wiped her forehead and cheeks. She took another drink from his hands. The last thing she wanted was for me to see her so un-dignified.

Those moments were long and horrible. I made myself ready to run for another bucket, but he asked that I wait with him.

"I should have never let her..."

She cut through the rest of his sentiment. Her voice was dry.

"My mother is stubborn," he said. "I told you that. Some things do not change. She needs a moment."

Soon-ja's color came back slowly. Finally she moved a little on her own. First she pulled the bucket close, and next she dunked her hand. She patted her face and wiped her hair. I could tell that she was embarrassed. Her deep breath

315

shuttered like after a good cry and she looked to us both and gave a nod.

After a brief exchange, Mr. Park asked me to empty the bucket. He filled it with the empty urn and its lid and directed me to her side. We helped her to her feet. With our arms under hers, she stood, and with us, slowly, she shuffled a few steps.

"Can we carry her, Mr. Park? Let me see if there is a chair..."

"She would rather die up here, Professor. This is one woman who will not be carried."

At the edge of the ridge, we could feel the wind. The entire of the tea field below was filled with villagers up to their ankles in mud. Soon-ja's hand tightened on my shoulder. From under the mountain, came the thunder of applause. In that moment, I knew that Min was finally home.

CHAPTER THIRTY SEVEN
THE FINAL CHAPTER

Boston's skyline. A city of few skyscrapers, studded along its edges with small islands, baseball fields, and marinas full of sailboats. I loved my city. I missed my city. The sky was big, and there wasn't a cloud in it for miles. The plane's shadow on the harbor as we skimmed into Logan brought me comfort.

I stopped in the gift shop for a bottle of iced tea and grabbed a teddy bear wearing a Sox jersey for Nick.

My father was waiting at the curb just outside the terminal in my car. They must have gone to my house first. He had the hazards on and the trunk open and was standing with a sign that said my name. It was upside down.

"You wanna drive?" he asked.

I dropped my bag and I gave him a hug. It was unexpected, but it didn't go un-returned.

"Sure," I said. "Were you waiting long?"

"Not even five minutes."

He always prided himself on being right on time, especially to the airport.

❖

A big sign that said "Welcome Home Daddy!" was waiting for me on the door. They didn't even let me knock. Nicky lit up, and my wife almost tackled me with hugs and kisses. It was less than a week, by about a day, but I missed them more than I ever imagined. With this thing behind me, there were a lot of questions I needed to answer - like *what comes next?* and *was this the final chapter for my career in higher ed?* - but no matter what, for once, it would come after them.

My parents came so I could take my wife to dinner. I was exhausted, but I couldn't think of a better way to catch up on the jet lag, which was all kinds of awful. I finally knew what she felt like working a day/night rotation and twelve hour shifts.

We went to that place in the South End, where we had our first date, and where we celebrated Nicky. She hung on my every word. I told her about the flights and long drives, the food, the village, Min's apartment in Tokyo, his letters, about Yoshi and Mr. Park. I told her about all the questions that I had, and why I was so hesitant, and scared, to return. Mostly, I told her about Soon-ja, and the things that I learned in my brief time with her. She listened and she laughed. Most important to me was that she supported whatever decision I was ready to make.

A handful of days later, she returned to work. It was sad to see her go, and she had a hard time being away from Nicky. She called every few hours to check on us. I thought it was very sweet, and I should have told her that.

❖

On Monday morning, I returned to the office. Spring Break had ended, and the early traffic at the first floor café was trickling back. Students were telling stories and ordering lattes, showing pictures from their vacations, complaining that they had to work, or griping that their parents didn't pay for them to go away. They seemed ready, though, and they seemed refreshed. Spring was in the air. I wasn't sure yet whether it was good for me to be back.

There were only a few messages in my inbox, and most of them had to do with project work, rooms for group advising, additions to the course booklet, or waitlist information. There wasn't a single student message, so it didn't seem like I missed all that much.

The first few days back were pretty quiet, too. It was good for me to ease into some simple student appointments, but it wasn't fair to them that I was divided. I couldn't help continuing to question whether this was what I wanted, and a big part of that had nothing to do with them.

To work with students, you have to be unrelenting. Beyond patience and know-how, you need to have a genuine interest and utter commitment to nurturing their development. Retention is a business-end word that means *bottom line*. Students are so much more than a number on a report, or a body to fill a bed. They represent the person in front of you, and the people and sacrifices standing behind them. They're depending on us for so much more than to be paddled through the system.

It's easy, and it's human, and it's very much *ok* to make mistakes. It's not *ok* to repeat them. I guess the thing that scared me the most was that the simple things along the way, or a single passing encounter, no matter what the intention, can have an impact. I can caution them about the amount of reading or the kind of math in a course, recommend the professor that will coddle or push them, or give advice on a major, and not see the fallout until a few semesters, or even years, have passed.

It's nothing to tell a student that something is "easy," but I owe them healthy challenges and authentic support, not just a write off.

Lord Katsumoto in *The Last Samurai* says "to know life in every breath, every cup of tea, every life we take, the way of the warrior." What if I couldn't sustain that level of intensity?

❖

For lunch one afternoon I found myself wandering past the usual fast food spots. Something brought me over to Chinatown. It took a lot to get me out of my rhythm, but I found a place doing Korean BBQ and hot stone rice bowls. It helped me to remember, and it didn't hurt that the food was fantastic. The kimchi wasn't as good as Soon-ja's, though I don't think it was about the cabbage alone.

I was hoping for a no-show after lunch, but my one o'clock arrived a few minutes early. Meeting with students was what I did best. It should have never felt like that; I shouldn't have been nervous about it, but I was. Almost two weeks back, and I was still so nervous that I would say the wrong thing. I was up and halfway to my door when a message rang in my inbox. It was another few seconds of diversion for me to miraculously figure out where my heart was leading. I was searching at every turn.

The email was titled "Help."

"Mr. Cahill, It's me, Ahmad. I need your help. I tried to suicide last night. I am with my Uncle now. Can you call me?"

Thankfully, I knew the campus protocol. I called the front desk to reschedule my student, called the Dean of Students, who would call the risk manager, and I called Counseling so they could free up a case manager. Sadly, I also knew the feeling. My heavy hand hovered over the phone, and my heart burst into my throat. This was not a task or to-do list item. This was not a time to coast. This was a person

321

and this was his life. This was his family's legacy. This was my thunderbolt, and this was my calling.

"Hello? Ahmad? This is Peter Cahill. I'm responding to your message. I am here for you. Where are you right now?"

— OWARI —

EPILOGUE

Six months passed before I received my first letter from Yong. I was sad to hear of the passing of his Grandmother, but happy to know that he was planning to move back to Seoul with his mother and begin High School. He continued to write every chance he got, and I would always respond. At some point, I got into the habit of including post cards if we took a day trip somewhere, and he always asked about my family. A few times, we sent each other small care packages of local candies and the like. He couldn't draw like his cousin, but he was ever enterprising, and quick to share his ideas on how to make a lot of money.

April came and went. I couldn't believe it had been a year. Nick was walking, babbling, and feeding himself with a spoon. Sort of. Carissa and I were expecting again. It was a happy time in our life.

One Thursday afternoon, after finals had ended and all the students were gone, I had a call transferred to me from the front desk. It was someone from the Advancement office. I never received calls from anyone in Advancement.

"Is this Peter Cahill?"

"Yes, speaking."

"Mr. Cahill, we have a Mr. Ken Park here, and he is wondering if you have a few moments to see him."

Oh shit.

"...Yes, of course. I'll be right up."

That elevator ride was an exciting one, if anything. The old me would have been nervous, or would have shied away from wanting to see him again. As it turned out, I had no reason to.

"Welcome to Advancement, Peter." There were handshakes all around. They had a full catering spread in the corner, and a coffee and tea station. Mr. Park stood at attention, but he did not shake my hand when I came around. He stood and he smiled and he bowed with respect. I gave him my return. I was asked to sit.

"Mr. Park has just finished telling us about your work with his son, who I understand was a student at your previous institution. You see, in most of these cases, Peter, families go to the institution where their student was actually enrolled. Mr. Park, here, has made a very generous offer to endow a scholarship in his son's name, but it's under the condition that you will be a part of the applicant review process. We can work with you to hammer out the details with your supervisor, and it would entail working very closely with Mr. Park for..."

324

"Absolutely. I agree, sign me up." I turned to Mr. Park. "Thank you so much, and thank you so much for thinking of me." The smile he gave told me that I was the first to thank him.

"Mr. Cahill, from my whole family, thank *you*."

❖

It took longer than I was expecting to close the deal, but that had nothing to do with dragging on the part of Mr. Park. I did finally get to see the General and the cut-throat, and it made me so happy to see someone put a few of our suits in their place.

I never was privy to the numbers, and that was exactly the way I wanted it to be. I *do* know that the amount was substantial. At our first meeting to discuss applicants, the Chair of the Board of Trustees was on the agenda. Her offer was an honorary Doctorate of Philanthropy for Mr. Park, to be given at next year's Commencement. Up until that point, I had never been prouder to be in a board room. But, sitting across the table from him, that sentiment didn't last long. He declined. Instead, he asked that they consider granting the honorary degree posthumously for a Bachelor of Fine Arts.

ABOUT THE AUTHOR

Andrew S. Cioffi works as a disability services professional at a local university in Boston, MA. By night, though, his dreams of dragons and samurai were calling enough to start writing things down. With a passion for great stories and great mythologies, he is equally inspired by comics, graphic novels, chambara films, progressive metal, and high fantasy of all sorts. Aside from hours spent enjoying the finest teas and pipe tobaccos, Andrew is an avid archer and skeet/trap shooter. His other talents include all things cooking and eating. But his biggest inspiration comes from his family. Born in Everett, MA, and well-traveled throughout the Greater Boston area, he now lives in Malden with his wife Christina and three amazing kids.

327

ALSO AVAILABLE BY ANDREW S. CIOFFI

The Painted Shogun – Book I
Dragon Festival, Harvest Fire (2013)

Mori No Akuma – Forest Demons
A Collection of Short Stories (2016)

Paperback and Kindle available on amazon.com
Mobi version available at andrew-s-cioffi.com